RESCUING
CLAIRE

RESCUING CLAIRE

A NOVEL BY

THOMAS JOHNSON

Scarborough House/*Publishers*

Scarborough House/*Publishers*
Chelsea, MI 48118

FIRST PUBLISHED IN 1991

Copyright © 1991 by Thomas Johnson
All rights reserved
Printed in the United States of America

Library of Congress Cataloging-in-Publication Data

Johnson, Thomas, 1949-
  Rescuing Claire / by Thomas Johnson.
    p.   cm.
  ISBN 0-8128-4012-7
  I. Title
PS3560.0386475R47   1991
813'.54—dc20   90-24101
                                                    CIP

Contents

1

At the Northern Lights

I WAS ENJOYING the sunshine, on the roof of Cabin 13, replacing some rotten shingles, when I heard the mailman's truck. It was one of those curious postal vehicles, white and blue with the blue flaking off, the steering wheel on the English side, the wrong side, looking lopsided and undrivable. Luckily, the driver was Snarro Knudsen (his friends call him Snow), was also curiously lopsided. He had polio as a boy, and his right leg is shorter than his left. His right shoe compensates for this imbalance with a thick slab of black rubber. Truck and man seemed perfectly matched.

Snarro (he insists he's named after a Nordic warrior-king) was a man afflicted by griefs great and small. He's the post office's Job. Despite them, he was a reasonably cheerful fellow. Perhaps this was merely a professional demeanor, the kind of bonhomie the post office expects (and so rarely receives) from its employees. His wife was dying of pancreatic cancer; his son—an alcoholic, and a brutish bully—was momentarily serving time in the Iron County jail for aggravated assault.

Snow got out of the truck and walked up the driveway. He stopped at the lodge; Fulmonar's wife was ready with a cup of coffee. He waved at me, and he cupped his hands and shouted: "Well it won't be long now, will it, Henry?"

What was imminent? Winter, the end of the season, his wife's death, his son getting sprung from the Big House? All were applicable.

"No, Snow, any day now," I answered, typical of me on a sunny day, full of hope and affection.

I returned to my work, to the gritty but vital details of innkeeping. I was a man passionate about maintenance.

I am half owner—with Ernie Fulmonar and his wife Pat—of the Northern Lights Lodge, on sparkling Lake LaPointe in Iron County, Wisconsin. In the summer we are strictly SRO, crammed to the gunnels with vacationers seeking the sun and silence of the north. Our reservation list for August includes America's premier tap dancer, a pardoned traitor, and a Nobel laureate. The reason for our success is that Lake LaPointe is the acme of North Woods bodies of water; and the lodge is heartbreakingly picturesque.

We run a clean and efficient operation: a main lodge with a small dining room, fifteen boats, fifteen cabins, a white-sand swimming beach. The cabins travel the arc of our little bay, weaving in and out among aspen and jack pine, connected by a red-gravel path. From the front lawn of the lodge—the site of our musicales and entertainments—the vista of our fifteen white cabins against the deep blue of the lake and the black-green of firs is profoundly calming, happy-making.

On Friday evenings in the summer we provide entertainment to amuse our guests and whoever else might be interested in soothing music: string quartets, Ukrainian polka bands, folksingers, wobbly-voiced sopranos, country-western aspirants. The lodge and its lawns could have been designed for just such events. The audience sits in a semicircle around the front porch of the lodge, listening raptly as anyone might, in darkness, on a moonless starry night, to lovely music. You would not think there were so many musicians and music lovers in these dark woods, but they are there all right, nursing old grievances or new dreams.

Fulmonar's wife brought me my mail and a bottle of beer. She climbed halfway up the ladder, so I didn't have to reach too far beyond the eave.

"Aren't you hungry yet, Henry? It's almost two. Why don't I make you a sandwich?"

"No," I said, "I'll make myself something when I'm finished."

Pat Fulmonar is a remarkable woman, the guiding force behind the order and elegance of the Northern Lights. She has been the place's Capability Brown. Mostly alone, she has worked on the grounds: the neat paths, the rock gardens, the sculpted shoreline. She has dug out boulders, uprooted trees, and built rock walls with little assistance and no advice from her husband or me. I suppose she is fifty or so now, but to me seems as lovely as a debutante. She is as slender and as sinewed as a ballet teacher. Old Ernie is a lucky man. I love her like a mother, although I'm just guessing at that emotion, being an orphan.

On the way back to the lodge, walking in her brisk, long-legged stride, she scoured the gravel path for weeds or broken glass. She is vigilant.

The mail, again, was scanty. A postcard from my wife. She is a classicist, an archaeologist, and is on Crete or some shard-encrusted hill in Asia Minor: digging, digging, always digging is Mrs. Fitzgerald. She missed me, wondering how I was. Lately she has been signing her letters and cards to me "Elizabeth," using her full name, not her nickname. I'm sure this usage has long-term significance, for these matters of style are to her state of mind what a drop in barometric pressure means for tomorrow's weather. Big storm coming. The two strongest possibilities: she wants either a baby or a divorce. Maybe both.

I also received a letter written in blue ink on expensive stationery from a long-absent friend. Knocked me off my stride. This was equivalent to getting a telegram from someplace a long way off, from Pluto. It was from Claire Cohen: the dark-haired lady of my embryonic sonnet. Having seen an article in her local paper (the Rochester, New York, *Clarion*), one of those escape-to-the-North-Woods-style features illustrated with a photograph of a bucolic, flannel-shirted owner of a rustic resort gutting fish and smiling at a blonde-haired tourist child—she decided to write. She had always wondered what had happened to me. (Not much, dear, and thanks for calling.)

Enlivened, I am embarrassed to admit, by lust—by the writer, a stringer for the *Milwaukee Journal* was gorgeous—I had identified myself as "H. Z. Fitzgibbons," a defrocked priest, cashiered by the Church. (Reasons unspecified, but libidinal torments were implied.) I had come here to the northern woods, far from temptation, to a hemlock cathedral, to offer the rest of my days as an acolyte to the Great Forester. I'm embarrassed to say that I actually used the words "hemlock cathedral," although I can't tell a hemlock from a warlock.

My problem: I have always erred on the side of excessiveness. In fact, I am not H. Z. Fitzgibbons; I am not, sad to say, a defrocked priest. It is possible I have traveled to the north for spiritual reasons, but not for the spiritual reasons I described. My name is Henry Fitzgerald. I am a man of property, a taxpayer, a relatively faithful husband, and an absolutely loyal brother. And with, admittedly, several notorious exceptions, an upstanding citizen. I am an orphan as well.

Claire wrote: "It took me a while to recognize you. I never think of you as actually *living* in northern Wisconsin. [Her emphasis.] I remember you in your apartment in Madison, in the kitchen, explaining how to throw a screwball. I don't think I ever really learned how, Henry. [She didn't.] I couldn't think of why this face, the one in the photograph, looked so familiar. Of course, the baseball cap gave you a real woodsy redneck look. But then, you never took a good photograph anyway. Then it hit me: Henry! I told my boyfriend about you, not everything. Some of that stuff, I suppose, I will never tell anyone. But I told him what we had gone through. I told him about what you and Norman did. He said you sounded like a weird guy. That's something a lot of people end up saying about you, though. Anyway, we had a good laugh about it. It didn't seem very funny at the time, did it, Henry? Six years have gone by awfully fast."

Claire's note, were I in a more active state of mind and not slouching toward wintery catatonia, would have infuriated me. History is being twisted into a false shape. I realize that people are entitled to a point of view, to a certain amount of therapeutic forgetfulness. Some distortion or a slight collapse of honesty is forgivable considering the intensity of feelings, the disappointment, the pain. But I haven't forgotten. It wasn't a funny moment for me, no reflective chuckles issue from my mouth. For Henry it was getting off the canvas with a mouth full of blood.

My brother Milton, as a result of the controversy surrounding the putative rescue of Claire Cohen (and other events that underscore my inconsistent acknowledgment of the moral order), calls me the Weird One. Hardly a person who knows me well will disagree with that assessment. Frankly, I am a bit strange. Not dangerous or cruel, just a bit odd. So what?

Clutching Claire's letter in my fist, I remembered a different version of myself. A quirkily contentious guy I was in my salad days.

In the autumn, the quality of the light this far north is astonishing. As if to make up for the radically shortening days, the light is richer and sweeter. Winter is coming; that's what I remind myself.

I will summarize the balance of her letter. Her current boyfriend is an M.D.; they have lived together for two and a half years. No children. No plans for any. Not even close to getting married. She taught school, having been certified by the State of New York to do so. She still danced, after a fashion, privately. She has a lot of gray in her hair, and she lost the tip of her left pinkie last year in a snowmobiling accident. The clear inference to draw: that she was, finally, happy.

Sure.

Sadly, it becomes necessary to set the record straight. With the season ending and winter coming, I have decided to construct a true narrative of the events surrounding Claire's peril, which events were highlighted, to my way of thinking, by the awkward affection Claire and I shared, my abandonment of her in an extreme moment; my sorrow at doing same; my disillusions; the discovery of a stalwart ally and boon friend, Norman O'Keefe; our discovery of a common enemy, Leonard Gent; the heedless and headlong attack on his house; our arrest and detention; our release and eventual triumph. In short, Claire's rescue.

Some persons, the kind of unhappy souls who put arsenic in aspirin bottles, have suggested that Claire's rescue was merely one of my nastier megalomaniacal fantasies. A harsh judgment, with perhaps a sliver of truth.

Claire had suffered a personal tragedy—several of them. A formerly true friend—I am that friend—had demonstrated a smarmy capacity for gratuitous cruelty. Eventually—and this is where the allegations of megalomania have some basis in reality—I came to believe that she had fallen under the influence of a notorious liar, a master of deceit. What happened? The simple truth, unrevised, unadorned, unbedecked by the gaudy gowns of invention, is my sole (and my soul's) concern, remember that. I rescued Claire; I had no choice. I stuck the envelopes in my back pocket and finished my beer. The sun was wonderfully hot.

After reading Claire's sad letter something occurred to me, something very troubling, and it was this: there are disappointments that may last as long as life.

2

I Am Born

THERE ARE TWO things that define me completely, govern my actions, and will undoubtedly settle my fate. First, I am an orphan. Second, I am moderately wealthy; that is, after this year's taxes I am about twenty thousand dollars shy of being a millionaire. The latter condition, near millionairehood, flows inevitably from the former.

My parents, Henry and Kathleen ("Hank and Kathy"), crashed in a small plane in the Brooks Range of Alaska during a storm. Their bodies were never recovered; the wreckage was never even sighted. They were geologists working for an oil company, Arka-Global Petroleum. I was six months old at the time; my brother was seven. The year was 1950.

Most of what I know of my parents, except for a few stories I've heard from my aunt of their meeting and courtship (at the University of Colorado, 1940, married the same year), is derived from snapshots of them in exotic spots: leaning against a truck in the Arabian desert; camped out next to a stream in the Rockies; aboard a tug in the Gulf of Mexico. My brother and I appear in only one photograph, taken only days before their death. The occasion, my brother tells me, was Easter Sunday. We were living in San Antonio then. The four of us are dressed for church. I am wrapped in a blanket and ready, as blanketed babies are, to go anywhere. My mother has on a dark dress (navy blue, my brother tells me) with a lacy white collar. She looks very young. She was young, only thirty. My brother is squinting into the camera, uncomfortable in his suit jacket and tie. Except for his cowlick, he looks much as he does now. The sun is shining in their hair. Two weeks later my parents will be dead. Is there a sadder snapshot in the world? I think not.

My parents were both quite handsome, in a rough-edged and raw-boned way. My mother had very beautiful, well-formed hands, however; that much is clear from this photograph. My father wore a bristly mustache and steel-rimmed glasses, probably thinking he looked like Teddy Roosevelt. He did. They were not delicate creatures: they looked as if they might live forever.

Recently, looking at these snapshots, Milton pointed out something to me that I had never noticed before: that the logo of Arka-Global appears in every picture except the last. It is on the side of a truck, on the funnel of a tugboat, painted on the flap of a tent. The logo is an amateurish thing. Since the headquarters were in Arka-delphia, Arkansas, it consisted of a razorback hog, wearing a hard hat, perched on top of a globe: "Arka-Global" is written on a banner that bisects the earth, like William Tell's arrow through the apple. Arka-Global went out of business in 1957, swallowed up by Texaco.

Milton and I each inherited a million or so. Perhaps because my parents' travels took them to many strange and dangerous spots, they had a great deal of insurance and had developed a complicated formula with Arka-Global for lump-sum payoff of their contracts (with interest and bonus) in the case of accident or death.

Since a great deal of money was involved, there was a brief and bitter struggle over custody. My parents' will had specified that we live with my mother's older sister, her only sister, in fact the only sibling either my mother or father had left alive. (My father had two older brothers who were killed in World War II, one at Monte Cassino, the other at Saint-Lô.) But our then surviving grandparent, Bridget Fitzgerald, a woman who strangled my father's parrot Ollie to death for soiling a damask doily (an horrific tale that is part of the testimony taken during the hearing), tried to win custody. She failed.

In the aftermath, a result, I like to think, of unreleased rage, she suffered a severe cerebral hemorrhage. My brother and I visited her only once more before she died. It was a gruesome interview, since the stroke had left her with half a mind and the color of cauliflower. Her room smelled like a subway station: of alcohol—they bathed her in it—and urine. She couldn't remember our names, and when she asked them of us, I answered, too frightened to say anything else, "Henry!" She turned to my brother, and he said, "Ollie." She gave him a look of venomous shock and sank back into her pillow, sailing into sleep or a coma. A parrot's revenge, my brother called it.

We moved to Mt. Pleasant, Illinois, a northern suburb of Chicago, an exurban paradise. Our guardians, my mother's sister and her husband, were Sally and Winston Duggan. Sally Duggan was fifteen years older than my mother and, I see now, resigned to, if not especially enthusiastic about, her responsibilities. Aunt Sally and my mother were not especially close. My cousin, Victor (whom everyone called Little Vic, a midwestern irony since he was a near giant), was away in college, Notre Dame, where he was captain of the hockey team. He was the cross-checking and fist-fighting specialist.

Aunt Sally was afflicted with gentility the way some people are afflicted with shingles: an itch that you can't ever scratch away. She had black hair, dramatically streaked with gray, and skin so white it was nearly transparent. She was an Irish beauty, much prettier than my mother, knew she was beautiful, and treated everyone with a kind of condescending formality. It is impossible to think of her in a sexual posture, mounted by my uncle, for example. She was delicate, intelligent, and fierce. I liked her the way you might like your kindergarten teacher; in fact, we had a very similar relationship, for the only things she ever seemed to say to me were "Why don't you take a nap, Henry?" and "Would you like some milk and cookies?" Milton took over the chief responsibility of my upbringing, and she gladly, if silently, acceded to the relationship.

In retrospect, I realize this taking on of two small children, one an infant, was an enormous responsibility. She had already dispatched Little Vic (with considerable relief, since Vic was a tyro alcoholic and womanizer) and was looking forward to a period of self-development, of travel, of leisured reflection. The day before my parents died she had written in her classic Palmer Method hand, in an azure ink, to the Chamber of Commerce of Charleston, South Carolina, for information regarding trailer parks, restaurants, and (she showed me the reply with her note still attached) "the general and specific ambience." Whatever the hell that means.

"Henry," she used to say to me, a thin hand on the top of my head, her bangle bracelet a cold reminder of who was the orphan and who was not, "no one can ever say of Sally Duggan she has not done her duty."

These words, I can assure you, on the impressionable mind of a parentless child, have a corrosive effect. I point no accusatory fingers, but this is just the kind of thing that leads to psychic malformations. I feel a lingering bitterness toward her.

My Uncle Winston, however, was not a bad guy. He was an architect. His father had been an architect as well, a talented one, who had actually trained with the great Louis Sullivan. Winston Senior's buildings were fine ones, elegant and harmonious. Winston Junior was carried forward with the momentum his father had established but with the certainty he was not of equal talent. Having seen what was left of his work, I reluctantly admit his professional skills were meager. His banks looked like gas stations; his suburban homes looked like train depots in a defunct Balkan state. His buildings were either too large or too small; they were clumsy and ill-lighted. Most of them have disappeared. But he was a charming fellow, and for a long time had more clients than friends, and he had many friends.

Ultimately, hubristically, he got careless and let greed and grandeur ruin him. I always think of him as the Illini Ozymandias. He designed a wretched house for the son of a Saudi petro-sheikh in Evanston, Illinois. The kid was studying at Northwestern and needed a place to crash on the weekends. It was a neo-Babbitt's dream job: get it built, buy off the League of Building Inspectors, take a kickback from the contractors, fill your pockets, buy triple tax-exempt munis, clip coupons in the Caribbean. (My uncle was never a man to shrink from felony in pursuit of profit.) This time, he went too far and got caught passing envelopes and twisting arms. He was never charged with anything, but he had outlived his usefulness to the pirates and profiteers associated with the building trades. His partners showed him the door.

Following his dismissal, he withdrew, sullenly, and went to fat.

Then, miraculously, he found his true vocation at his club, Chestnut Hills Country Club. (I always thought it should have been called White Vinyl Belt Country Club, since there were infinitely more of those on the grounds than either chestnuts or hills.) His real genius, he saw, was seduction. Not of the ordinary fleshy variety, but of luring from the wallets of relatively (and recently) well-to-do men (car-lot owners; speculators in slum real estate; arsonists compensated by insurance companies) sufficient funds to keep the club solvent. He saved the club from Chapter 11.

Despite the new layers of flesh (forty pounds of it), he was a striking man. Tall, gray-haired, with shoulders that could support a pediment, his days were a fury of five-foot putts and heartfelt conversations with prospective members.

"Your daughters, Bobby," he would say, for example, to Bob L. Lawrence of Bob L. Lawrence Chevrolet, "are lovely girls, real beauties. They'll love it here. They'll meet the right sort of people."

(The sordid truth is that they looked like they had just turned professional after an extended period of backseat amateurism.)

Uncle would grab a sap like Bobby by the shoulders and, looking him in the eye, make a sincere plea: "Please join us, boy, we need your help, we need your business sense to keep this place happy and profitable. Can we count on you?"

Of course, Bobby accepted and rushed out to buy his pastel polyesters. My uncle's irrefutable deduction: social climbers can't resist flattery, even auspiciously insincere flattery.

As membership chairman, my uncle was granted sweeping powers—he was the Caliph of Parvenu Park, so there was no need for any other subsequent interviews, inquiries, or investigations. If you were accepted by my uncle, you were accepted. He did not actually associate or socialize with new members ("emergency" members is what he called them). In fact, the last thing he ever said to them (this while folding the check and putting it into his wallet) was "the course is closed on Monday."

He would write a note to the club manager, enclose the check, and settle down for an afternoon of gin rummy, sitting in the greenish haze of the Men's Grill like the king of a very small country, calling for vodka martinis by raising his glass and saying to no one in particular (for he was a true democrat): "Yes, I'll have another, thank you."

I was a silent, shy kid, but not unhappy, considering the circumstances. I occupied most of my time with sports and books. I could have, but did not, teeter on the edge of moral oblivion. This is the result of my brother's wise counsel and firm hand. For, despite the abundance of creature comforts, I realize now I could have been one of those desperate, haunted creatures who robs gas stations. I could have been a child molester or doper. I escaped that unhappy end because I believed my fate was elsewhere, in great accomplishment, in acts of tenderness and courage. Having endured silence, my own and others, I went to college resolved to be at the center of things and not to drift, as I had, into quiet corners and empty rooms.

In my senior year in high school, I applied to and was accepted at the University of Wisconsin, where my brother had attended law school. Milton entered law school in his junior undergraduate year, a real shooting star, a phenom, like Bob Hazle, the Hondo Hurricane. He was an intensely political creature (for a long time he was a Trotskyite) and aggressively defended the wretched of the earth. His practice was a moral and political success. Milton is intelligent, honest, and utterly lovable. When I enrolled as a freshman, he was already becoming a local hero. It made things a lot easier for me.

On August 28, 1967, a day so hot bees could not find the courage to buzz, I kissed my aunt and uncle goodbye and took a cab to O'Hare. I resolved, driving along blacktopped roads that were as soft as taffy, to leave behind me forever the dispiriting circumstances of suburban Sundays, country club lechery, and the well-intentioned ambiguities of my guardians. I had in my jacket pocket the dog-eared photograph of my parents. Protected and encouraged by this talisman, I set out.

3

The War Is Not Quite Over

LATELY, I HAVE come to recognize, and a bitter recognition it is indeed, that my undergraduate days were a callow epoch, a period bracketed by my arrival in Madison and my meeting Norman O'Keefe, five years more or less. Here's the thing: a certain callowness was a necessary condition for the dreariness of the historical moment. The war in Vietnam was a callowness factory, giving a lot of guys a twitch, a tic, or a tremor. Remember Mel Laird, for Christ's sake, remember Robert McNamara? I admit it, those fish-eyed bastards clenched my colon. Dread filled the air like farts in a chili house. Ah, but, like most college-age white boys who didn't care to go to Southeast Asia, everything worked out pretty well induction-wise for me. I wasn't drafted; my number in the lottery was 342. I had nothing to worry about.

Still, in the months prior to the lottery, I had been thinking about my options, given the worst: jail or Canada. I had come to no firm decision. I had been told, and believed, stern and joyless men plotted the extinction of Communism and to that end dropped bombs on babies and old women.

In my own city, in Madison, in the middle of the midwest, the night sky was filled with fire and smoke. And in my own sedate neighborhood, in which still lingered little old ladies of extraordinary

delicacy—hothouse blooms who had retired from their jobs as teachers of Latin or heads of rare book rooms—windows were shattered
and students yahooed and scurried among tear-gas bombs. In pursuit
were ranks of National Guardsmen and jump-suited redneck sheriff's
deputies bussed in from the country corn towns and wide spaces of
rural two-lane blacktops. Goddamn it, things were gas and sorrow.
Nothing was working out.

And what did I do?

I marched. I expressed my anger and confusion in what now seems
a series of random and, unhappily, insignificant ways. Not much
else. The easiest thing to do, very possibly the wisest.

Of course, I read the papers. Even if you were lucky enough to
evade induction, you couldn't evade history. Battles raged, bombs
dropped, a new body count was announced every day. Very sad stuff.
Milton developed the nasty habit of phoning me very late at night,
juiced up into Nix-o-somnia. Not trusting me to ferret out the ugliest
facts for myself, he filled me in.

Milton wrote letters to periodicals and television networks trying to
rend, he said, the tissue of untruths, contradictions, and lies that
covered the country. Lies, he said, were fouling the city air; lies were
polluting streams and rivers. Lies were entering the food chain; we
would soon be eating and excreting lies. These things roiled the
smooth surface of Milton's spirit. Milton was in despair, and he could
handle that in very small doses. After all, he was an orphan, too.

"I wrote a letter to Nixon yesterday," he told me one night about
midnight, the day of the Kent State shootings, at the absolute end of
his spiritual tether. "I said that I was on to him. I was keeping track
of what he was doing. He could give everyone else a little blue pill to
take—that was a kind of metaphor, Henry—but I wasn't swallowing
mine! Let me read it to you: 'I am out here, Nixon; one false step and
I'll throw you to the coyotes. You remember Mussolini, Nixon?
When we're done with you you'll wish you got off as easy as that son
of a bitch. Imagine your arms torn from your torso; imagine your
tongue coated with acid and excrement.'" He paused there, as if
stunned by the depths of his hatred.

"By the way, Henry, since I could get disbarred for this, I signed
your name."

My brother banged tables and shattered china. He howled. He swore foully. He broke down at dinner tables and wept; large tears filled with bile and blood fell onto the linen tablecloths of his hostesses. He shrugged off comforting arms; he closed his ears to consoling words. Old Milton was right on the edge. One slight error and a fall into oblivion. I calmed him when I could, stood by him when I couldn't.

The true fact of the matter is that the war in Vietnam was grist, as the saying goes, for Milton's psychological mill. Milton graduated from law school in 1964. He was a boy genius in the law. His law boards were towering; he was footnote editor of the Law Review and clawed his way to the editorship. He was courted by the partners of well-known firms. But he shrugged off the glad hands. He wanted to help people. "Helping people" has always been his fiercest ambition. He married his wife because he wanted to help her. She had had a nervous breakdown during their courtship, and during one especially bleak period believed herself to be Sonny Liston's daughter. They're divorced.

After he graduated from law school, he opened a law office in a basement, a space beneath a Marxist bookstore. Milton was serious, for a time, about World Socialism. I mean *really* serious. Big brotherly criticisms accompanied any manifestation of my lack of political will. And then, just as he began to undergo his first true crisis of the spirit, just as his marriage was becoming burdensome and his practice disillusioning, Lyndon Johnson escalated the war in Vietnam, saving Milton from drowning. He was rescued from self-contemplation (Milton is a virtual encyclopedia of unresolved psychotensions and tics) by bullhorns and arm bands and rage-choked middle-of-the-night phlegms. He was strengthened by teach-ins and the interminable babble of protest. He became his old contentious self, headed for some Finland Station of the soul. (I'd love to have a painting of Milton amid a sober crowd of softcore protesters, as well as Weathermen, Yippies, Communist Youth Leaguers done in the heroic Soviet Socialist Realist mode.) Despair was his element, and he was held aloft in it, the way a kite is held aloft in the wind. He defended draft evaders, window smashers, arsonists, police beaters and baiters, Quakers who smeared blood on files and floors, seminarians who chained themselves to troop trains or the doors of induction centers. The whole suffering universe of protest.

In court he was magnificent. Milton looks like he could be a millionaire; in fact, he has increased his holdings considerably. He is solidly built, a little heavier than I am, a middleweight having a hard time to stay in his division. In those days he still had most of his hair, and he combed it straight back, revealing a high, intelligent forehead. His eyes are violet (like my mother's), and his hands are as delicate as those of a safecracker. He has a grave demeanor; Milton's a serious guy.

Milton didn't like the unkempt blue jeans and workshirt of your archetypal movement lawyer. Expensive tweeds and flannels, silk ties, English shoes (Milton was a bit of an Anglophile, I'm afraid): that was his style in those days. Fancied up, the impression he projected was one of sobriety, balance, and compassion. Deep in his great heart, though, he was a nasty, street-fighting dude. He is actually a tough guy. Some cheap advice: don't get Milton pissed at you.

In court he rose to question a witness with glacial slowness, smirking at the prosecutor. When he delivered his summation he would turn and look at the jury with a deeply felt, sorrowing glance. Garage mechanics and housewives, retired accountants and efficiency engineers—the meat and potatoes of jury lists—could feel, I'm sure, the subtext of that glance (automatic weapon fire, body bags, streets full of angry and confused Americans); they had seen it nightly on the evening news.

His was an extraordinary presence in the courtroom. His world— the blond furniture, the blood-red briefcase, the yellow legal pads, the bailiff's pressed uniform with the jewel-like badge gleaming on a shirt of navy blue—suited him perfectly.

"Ladies and gentlemen," he would begin his summing up, "you must now consider the innocence or guilt of my client."

This was the way he always began. No anger, no histrionics, no bad acting. This was a conversation among civilized folk about horror and so on.

The eyes of the jury would follow his gesture as he pointed a teeth-scarred pencil at his client (feverish pencil chewing is symptomatic of his repressed anxieties), the young hero of the revolution, for having thrown a brick through a library window.

Poor kid, Milton had you thinking, damn bad time he's having.

And, of course, what you saw was not a frightened, drug-buzzed netherwit, but "a sincere young man whose zeal we must condemn, whose sense of responsibility is not yet fully developed, yet whose courage we cannot fault. The war, after all, has done this to us. This young man should be sitting in the library studying physics with his girlfriend or practicing the oboe in a music room. Why must he be in the streets, outraged? Why must he confront the police? Why must he oppose us, his elders, for no reason except a blind and incorruptible insistence that, by God, *something is wrong*. Well, my friends, something is wrong, and must be called wrong, must be exposed, defeated. What has turned this boy against us has been the war makers, the bomb droppers, the liars, the scoundrels!"

Here usually came a pause while the prosecuting attorney objected to the tone and language of my brother's summation. He was generally sustained.

Slightly chastened, Milton would stand in front of the panel then, looking at each juror, trying to meet his or her gaze. Most would look away.

"Find him guilty. But guilty of what? That he saw lies and called them lies? That he saw wanton and vicious destructiveness, and he spoke clearly those words? That he was not fooled by lies and stood on the streets and confronted those lies. Find him guilty, ladies and gentlemen, if you must, if you feel the law commands you. But as you deliberate, try to remember of what he really stands accused. Not of breaking a window, but of smashing silence."

One of the ironies of Milton's political milieu is that he actually didn't care much for his clients.

"Pimple heads, Henry," he said. "You know, I'd love to defend a real desperado. This misdemeanor shit is beginning to get me nervous. Sometimes, Henry, I think I should have tried to qualify for the Tour." (Milton shot a 67 at Pebble Beach in 1970; he's right on the edge of being a serious golfer.)

"Aren't you interested in justice?"

"Justice. Justice. Henry, grow up, will you. Justice doesn't exist.

Deception exists. Deceit. Big guys are pushing little guys around. Bullies are walking in the street trying to keep the peace and maintain order. I like to stir things up a bit. Throw a ball bearing into the gears of justice. That's why I get in the newspapers. I harass people; I enjoy making a modest amount of trouble. That's all."

Making trouble, Milton became a minor celebrity in Wisconsin, sort of like Liberace's brother. People liked Milton, regardless of their (or his) politics. He made jokes, he passed out Cuban cigars, he bought the house a round. He chatted up everybody, so I suppose it is not surprising that he knew Claire Cohen.

I met Claire shortly after I shaved off my beard, January 1972, my second senior year. I have two photographs taken in that period, one in the fall and in the other in spring. The autumn picture shows me as hairy as Jim Bridger. In the spring—Lake Monona is ice-free over my shoulder and a sapling exhibits buds—I am as smooth-faced as Apollo.

We were drawn together—Claire and I—because of her old boy-friend's politics and my brother's vigilance in protecting the wrongly (or rightly) accused. Claire swears we had met earlier. That I had stepped on her hand during a sit-in at a dormitory cafeteria—she the sitter, I on my way to get more milk. She also said we met again in the basement of St. Francis House, a center of Episcopal radicalism, during a speech by a radical Episcopalian. She said I was trying to look up her skirt the entire evening. This, frankly, sounds plausible. She said she called me a "voyeur" and stormed out. It seems like I should remember that, but I don't. I now freely confess to trying to look up girls' skirts whenever the opportunity presented itself. I am not alone in this.

Sometime in early January of 1972 and Milton and I, on our way to lunch, found ourselves on the edge of an anti-war demonstration sort of waltzing through the rabble . Habit had made both Milton and me somewhat reluctant standers-in in anti-war crowds (tear gas was apt to explode in your face), and we were working our way across the Library Mall toward State Street. It was a cold but very bright day, and Milton and I were chatting about some land he was going to buy in Bayfield County: seventy-five acres close to Lake Superior. As a sort of predemonstration warm-up, a blue-grass band was playing on the Memorial Library steps. I recognized most of the musicians. One often saw them on a street corner standing behind an open mandolin case. Most of them had dropped out of school and were supporting themselves as minor-league marijuana salesmen or janitors in state office buildings. They had always looked to me like people you wouldn't trust with large (or even small) amounts of money.

They played several tunes: mandolin, fiddle, bass, and two guitars moving through and into nasal laments, broken hearts, broken promises, misappropriated lucre, and so on. The cops—who knows where they were lurking?—moved in without subtlety. Eight campus cops, clad in olive green, big guys in battle dress, scooped them up, instruments and all, and carried them off. Permitlessness was a misdemeanor under the modified condition of hostilities that prevailed. A minor scuffle ensued, screeches of the sound system and electrified and unelectrified shouts of "Fuck you pig" rising. It was over in minutes.

"Let's go, Henry," Milton said, grabbing my sleeve.

"Go where?"

It was a pointless question, for I knew the answer.

"To get them out. This is a goddamn outrage. Jesus Christ, these bastards are beginning to annoy me."

"Hey, Milton, let someone else do it. You need a rest."

He looked at me. I recognized the stare. It inevitably preceded a diatribe. Almost always something was said about fascism and Richard Nixon, the need for constant vigilance. Serious stuff.

Truthfully, I didn't really care. Musicians, as far as I was concerned, pretty much deserved what life dealt them. If this included a stretch of hard time, who was I to step pointlessly in front of destiny's juggernaut?

However, a strange mood came over me. These moods, I knew, almost always preceded something amusing. (Call them premonitions.) What the hell, I thought, and trailed after Milton through a long brown avenue of plywood. (Over the years, State Street merchants had lost their broken-window insurance, so on demonstration days they tacked up half-inch plywood to deflect rocks. State Street—

fairly funky under the best of conditions—often looked like
Galveston after a hurricane.) We chugged up toward the State Capitol, bright as an Alpine summit, sparkling in the winter sun.

Our destination was the City-County Building—a fortress of cement, steel, and copper-colored glass. We intended to bail the boys
out, to pluck them from the steel jaws of capricious justice. My
brother was a Bulwark Against the Dark Night of Nixon. Unfortunately, his services were unnecessary. We discovered, upon arriving,
that no charges had been filed. The band, the Windy Mountain Men
(a name subject to several interpretations), had been dumped on a
sidewalk, given a series of summonses, and scolded for being perpet-
ually out of tune. The only casualty was an instrument: a guitar neck
dangled in a tragic posture.

Milton began a low-level howl about a block away. He was breathing hard (we alternated a kind of slouching-toward-Bethlehem jog
with leaning-against-parking-meter gasping). Milton was not in good
shape. Plumes of breath bounced out of us in the cold; perspiration
ice was frozen into my hair. He pointed at the equipment and then
at the cops. I believe he was disappointed that charges hadn't been
filed.

"Cocksuckers," he yelled at the receding cops, "fucking brown-
shirts. Goons."

He gasped for breath, and then surrendering to the absurdity of the
moment, laughed a little.

"Well," he said, "another good fight won in a just cause. They saw
me coming, I'll bet, and that scared the shit out of them. Henry, take
the victims' names and numbers, we're going to sue somebody."

He strode off, a happy warrior, his blush dimmed down to pink,
looking for a public official he could badger into an apology.

Irony was not then foremost in my mind. True, at the moment, I
was not especially *enragé* or *engagé*. Helpful is mostly what I meant
to be. I was dragged into this thing, if not exactly against my will, at
least tangential to it. But I undertook my task diffidently: I went up to
the gallant martyrs one by one, took their names and numbers,
uttered small tokens of consolation or outrage. They were still a bit
traumatized. I used a paperback copy of *Heart of Darkness*, writing
on the title page in the space between "Darkness" and "Conrad."

Nicky "You Should Go to the Dentist" Waller; Danny "Fat Lips" Donohue; Eric "Lump on His Eyelid" Stein; Harry "Hat Rack" Goldman; Lloyd "Excessively Short" Johnson; Milo "The Mad Bohemian" Plagonika: their names, including an informal descriptive monicker of my own invention. Two things distinguished these musicians from the normal course of humanity: one, except for "Hat Rack" Goldman (who crowned the appearance of utter perpendicularity by wearing a very large—ten-gallon-plus—black cowboy hat), each of the band members wore a Marlon Brando, "Viva Zapata" mustache; second, each of them had a hard time remembering his telephone number. That's untrue, just kidding. Nicky was the leader, and he rushed off to get his van.

A young woman suddenly appeared, as if she had dropped in by hot-air balloon, flushed from exertion. (In fact, she had followed the trail from the Library Mall to the City-County Building—maybe three-quarters of a mile—that Milton and I had blazed. She got a late start, not actually having been on the Mall, but getting an urgent message in the Union Cafeteria.

"What happened to you?" she demanded of Lump on His Eyelid. (He'd been poked above his eye with a nightstick.) "And where's Nicky?"

"He went to get his truck," Lump answered. "He's all right."

I liked the way she looked. She was dressed in blue jeans and a blue-hooded sweatshirt. (Blue is Claire's favorite color.) She wore a blue-and-white bandana around her neck—a primitive gas mask—and it was tangled into a silver neckchain. She was agitated, and there was something childlike in her frustration in getting the chain untangled. Attractive young woman, I thought. New to me; never seen her before.

"Let me help you with that," I said, seeing her frustrated efforts.

"All right," she said crankily, "but don't break that chain, it's very old."

She was irritated at the complexity of the entanglement. But I thought she was being unfairly irritable. I was simply being helpful.

"Put your arms down," I said. I stood in front of her as if we were about to dance.

She had thick black hair, as thick and as wavy as a night at sea, which she wore pulled back in a ponytail. During her run, a few strands had worked loose and fell across her face; several of these contributed to the bandana-chain tangle as well. (When things happen, they happen quickly, don't they?) Her eyes were deep brown. She was slight, but, standing so close to her, I could feel the kind of coltish energy she possessed. Supple in a dancerly way, she was in fact a dancer. I was quite attracted to her. I'm not a believer in love at first sight; basically, I had the old twitch in the groin: sex was what I had on my mind. In my early twenties, I almost always had sex on my mind.

She smelled of cigarette smoke and baby powder.

"Who are you?" she asked.

She emphasized, somewhat coquettishly, "are."

I was bent over in the vicinity of her chin trying to untie the knot in her bandana. I whispered, like the as yet unindicted conspirator I was.

"An outraged bystander," I answered. "Outraged, by the way, is a barely adequate description of my inner turmoil."

A lengthy, scrutinizing pause followed. Sniffing the air for the odor of sarcasm, Claire tried to creep away from me, but I pulled her back.

"What happened?" she asked.

"Fascist goons beat up blue-grass saints," I answered, "that's what the papers are going to print tomorrow anyway. Look, I'm taking names. Are you a witness? Let me lay a couple of concepts on you: lawsuit, major out-of-court settlement. We could squeeze some heavy bucks out of the university."

I was well on my way, then, floating along the riptides of weirdness.

"Look," I said, "here's the scoop. I think I can trust you. I know of a fifth column, a silent, secret group of heroes who are eliminating the type of down-homey suburban frauds the Windy Mountain Boys personify. Cultural commandos, I call them, who are confronting upper-middle-class poseurs who arrogantly imperialize genuine folk ways. Nasty business. Many innocents will be washed away. But there you have it. The truth, lady, isn't a pretty thing. Sometimes it wears steel-shank boots and carries a blackjack. White boys with beat-up guitars and phony Okie accents will be stomped into the consistency of marmalade. It has only begun."

I undid the complicated knot in her chain and stepped back, triumphant.

"There," I said, "another success."

I guess I shouldn't have been surprised when she tried to make a hasty escape.

"Thanks so much. I'm afraid I'm going to have to find Nicky," she said. "I'm sure he's upset. He takes everything so seriously."

"Whether they are serious or not," I said, grinning like Prince Drexel the Loonie, "there will be no one to protect them in the days to come. No one."

"Thanks for your help." She edged away.

"Your name, please, and number. It's for a potential lawsuit. Your testimony could be crucial. We have to struggle against Moloch." I was getting pretty wound up.

"If you have Nicky Waller's number, you have mine. We live together."

This is a message and a warning to me. Don't get so fresh because you are talking to a woman in love. Unfortunately, I had just talked to Nicky. I didn't like him much, having heard him whine about his amplifier. (I thought he was a surly shit.)

She turned away, moving among the band members, offering what solace she could.

Milton returned. He had found no one to share his outrage and in fact was getting a little bored. (The lack of criminal charges was what bummed Milton out; criminal charges were what put lead in his pencil.) He gave me the old "let's bug out" sign, but spotted Cohen just then. He went up to the dark-haired beauty and put his arm around her slender waist. I suppose they knew each other from some nutball anti-war thing—Dancers and Lawyers Against Asian Hostilities. Combinations like that were always springing up and then dissolving, the result of some passion or pique.

He turned her around and pointed at me.

"That's Henry, my brother," I heard him say.

Did clocks chime the hour? I think so. Those bong bongs might have been my libido kicking in, however.

He led her over and introduced me.

"Oh, my God, you're the guy who wears that unbelievably ratty pair of khaki shorts in the summertime, aren't you?" she said. "They're disgusting. Did you know that?"

Thank you, dear, and did you know your tits were lopsided? Disgusting huh?

"They're just getting broken in."

For my part, I must have been spending a lot of time in a trance because Claire was utterly new to me. It seems impossible I wouldn't have noticed her.

We smiled at each other tentatively.

She grabbed my hand and shook it, power-to-the-people style, as if we were going to Indian wrestle. She had the hold of a bar clamp, vise-grips, boa constrictor. Strong, anyway. I felt like I was going to have a nosebleed.

4

Claire Cohen

SO COMMENCED MY relationship with Claire Cohen, dark-haired Claire Cohen, quiet Claire Cohen. Milton and I left her standing in the cold comforting and consoling her badly whipped boys. Curiously, I turned back as we walked away, hoping to catch a final glimpse of her. (Maybe I wanted to confirm her presence in the phenomenal world.) She stood out from among the others, swirling along the edges of that ugly knot of musicians, never at rest, offering what encouragement she could. She was in the sunlight, and the sun caught her delicate neckchain, magnifying its importance. The sun was reflected in the tiny hoop earrings she wore. She chose that moment to look up, too (telepathy, electromagnetic brain waves, destiny, etc., are all possible explanations for the mutuality of our attentions). Her gaze was surprisingly affectionate. She waved, and I responded with a snapped-off Sugar Ray Robinson jab.

"Henry," my brother said, "I don't have to tell you this, you having just recovered from Lily Campbell. But I will. Don't even think about Claire. I know she's your type, but don't."

"What?"

"I just had this ugly premonition, Henry. In advancing your friendship with Claire, exercise caution. She's an odd girl."

Milton is only too aware of my archetypal affinity for small-breasted, dark-haired women. He neither shares nor commends me for my tastes. Similarly, I find his penchant (pathological obsession is closer to the mark) for bosomy blondes equally mystifying.

"What I'm saying, Henry, is Claire and her boyfriend are complicated. Nicky, frankly, is slightly south of the slime level, but he's been good for Claire. Before they were together, she was really off the wall. Dangerously so, Henry; she ran with a nasty crowd. Take my word for it. I know her well enough to see she's still in a bit of a turmoil. You, of all people, don't need turmoil."

"Tish tosh," I said grandly. "I don't believe it. Nothing is complicated. She's pretty. I am notoriously pleasant to pretty girls. In fact, I am pleasant to people in general. Good manners, you'll remember your aunt saying, are a mirror of the soul."

"Turmoil, Henry. Happy feet at three in the morning. Just remember your capacity for irrational behavior. She's difficult."

"Claire is already a fading memory."

I was feeling a bit set upon. Did I deserve this? Okay, so the bitter conclusion of the Lily Campbell thing was two days of lachrymose drinking and quite a large pool of bourbony vomit on Milton's stove. One strives to learn from one's mistakes.

"Oh, sure. I saw that look you gave her. I've seen it before. Just remember, Henry, when you hit bottom, and you will, you heard about Claire here first."

We walked along the perimeter of the Capitol Square. The Square, which was downtown, had once been crowded with shops and shoppers. Lately it had developed a bad case of the shopping-mall blues, and now many of the storefronts were vacant; badly yellowed for rent sign clung to shop windows. The afternoon light was nearly gone. We walked silently in a dismal wintery twilight. Depressing time of the day; the hour of the broken heart. Milton had lost his gloves, and he kept his hands in his pockets. He was hunched over like an old man with a bad stomach.

"Suffering Christ, it's cold," he said.

"What's so complicated?"

He laughed, a wicked, wicked cackle. He didn't answer.

"She's pretty," I said. "I like her."

Fatal words. But for months (a kind of phony-war interlude), libidinally speaking, things between La Cohen and me were on the back burner. Time passed. The distasteful history of a distasteful epoch rushed by. I plodded along, Good Citizen Fitzgerald, like the shovel-and-scoop man at the circus: dogged, diligent, but well separated from the frolic and the glitter.

The war went on. Protests simmered like tomato sauce in a tiny trattoria. The cold winds howled. I went to class according to my own lights and inspiration (which usually meant with fair regularity); Claire went to class punctually, assiduously attending each session. In her entire class-going life, she had never missed a day of school, except for when she was prevented from entering an economics class by a line of Weathermen. Even then she stamped her foot in irritation.

I engineered meetings with Claire in the library, having discovered I could regularly find her there alone, in the first-floor reading room, reading. She sat near the window, at one of the bowling-alley-length library tables, intent upon learning. When it seemed appropriate, I sat with her, pretending to study but actually just staring at her.

Claire was almost always dressed in some version of her dance major's costume. Blue jeans (the knees patched with a darker blue denim) and a leotard the color of a good painter's palette: Japanese orange, Florentine blue, magenta, cobalt blue. Her hair was usually pulled back, and she wore her neckchain (a family heirloom; birthday gift from grandmother) as her singular adornment. She seemed beautiful to me. But, frankly, I was one of the few persons who thought Claire Cohen a beauty. A languorous afternoon with her in the library left me stupefied with dumb lust. (Is there another kind, though?)

In the odd moments we found to spend with each other, alone and out of the way, secluded from the gritty details of what Claire liked to call her "real" life, her Wallerian life, we made small talk, genially, affectionately. Mostly we behaved ourselves, although occasionally we strayed from the paths of righteousness. One snowy Friday afternoon, in the teeth of a Great Plains blizzard, we got liquored up on three pitchers of skunky beer at the Hasty Tasty, way in the back by the pinball machines—hiding, really—and ended up wrestling each other in a series of icy snowbanks on the way home. Claire avoided me for a week or so, trying to teach me a lesson. Just what the lesson was eludes me now. I guess it was that she recognized there was something inappropriate about her and me. After my week on Elba, she demanded a rectification of circumstances, a clarification of absolutes. Henry was going to have to keep his distance. To that end she had a plan.

"Why don't you call me at home, Henry?" she asked me. "Nicky will feel better about my talking to you if we were more normal friends. Like if we went out for dinner as couples. With Pixie. We can't have any more of these little kisses and squeezes."

Malice is my true métier.

"I don't want him to feel better, Claire. I don't like him. I like you."

"Maybe you're right, Henry," she said, snapping shut a text resignedly. "I guess basically I like things the way they are. What are they, anyway?"

"I guess I'm your assistant boyfriend, Claire," I said, with the bitterness unhappy insights bring. "The only thing is, I'm not getting my duck wet." Getting one's duck wet. Lovely phrase, that.

"And you won't either, Henry. I live with Nicky, and I love Nicky."

"Sure you do. Please don't break my heart with that shit, Claire."

She took that personally and bolted the library, leaving me to be admonished by the Taiwanese chemistry majors who filled the reading room and traditionally tried to peer down her blouse on the way to the pencil sharpener.

She never said it, but the clear indications were she was miserable. I didn't take it all that seriously. Almost everybody I knew was miserable, including me. But sometimes, sitting at a table in a drugstore cafeteria or at the Union, exchanging particles of studentish non-information, I sensed in a too-long glance or an awkward wave of her hand that Claire's unhappiness was structural and not circumstantial. She was seeing a therapist, recording her dreams, and reading Baba Ram Das. Something, Henry, I told myself, is not quite right. She was seldom with Nicky Waller. When I saw them together, an ancient antagonism sprang up between Nicky and me. He had the look of a bad mechanic in a small town. (What? Am I supposed to be charitable toward this zombie?) An ugly situation was evolving. He wore a fringed leather coat, the kind Custer made his last stand in. Before he came to Wisconsin, he hadn't been west of Newark, yet he wore cowboy boots. Have I mentioned I didn't like him?

Claire's uneasiness when the three of us were together—her moments of awkward sadness—made us all uneasy. Something unseemly, you'd have to be a fool to miss it, was happening between Claire and Henry. The cashier in the cafeteria saw it. Despite my basic instincts of well-intentioned politeness, my distaste for Nicky was obvious. (Okay, I suppose I was rude as hell to him.) Claire became the sole focus of my attention. Of course, Nicky's dislike for me was accelerating nicely as well. Because I played tennis regularly and often had the handle of my racket sticking out of my rucksack, he took to calling me the Club Pro. He did this behind my back, and eventually, with a smarmy smile, to my face.

Claire and I passed January, February, and March this way—bitter months in the north country—within an igloo of depeening cordiality. Except for our one blizzard-madness roll in the snow (a calamitous drop in the barometric pressure stimulates Claire to excess) things progressed platonically: no stolen kisses, no furtive hugs, no forbidden fondling. I had a serious girlfriend, Airy; she had a very serious boyfriend.

And then it was spring. How pleasant it is to say that! After a dark winter made bitter by a series of wind-driven storms, the sun was suddenly higher in the sky. With hardly any effort on my part, the snow began to melt into deep, black puddles; and even the puddles dried up, and it was nearly the vernal equinox. Release from frustration. Creatures who a few weeks before had been indistinguishable from large woolen clouds, declared themselves to be women: lovely delicate arms and legs; breasts bursting out of shirts, popping buttons; fine white necks meant to be breathed heavily upon. Women—I discovered this every spring—are a temptation and a mystery.

I had a sense of inevitability about Claire, that we were being drawn together by megaforces, large historical and sociological trends. Every worm will have its day, as my uncle used to say (a

confusion of homilies that suggests the wider and deeper confusion of
his life). I believed him. Every worm, I used to say to myself when
I saw Claire, every worm will have his day.

March and April are traditionally good months for me. Spring
training. This year seemed to be an exception. First, I stubbed my toe
early one a.m. and it turned a purplish black. Second, I began to hate
my apartment. Its arrangement suggested a badly designed Pullman
car—it was a railroad flat, after all. The living room was furnished
with remnants of the previous tenants' miserable lives: the ancient
widow's yellowing lace curtains, her urine-stained sofa (in her last
days she became incontinent); the sad poofter's (a record-store manager) California-redwood-burl coffee table, with its inky shadows of
neglected cigarettes; and now my books and desk. The former piled
beneath the windows, unevenly and irregularly, looking like a low
range of mountains in autumn, and the latter a neat sawhorse-and-
plywood affair upon which, sedimented like the many layers of Troy,
rested data related to my economic, educational, and spiritual strug-
gles. The bathroom and kitchen were connected in sequence like a
parade of circus elephants, tail to trunk. A snapshot of these two
rooms—thick veins of missing plaster, and those black dots you see
aren't raisins but roaches—would represent my late winter mood.
Depression before spring I had. I like the fullness and exuberance of
bad weather and of good. The lukewarmness, half-heartedness, non-
sanguine, undecided, drizzly, worn-in-the-elbows wintery shit was
making me nuts. My toe hurt. I had to soak it and then prop it up on
a pillow. The doctor thought I'd lose my nail. I felt like I was hiding
from the Gestapo in the crawl space underneath a spice warehouse in
Lyons.

Finally, in late April, when girls began to appear in T-shirts (My
God, Milton, nipples! Nipples!) I felt better. I'm not suggesting cau-
sality here, of course, but a relationship too strong to be merely
accidental. Well, things happen, as my friend Bob Birdwhistle always
reminds me; things happen.

On the morning of April 25, 1972, the old Claire Cohen–Henry
Fitzgerald ball really got rolling. I was sitting on my sofa reading the
sports page. Baseball season had recently commenced and I was
absorbing box scores the way a plant absorbs sunlight—to put it to

some purposeful future use. I was called from my concentration by a timid, twittery rapatap-tapping on my door. The fragile glass panel in the door, which shook when a heavy truck passed, rattled with the tapping.

I was sitting on my sofa starkers, just having popped into and out of the shower, a towel covering my privates. Clearly I wasn't expecting company and I was antagonized when it arrived. In fact, I was feeling cranky as hell. I assumed it was my landlady, a voluptuous ex-Carmelite nun, who was always trying to catch an indiscreet glimpse of me. No kidding.

"Sister Lawrence," I said, using her religious monicker, "I'm on the phone." (She hates it when I call her Lawrence.)

"It's me, Henry."

"Who?"

"Claire."

I thought she said "Lar," a diminutive of Lawrence by way of Larry, and was ready, at long last, to give my landlady an unobstructed view. I stood up, atingle.

"Cohen," she said then.

"Claire Cohen?" I asked, stupidly. "Claire Cohen the dancer?"

"No, the brain surgeon. How many Claire Cohens do you know?"

Was that a trace of sarcasm in her voice? Sharpness in my pal Claire's tone?

"One, just you. Just a minute, Claire. I have to put my pants on."

My customary equanimity had dissolved. I was flustered. I regret now that I didn't just rush to the door in my condition of utter undress, throw it open, and let Claire have her way with me. I was pointlessly polite (and I, laughably, had believed being polite could never be pointless). This nod to propriety slowed down the steam-building part of our relationship. Surrendering to a wave of lust might have resolved everything early on.

I dressed in what I thought was a mad rush; I left Claire outside, on the stoop.

"If you're occupied with something, Henry," she said, irritation creeping into her voice, "I can come back another time."

Clearly, Claire did not appreciate being left standing on the doorstep. Desirable women (she knew *I* desired her, at least) are hardly ever made to wait for anything or anyone. This insight, by the way, is a product of much bitter experience.

"I'm here," I said, throwing the door open. "Sorry."

Claire was dressed for spring and to create a vivid impression. Her hair was clean and fragrant (I sniffed it; it smelled like sunlight). She wore it down, not pulled back and engineered with barrettes, bobby pins, rubber bands, and other gadgets. Standing in the doorway, she seemed to carry with her the freshness and brightness of the day. Behind her, over her shoulder and across the street, the sun shone very brightly on car windshields and a set of steel wind chimes. The world seemed full of bright and transient objects, and she, Claire Cohen, in a sunset red sweater, was among them, the brightest and least permanent.

"At last," she said, without malice.

"Sorry, I had just come out of the shower."

We looked at each other the way men and women do.

"So," I said. "To what do I owe the pleasure?"

"I've come to ask you a favor."

"Anything." I was ready to fight Achilles, Hector-like, had she asked me. Hormonally, glandularly, brain chemically, I was fully cocked and ready to fire.

"Come to my dance class with me. It's a real emergency, Henry."

The thought of taut, lovely women, flushed with exertion, dewy with perspiration was not unpleasant: smooth arms, finely muscled legs, thighs and rear ends, with the leotard sliding up just a little past absolute decorousness. Henry had spring fever.

We were still standing in the doorway; Claire in the sunlight, I in the shadow. We both had our arms folded across our breasts, intent upon self-containment. Claire's words passed through me like gamma rays. She ran her hand through her hair—slight anxiety, perhaps?—and it fell smoothly back into place. I grabbed her forearm and tugged her gently into my living room. She passed directly past my chin, beneath my nose. She resisted my pull a bit, and I was rewarded with a pleasant fish-catching sensation. She wouldn't come into my living room more than a foot or two despite my exertions. She stood timidly, poised for flight. She didn't then know how harmless I was; I didn't even know how harmless I was.

"Will you help me?"

I wasn't sure of what help I could be in a dance class, unless she wanted me to waltz her about the polished floor of a hotel ballroom.

"I don't know, Claire. Let me think. Boy, I've got a lot of odds and ends to do today. Laundry for sure. I'm down to my last pair of shorts. Do you want coffee or something?"

I was delaying my answer. I didn't want to seem too easy, too eager. I tried and failed at looking pensive. Claire checked her watch. She wanted a decision, pronto, and wasn't much interested in my pensiveness (not a quality she highly esteemed in her men friends).

"No coffee thanks, Henry. I don't have very much time. Look, doing this for me would be a real favor. What do you say?"

"Of course, I'll do it, Claire. I was only playing hard to get."

"I don't think you're hard to get. That's one of the last things I'd think about you."

It's hard to disguise my essential nature, which is profoundly lap-doggish. For a taste of something sweet (I was thinking about the smooth, fragrant skin just beneath Claire's ears), I'd do more tricks than Trigger.

"Good. Do you remember I told you that I was practice teaching in a high school this semester? Anyway, I have to teach class today, and I need someone to operate the record player. I can't really do it myself. The person who usually does it is sick, and I can't find anyone else on such short notice. Nicky says he's too tired. I was passing by, and I thought I would ask you. I know it's a real imposition."

I smiled at the thought of Nicky Waller, that cadaverous moron, stretched out, like Camille, too weary to put records on a turntable. (This smile is emblematic of a venomous aspect of my personality I don't care for.) I also thought that her pretext for getting me to come along was transparent. Surely, there was a simpler solution; one more congenial to her boyfriend's low opinion of my character.

"When do you want me?" I asked, struggling to suppress a smirk.

"Right away. In fact, we should be on the road right now. I'm going to have to really hurry to get there on time."

"How do we go?"

"My car," she said proudly, "is around the corner."

It was indeed, and just barely: a sky blue Volkswagen which had carried more than its allotment of the *Volk*. It listed ominously to port—badly beaten up shocks and springs—like a torpedoed destroyer.

Claire had an unseemly pride in her car. She allowed no one else to drive it, for good reason, I admit. I didn't especially relish the thought of strapping myself into what was left of the driver's seat and wrestling with this mass of momentarily joined pieces as it hurtled itself through city streets. That Claire was its mistress—knew its vanities and quirks as well as she knew her lover's body—was pleasing to me. I actually thought I was going to enjoy being driven by her. (I hate automobiles myself, preferring to walk above all other forms of getting from Point A to Point B. Automotive-mechanic chat gives me a stomachache.)

Claire was not a careful driver, she was an instinctive one (especially if you assume some sort of death wish). She kept us moving forward, toward her teaching assignment, when common sense and the lessons of history insisted we could not. At last, we stopped, abruptly, at the rear of a ruin, a school building that had been abandoned for several years and had been repeatedly vandalized. Now it was barricaded at obvious points of illegal entry with sheet metal and plywood: Fred Hampton Alternative School. Its reopening had been half-hearted; hardly anything that was broken had been fixed. The place had a kind of final-hours-of-the-Third-Reich look. I found it depressing. Basically, the smashed window glass had been swept up, and new urinals had been installed to replace the ones ripped off the wall and smashed.

"Pretty gloomy, huh?" Claire asked.

"In the Führer's bunker," I said.

Large chunks of plaster had fallen off the wall; water damage was epidemic, exposing rotting wooden lath. A disapproving look must have been on my face. The walls, where they were intact, were painted a creamed-corn beige. This is where Claire taught, but what manner of person would choose to go to school here? Pretty much your garden-variety midwestern teenage desperadoes: indiscriminate drug and alcohol abusers; aspiring Guevaras; welfare mothers not yet fifteen; beautiful young women who had attempted suicide; margin-

ally retarded pyromaniacs; the dizzy, the unsocialized, the unfo-
cused. No pep bands or chess clubs in this joint.

Claire walked a little in front of me, smiling and waving at familiar
faces. I carried the record player and the records. She pulled me
along like flotsam in a tide through hallways lined with battered
green lockers. She strode through the school like a Medici through a
Renaissance cathedral: sleek and powerful. This was a new Claire to
me. She was as unambiguous as the winter wind. Claire was eager to
teach geeks, deadbeats, nose pickers, lump prols what it was like to
dance, to move to music, to free themselves from the sad encum-
brances that bound them to the earth. Hey, you awkward and gravity
bothered, Claire was telling them with her singular grace, transcend
yourselves. So I imagined Claire's effect, anyway, in my rapturously
goofy state of mind. (I was already nose deep in Cohen admiration.)
I trudged behind her, happy to be carrying her music.

5

Claire Among
Schoolchildren

THE GYM: I could have wept tears of joy. I love gymnasiums; the smell of exercise, of ammoniac perspiration, bacteria-laden foot skin in crusty sweat socks. Fred Hampton's gym smelled heroic, epical, Homeric.

"This place is awful, isn't it?" Claire asked, crinkling her face into an extreme frown. "There was a massive leak last summer and everything is rotting."

She smiled at me, a little shyly; I smiled at her, not so shyly.

"You can plug the player in over there," she said. "Just set it on the floor. I'm sorry there's no table or chair. Everything is pretty primitive."

I found the outlet and sat the record player down near it, popped off the cover, and inserted the plug. I turned the power knob and a red light came on and the machine hummed, majestically. I engaged the turntable to make sure it worked. It did turn, although it wobbled a little, making a slightly eccentric revolution. I sat back against the wall. I crossed my legs—with the records in a neat pile to my left, the player alive and well to my right—and was ready for any contingency. Okay, let's have some dancing.

"Why is it so dark?" I asked, an innocent in the alternative-school milieu.

Claire smiled at me as if I were brain-damaged. (Actually, she wouldn't even have smiled at someone who was brain-damaged like that. I felt patronized and I, Henry Fitzgerald, do not enjoy—or merit—patronization. Beneath my surface calm I was annoyed. A barely noticeable rippling of my jaw muscles would have been the only indication.)

"Money," she said.

I assumed by that she meant the lack therefore or perhaps its allocation to enterprises considered more worthy than the renovation of the gym: for example, macramé frames; empty bottles for Molotov-cocktail-making class; special instructors in the History of Revolutionary Speeches; Anger-Elimination seminars; Environmental Abuse clinics.

Of the fifty lights I deduced were in the ceiling (five rows of ten each) seventeen were actually lighted. The result: semidarkness. The gym was a vast space, two full-size courts laid out side by side with the roll-backable bleachers rolled back (they climbed the walls and looked like flattened Venetian blinds or a vertical xylophone). The glass backboards were still in place, but the rims had no nets. The hardwood floor was buckled and warped, with a depression near the center. It looked like a fallow field into which a small meteorite had fallen. The relative lightlessness (and the fact that the narrow windows at the top of the north wall were bricked up) created vast areas of darkness, like the map of an ancient cartographer, amid patches of dusky light.

Claire stood in the middle of this light and dark unchanged, wearing her jeans, red sweater, and sneakers. She looked at me with an expression of triumph (over whom or what?).

"Thanks for helping out, Henry. You're great."

"No problem."

"I'm going to change now."

"Fine. I'll be right here. Or should I turn around?"

"That's all right. I'm just going to take off my clothes."

No problem, I thought, that is absolutely okay with me.

So she did. She sat on the floor and untied her shoes, slowly, smiling to herself. She pulled them off and set them together to one side. She stood up and unbuckled her belt. (Ah, Milton, a woman can take a long time—an eternity—to unbuckle her belt.) I was staring at her. I could not help myself. What am I supposed to do when a pretty woman begins to undress, take a walk around the block? (Milton, if erections had a human voice, mine would have been pleading for immediate release: "Please, please get me out of here.")

Belt unbuckled, she zipped down her fly. I have been unzipping my fly (boy and man) for over twenty years; seen it done in bedrooms and locker rooms thousands of times, but this downzipping was beyond perfection. Next, she pulled her pants down to her knees. Just plainly pulled them down. I thought an artery had exploded in my neck. She was wearing a leotard beneath her pants, of course, but that seemed beside the point. She stepped out of her jeans, folded them nicely, and put them on top of her shoes. A very tidy soul is Claire Cohen. She looked up and smiled. How she was enjoying this! She grabbed her sweater crosshanded at the bottom, and with a swift snap (sail in a storm, flag in a strong breeze, whip on a horse's flank) was left with only her leotard (also black). Claire in black with her hair worn down, falling on her shoulders in a field of light and shadow. She spun around once or twice, just for the hell of it, just because she had a pretty body. She was a lovely girl.

"There," she said, "I'm ready."

My voice was barricaded behind a wall of lust-induced phlegm.

"Right," I croaked at last, "I'm ready too."

"Do you have the time, Henry?"

"Almost ten," I said, looking at my watch, "three minutes to ten."

She smiled again and turned away.

"We could have some lunch or something after this, Henry. We should have a nice long talk."

Or we could rip off our clothes and roll around on the locker-room floor. A suggestion, regretfully, I didn't articulate. The sex endomorphins were bing-binging in my brain. She walked to the edges of darkness, barefoot (the stirrup of her tights edited out her arch, leaving only heel and toes).

"When does class begin? I haven't heard any bells."

"Oh, Henry, there are no bells here. They are strictly forbidden. Classes start, more or less, on the hour. But sometimes they start a bit later. Some irregularity is acceptable."

A wild understatement.

"No one cares?" I asked.

"No one seems to."

As we spoke, faces began to advance out of the darkness, out of odd corners, the junctions of dimensions, down off the ceiling; her class appeared like Hamlet's father's ghost.

The boys were slight, shy creatures for the most part: blond hair worn long in thin strands that hung across their shoulders and backs. They looked like the survivors of a forced march. Many had dropped out or had perished along the way, and these remaining few radiated the ineffable sadness of a totally defeated army. There were ten of them; they wore patched blue jeans and work boots, which they kicked off into a pile. To me they seemed like the milky white creatures found in the depths of the ocean, near volcanic crevices. I cannot imagine what I seemed to them, except alien. Claire called the roll, gathering them in like a Siren (no wax in the ears; no tied-to-the-mast bravery for them).

The girls, however, were uniformly pretty with clear complexions and expensive haircuts. The boys were drones and gofers; the girls were on their way to becoming charter members of the dilettantery, dabblers in the arts. (Sadly, a little like Claire herself.) These young women—they would never be more beautiful than now, at seventeen—wished to be taught how to dance. In that they were charming. I believed the hour was going to pass much too quickly.

After roll call, Claire began to organize her class—almost an even split between boys and girls—breaking up the gender-centered clumps and nodules of dancers, pulling them into two lines. Claire tugged them into an awkward balance and a rough symmetry. She positioned herself at the left end of the two lines, turned to face them, hands on hips like an anxious football coach. She waited for the small talk and the giggling to stop.

At last, they seemed ready.

"All right," she said, "let's start with some stretching."

Claire stretched her body upward, arcing her arms above her head until she was taut, catlike, on tiptoe. Her movement was astonishingly quick and smooth, like the burst of light from a flash bulb. Her students—except for an extraordinary girl quite near Claire—were not nearly so smooth and unforced. Their arcs were disfigured, crooked elbowed. Their balance was only provisional, and somewhere along the path of this movement they toppled forward, awkwardly.

Claire said nothing and corrected no one. A fat boy in the back, a self-exile to the dark area, was encouraged to come forward.

"Andy," Claire said, "I'm losing you, aren't I?"

Andy smiled hopefully but seemed ready to acknowledge the fact that he was lost. He had a sleeveless leather vest on and no shirt. It was much too small for him, and the bottom was creeping up over his belly. The arm holes had dug into his shoulders, leaving two reddish circles.

But Claire did not abandon him. Come out of the darkness, she said to him. There was no question she would be obeyed. When Claire called you out of the darkness, you came. I see that now. It was then that I realized Claire possessed a sort of irresistible energy. Despite the sincere counsel of family and friends, I wasn't going to be able to resist her. She bent down and stretched forward, loosening her back and hamstrings. A lovely body had Claire. I was so aroused I almost floated. Claire grunted energetically. She bent lower and lower until she seemed planted, permanently. Then she sprang back up.

Claire looked at me and smiled. She pointed at the records.

"Okay," she said, "you can put on the first one."

The music commenced with my dropping the tone arm on a spinning record. At first I did it too heavily and there was a millisecond of chaos and noise. Heads snapped and shook themselves at me, unhappily. Claire had chosen mostly chamber music: Vivaldi, Bach (the old man and some of his sons), some Mozart. She also included Miles Davis—playing with one of his old quartets—when he was in his melancholic mute epoch. Very sad stuff. Mostly, though, on a cheerier note, we hopped back and forth in the Baroque and early Classical modes.

I didn't have to play the entire side of each album. Claire told me

when to stop and when to change; when to volume up and when to
volume down. J. S. Bach, as far as I was concerned, was the champion. Even an old record on a tinny record player filled the vast space
to bursting. I can't listen to Bach without smiling—even in the
blackest moment—and Claire's dancers must have felt the perfection,
too. They seemed almost graceful as they scampered, capered, and
leapt to one of the Brandenburg concerti. I almost got up and scampered about with them but remembered my responsibility resided
here, on the floor, directing musical operations. I wiggled my feet
instead, vigorously. I looked up in the midst of my most energetic
feet-wiggling passage to discover that Claire was staring at me, a
strange, tender expression on her face. We both turned away.

Claire led her class quietly, gracefully, with attention paid to a
sequence of steps. She was a fine teacher and a natural leader. Somewhere in the randomness of the movement, buried beneath awkward-
ness and timidity, was a pattern. Claire had choreographed a dance
that these twenty would be performing; it was this they were rehears-
ing. I figured that out for myself, although it took an intuitive leap to
do so. Claire moved in and out of the two lines of dancers, through
the dusky light. In this moment I believed (and believe still) Claire
was at her best. Dressed in black, I will now remind myself, she had
no part of blackness or extinction. She stood out of the darkness.
Much later, a solitary walker on a wintry country road, I was cata-
pulted into action when I remembered Claire in that awful twilighted
gym.

Finally, the music was exhausted. I had a headache from lifting
and dropping the tone arm, trying not to jab the needle into the vinyl.

No bells rang to signal the end of the hour. But at 11:00 everything
stopped. A circle was made around Claire: bees around their queen.

"Next time," she said, "I'll show you more. I think we're getting
better, but now we have to start getting serious. Okay, you can go."

And they disappeared, scuttling away, as confused as crabs after a
storm, all directions available and attractive. A few, mostly girls,
hugged Claire as they receded. I wandered over to where they were
standing, hoping they might want to hug Claire's assistant as well.
None did.

"What do you think?" Claire asked, after we were alone.

"About what?"

"About them. About this."

"I wish I had had a teacher like you when I was sixteen."

"Is that a compliment?"

"Of course."

I packed up the records and put the top back on the record player. She was disappointed that I was not excited. She dressed, but I had my back turned. She seemed sad.

"You didn't like it, did you?"

"I thought it was great, Claire. I didn't mean to let you think anything else."

She pouted. And pouting, she looked like a pretty—but ordinary— college girl in a red sweater.

"I thought you were exquisite. You're the best thing about the class. But I think most of your students—especially the boys—are about to fall off the edge of the earth. If Alcatraz were a state of mind—like depression—they'd be serving some hard time. They seem like bugs just waiting to be squashed; they seemed doomed. They're cannon fodder. Is that cynical?"

"That's pretty depressing."

"I didn't mean to make it so final."

She turned away and walked toward the exit. She had the records under her arm. I followed her, alarmed at my outburst. What made me so judgmental? Just instinct. I followed her, in silence, through the hallways and out the rear door. We found her VW and lurched back toward campus. Our route took us along Sherman Avenue, which bent around the lake. Between the substantial houses—products of enterprise and thrift—I could see the silver spars of sailboats, protruding from cadaver gray tarpaulin. One boat was in the lake, which was blue and iceless; it seemed the paragon of sailboats, a white so sharp it hurt the eye. Despite the fact that Claire was being a little sullen—nursing a grudge—I felt well, although a little over-stimulated.

Annoyed, Claire is the master of monosyllabic conversation. It was astonishing what anger a two-letter word can express.

Finally, we made the turn onto Gilman Street, just above James Madison Park. That short, acute hill was a profound challenge for

Claire's battered car. Happily we achieved the summit and plunged—coasting with the clutch disengaged—down the back side of the hill, past her apartment and toward mine.

She pulled to the curb, pleased, despite herself. I had trouble with the door latch (opening it involved a jiggle that I hadn't mastered), and she had to reach over to help me. First, though, she grabbed me around the neck and hugged me savagely. My nose was welded to her cheek. She let me go just a little so she could kiss me; I kissed her. So far rough parity in the passion department prevailed. However, when I tried to slide my hands forward—from her back to her chest—in order to place them squarely on her breasts, she clamped them down, pinioned them in place about midway with a fierce squeeze of her elbows. Henry was not going to cop a quick feel. Then she kissed me again, this time more tenderly. A lot of interested folks walked by, goofy smiles on their faces. Some even rapped encouragingly on the windshield. It was spring, everybody was a little juicy. Then, as if we became aware of the consequences of desire (the long-term emotional ones, not the short-term tumescence), we looked at each other carefully and with deep emotion.

"Okay, pal," she said, "last stop."

Claire was flushed a bright pink. She pointed to the door, the world beyond her door, with a trembling forefinger.

"Hit the road."

I got out. What choice did I have? I was going to lean over and say something to her, but she slammed the gearshift upward, into first, and blurted off in an effusion of moon blue exhaust.

"Ah, shit," I said, master of the bon mot.

It was just before noon; I was horny as a seven-day cyclist (assuming they have no outlet except determined exercise). Claire abandoned me in the bright midday sunlight. But I was not downcast, quite the opposite. Oh, confusion and ambiguity, elements essential to my well-being, were growing, hourly, like yeasty dough in a hot kitchen. Things happen, I reminded myself, things happen.

6

A Short History of Abomination

I FIND IT hard believing to what depths certain scumboids can fall. Milton has told me stories of human behaviors, sexual practices, violations of taboos so bizarre, cruel, and destructive that I felt sick and had to sit down and hold my head in my hands. One of his clients found it pleasurable to put safety pins through the nipples and tender stomach flesh of fourteen-year-old whores. And worse. Yo, Wayne Leach, you out there? Be not deceived, pal, you haven't gotten away with anything. Your punishment has merely been delayed until we can think of something especially horrific, something particular to the nature of your evil.

In the afternoon, hyperstimulated by smooching Claire, I played tennis with my upstairs neighbor, Noburu, a visiting professor of literature from the University of Oregon, a nisei Jamesian, a samurai scholar, a truly odd duck. Frankly, he's a lot better than I, having been the number-one singles player at UCLA in 1957, but I beat him up. I drove him around the court like a beer can in a big wind. Winning the first set 6-2, I won the second with a topspin forehand that ticked the net and skipped on the baseline just beyond his desperate reach. At love, six zip. Outraged at my dumb luck, he ignored my attempt at a handshake and rushed to the locker room to stand under a steaming shower and sing "Stand by Your Man."

But sullen rage was not Noburu's style. He is a sweet man, really, a titan among pygmies in my estimation, although envied and disliked by most of his colleagues. Could that envy and dislike result from the two hundred publications he lists in his *Curriculum Vitae,* or his Guggenheim, or the fact he smokes disgusting French cigarettes at faculty meetings?

"Henry," he said, toweling off, his good humor restored, "nice match."

"Once-in-a-lifetime stuff, Noburu," I said. "You'll destroy me next week."

"Yes, probably. By the way, who was that popsie I saw you struggling with?"

"Excuse me?"

"The one in the Volkswagen, Henry. The girl who was licking your teeth."

"Oh, just a friend."

"Old Hard-on Henry: answer to a lonely coed's prayers."

"Fuck you, Noburu, I hear you dragging those cocktail waitresses up the stairs at night. Are you reading to them from *The Golden Bowl* or bending them over it?"

"You're right. Just kidding, Henry. I was just surprised. I saw Airy in the library the other day. She was kicking the shit out of a librarian. Willful young woman. It would be too bad if you did something, you know, stupid and ruined everything. Just tell me to mind my own business, Henry. But I like you both."

"Noburu," I said, "it's spring. Things happen. Didn't mean anything."

"Sure," he said, "I understand."

Maybe he understood, but I was still a bit fuzzy. Reality crept back into the locker room on slippery shower clogs. *Willful* was a woeful understatement.

We rode the campus bus together back to the Union, in gloomy silence—pondering, I suppose, our infidelities—and we parted with a cursory handshake. I was on my way to meet Airy Elder, love of my life, et cetera. She had been off to Chicago the day before with her mother to pick up a few frocks for her trip to Greece this summer.

Dog that I am—groping with the Other Woman in a parked car—I still hoped she had a little something for me.

Airy Elder: small and blonde, delicate features and lovely skin. Her nose had been broken in a toboggan accident as a child, and it was no longer perfectly straight. And there was a small bump and a tiny scar across the bridge. Her scar is only noticeable in the summer since it doesn't tan, and the half moon of whiteness appears like an arc of current. She's a small woman, with perfect breasts, truly perfect. (There are times when I think all that matters to me are perfect breasts.) She never wears any underwear, except a T-shirt, but if she catches you checking out her tits, she'll whomp you like a linebacker. I hate to admit it, but she's a little on the grim side. Her grimness is something I used to find interesting but which was becoming sort of a burden.

I love Airy, that's the truth. Absolutely mad about her. She is intelligent, forthright, independent, cunning, courageous; she lacks nothing. The thing is, she isn't sweet. She's not a Honey, a Dear, or a Darling. Quite the opposite. She has a photograph of Vince Lombardi on her dressing table, with this dedication: "Best Wishes to a Tough Little Lady." Airy is the female equivalent of Big Daddy Lipscomb.

I met her at a cocktail party for a minor-league religious activist—a midwestern William Sloane Coffin—and his hard-drinking wife. He was always on his way to or from a conference on American war crimes. He was an Honorary Albanian, I think, or maybe he had been awarded The Order of Brezhnev by the Czechs. This time he was raising money for a defense fund because he had gone to North Vietnam without a passport, and he was about to be indicted by a federal grand jury.

The party was at her parents' house, a very large Federal-style demi-mansion high in University Heights. Her father is an economics professor, a former holder of a John Bascom chair (very big stuff), and filthy rich as a result of insightful trading in public stocks. Ralph hates me. Of course, he really liked her old boyfriend, Alvaro, the Argentine MD. Ralphie was all set to buy a finca outside Buenos Aires—Airy's dowry—when Alvaro ran off to San Francisco with a guy named Jerome, who made his living as a cat-show judge. It's an odd life we lead in the midwest; it can break your heart. Anyway, Milton, who is a fixture at anti-war cocktail parties—he's at the top of everyone's Nixon Loathers list—dragged me along because he wanted company.

What I discovered at these events is that Milton's connections, the infrastructure of confidantes, colleagues, informants, and favor-traders he carefully cultivates, is impressively comprehensive. He seems to know everyone with a bit of power in the state of Wisconsin and has become a repository of sordid tales, vital truths, corrections to and accurate versions of the complicated tales told by devious men. When he enters one of these quasi-political soirées, bellies churn and cold sweat trickles down spines. The guy has dug more dirt than Mr. Greenjeans.

At the Elders' affair, I tagged along, Boswell to his Johnson, more or less silent, observing, making mental notes, forming conclusions. He introduced me about accompanied by sticky handshakes and thin smiles. He introduced me to the Elders, Ralph and Helen, my future in-laws, Mom and Pop. Ralph slapped him on the back, and Helen planted a crimson kiss on his cheek. Milton slid across the room, abandoning me, to mingle with the toilet king of southern Wisconsin and his wife, Lola, whose finest moment was snubbing Pat Nixon in a lady's room in the Palmer House.

The Elders asked me the dirty details about my current status. Cocktail-party chatter mostly, and I lied like a rug. My answers were: med school, the Peace Corps, and "harmony among the races." I've forgotten the questions. Ralph and Helen were perfectly cordial if somewhat overdressed folks, I thought to myself, always willing to overlook a bit of gaucherie. For my part, I was handsomely turned out: blue suit, white shirt, and a red tie. My hair was clean; my beard was trimmed. Had I not had so much to drink, or perhaps had I not drunk it so quickly, I'm sure I would have made a more favorable first impression. As it was, jostled by a herd of pacifists on the way to the buffet (just off a hunger strike and ravenous), I spilled my drink—a corky red wine—on the front of Professor Elder's shirt. I felt bad about it, but what the hell, if you don't want something spilled on your shirt, you shouldn't have a cocktail party. Argue with that logic.

"Christ, I'm sorry," I said. But was I? Strong evidence suggests, although the psychological data needs further analysis, that, inwardly, I was gleeful. Mrs. Elder gave me a stern glance, the first of many, I'm afraid, and prevented me from trying to blot away the offending stain.

"That's all right, Mr. Fitzgerald," she said. "I'll fix things."

Believe me, that old babe could. She was a veritable Arnold Rothstein for Christ's sake. Sobered by my contact with her, I turned away to replace my drink: I needed champagne. The swill they were passing around was barely drinkable, and I thought, with a little luck, I might find the secret cache of Moët. Stung by my faux pas, I slumped barward. What noise! What smoke! The cream of an academical generation were making tiny talk, feverish with rotgut sparkling wine. I was suddenly overcome by the urge to pee and tiptoed to the rear of the house, hoping to find the toilet.

Departing the happy-making, I found myself in a corridor lined with doors. Only one was open sufficiently to invite entry. Inside it was cool, dark, and nearly empty: the Florida room. (I discovered it was called the Florida room in another incarnation, not as a party guest but as Airy's date.) Only the wall sconces were on, dimmed down to a glimmer, and a Beethoven piano concerto was tinkling out of the ceiling. The whole effect, I thought, was that of a waiting room in a very expensive dentist's office.

"Hello," someone said, startling me, "you're Milton's brother, aren't you?"

The voice belonged to a blonde, sitting on a sofa, her legs tucked beneath her, and her arm draped on the backrest. She was smiling at me. She looked pretty (although who could really see in the dark?), wearing a black sweater and tortoiseshell glasses. She was nicely self-contained. Ever the optimist, I smiled back. This was Airy Elder—Elizabeth Elder—the most intelligent person I've known.

"Yes," I said, "Milton's brother."

Her parents called her Airy either for her early precociousness ("she was like fresh air in a stuffy room") or her tininess as an infant ("she was light as air"). I was never able to get a straight answer. Airy, according to my reckoning, is not airy at all. She is down-to-earth, sensible, knowledgeable about such diverse topics as when to plant tomatoes in the tropics (never) and what is the best way to get from

Bal Harbour, Florida, to Bar Harbor, Maine (85-foot yacht). She's a very tough number.

Sitting half in darkness, toplighted by the sconces, she was a very arresting sight. Airy, I will tell you now, has always succeeded, academically. Romantically, she is one of life's losers. Her taste in men (I was the exception that proved the rule, I hope, but perhaps not) is execrable. She seemed to be alone, but I suspected some overearnest shlump was off fetching her a shrimp puff. (Actually, Michael Cox, a cineaste, expert on German Expressionist film, was retrieving stuffed mushrooms and club soda. The guy skeeves me, as Birdwhistle's wife says, truly skeeves me.)

"But I've forgotten your name."

"Henry."

Anyway, it all started there. In other words, and despite my faux pas—spilling wine on her old man's shirt—we became an item. By the time I met Claire, Airy and I were solidly encoupled, asked to weddings with the same engraved invitation. I was not unhappy, at least regarding Airy. She gave me plenty of room and forced me to give her the same. She was orderly, direct, and goal oriented. I was none of those but was trying to get with the program. Then I stumbled across old Claire Cohen and somehow began to doubt the long-term potential of Airy and me. Look, I know I'm cheap.

Eventually, without ever announcing her intentions, Airy began to form plans regarding our future. Foremost among these plans was a career for Henry. In her own reserved fashion, she loved me and wanted to be proud of me. She wasn't going to settle for a deadbeat.

"You have to make plans, Henry." She was after me to explore some options no matter how tentative. I wasn't so sure or so ready.

"You can't just drift in and out of these fantasies: graduate school, law school, or whatever. You should make a plan, Henry, and then try to follow it. I mean, I have a plan. Maybe it's not the best, but I'll find that out. You're just so unambitious."

She struck paydirt with that one. I was a prime example of unambition. I needed to be roused from my stupor. Clang a bell or rattle some pots, because Henry had to get motivated. Do anything, Henry: that was what I said to myself, do something. But what I wanted was still in formation, not yet having settled on a large house or an expensive set of golf clubs. I wanted something else.

It was at the confluence of these streams, then, that I sat in Larry Frick's BurgerTowne—a homage to Formica—having been shaken to my Plantar's wart by Claire Cohen, having whipped Noburu, waiting for Airy Elder.

The lunch crowd had departed, and the waitresses were sweeping beneath the tables and chairs, refilling ketchup bottles and saltshakers. I had gobbled down a double cheeseburger and read *The Capital Times*. A feature story in the green section reported Slinkie-like ripples of religious fervor moving through the general population. Armies of men and women—devotees of guru, swami, visionary—turned from the world's body. Fantastic hypotheses were confirmed by candlelight; secret longings found their consummation. It was possible, according to the paper, for a man to make a million dollars—quickly, by manipulating paper—and then in the middle of the night in Lincoln Park in Chicago be struck with a holy vision so intense that he shucked off his old life and emerged into the new, utterly transformed.

Personally, I was going to stick to Sydney Omarr. Today, for example, something was in retrograde and, reading between the lines, I could see I was in for a rough time. No long trips for Henry, period. I was sipping a Coke, becoming annoyed at Airy for being late, when a shadow fell across my table. A figure, a smallish man, interposed himself between me and the bright light pouring through the plate glass. Already in a testy mood, this was too much. I looked up, furious.

"Hey," I said, "you're in my light."

"Son, don't I know you?"

I don't like to talk to strangers.

"No."

"I think we've met before. Can I talk to you for a moment?"

"About what?"

"Your destiny. It may change your life."

Bingo. Just the conversation I was looking for. I decided to talk to him and, if there were a problem, to blame Airy, who after all started me down this road. She's the one who's obsessed with my future. He took my silence as a form of approval. I suppose it was.

"Leonard Gent," he said, extending his hand.

A polite boy in a raucous time, I shook it.

"Henry Fitzgerald."

Gent was almost handsome: solidly built, dark, finely featured. His good looks in the end were betrayed by a bit of an alcoholic's bloat, a chubby jowl, and a chin with its half-chin companion. He needed some sun: his skin had the waxy pallor of a corpse. Gent's hair was black, and he combed it straight back, dressing it with shiny teenage hair gook. He probably once had a pomaded pompadour, a man of the Fifties, an Ike liker, an Elvis maven. He clung to this particle of his youth by not abandoning Brylcream.

His clothes were modified junk-shop workingman's garb: heavy charcoal gray trousers a bit tattered in the cuff; a white permanent-press shirt buttoned tight to the neck. He didn't wear a tie. His outercoat was an olive-drab parka—army surplus, designed for DMZ duty in Korea. It fell well below his knees, which made him seem even more beaten up, down and out. This was just before he commenced his street-corner sermonizing era. He was trying to be one of the boys, a man of the underdogs, a person of the people, one of the Brotherhood of the Barroom. But he wasn't like them at all; the son of a bitch had had a vision. He bristled with vulgar energy. Passivity, six packs of Budweiser beer, and long winter evenings crouched in front of the T and V weren't on Gent's agenda. If he had any more juice, he'd be totally out of control, a mass murderer, this year's Richard Speck. From the start, Gent scared the shit out of me, especially when he gave me that sidelong stare, the Gent Eyeball— the lascivious look that hypnotized the just and the unjust in equal numbers.

"Henry"—right away we're on a first-name basis—"I'm a religious man. I believe in repentance and grace. You follow me?"

"Sure."

"I used to be a sinner. A bad one. I led a life of degradation and folly, and now I'm trying to help others, young people, rescue them from the streets of our great cities and our tiny towns. Pull them away from temptation, from drugs and booze. Free them from the terror of the dark alley, the pimp's promises, the phony high. Do you hear what I'm saying, Henry?"

His hands were clasped together in an amphetamine-white grip. This was pretty good actually: "the dark alley" riff was effective.

"I think so," I said.

"You know, Henry, I sat here for a long time watching you. You seemed lost to me. You seem the center of a vivid unhappiness. Pain and confusion, that's what I saw in your face. And you know what I think?"

"What?"

"It's only going to get worse. I repeat, you seem unhappy."

"I'm not unhappy."

"Yes, yes, yes you are."

Here I began to get bored. He was going to have to do more than this to keep the ball in play. I began to put on my jacket.

He stared at the floor.

"Henry, Henry. Do you know what a blowjob is?"

"Pardon me?" I was going to give him a chance to retract his impertinence before I hit him with a ketchup bottle.

"A blowjob, fellatio, you know."

A longish pause ensued. He gave me that Hypnotizing Cobra Look, and it made me squirm.

"Listen, you creep . . ." I began but could not finish.

He began to speak, fluently and with great sincerity. It was his Oral Sex in Lincoln Park Rap, a routine which I was to hear again and again in various venues. I realize now that he must have practiced this speech before the mirror, and I suspect that I may have been the first awestruck auditor. He probably sought a harmless-looking person to road test his pitch on. That most harmless-looking of souls? Henry Fitzgerald. Do I know what a blowjob is? Do I listen patiently to the sad words of a devious man? Of course.

"Good," he said, "you at least know what I'm talking about. Henry, In Chicago on 7 June 1969 I was wandering about Lincoln Park looking for sexual gratification. You know what I'm saying, I was willing to pay some young kid to do it. Or I was willing to pay him in kind. Shocking, isn't it, Henry? I can see your disapproval. I did a lot worse than that, believe me."

I wasn't especially shocked. I just didn't feel like talking about Leonard's odd sexual habits just then. I wanted Airy to show up so I could go home. It had been a long day. Christ, I was low.

"No, Leonard," I said, "I'm not shocked." The world can be such a sad place, filled with silly, vile men like Lenny Gent. Titans of the perverse; gutter nutballs. And I thought of my father then, of his solidity and strength, of the great things he dared: of treks into the wilderness, of flights over sunlighted mountains, of loving a virtuous woman and two small sons. I felt I had sunk to a very low state to sit and listen to this shabby and ill-mannered hillbilly talk about his evil obsessions.

"Can you guess what happened?"

"You were arrested, sent to jail, and raped by a pack of sodomists."

"I'm being serious."

"Gang rape in prison isn't serious?"

He ignored my question, which I thought fairly apposite.

"I went into a toilet in the park, Henry, near a bandshell. It was dark and dank. I had been there before. A lot of men meet there in the darkness, Henry, sad men, lost men, hungry for human contact. It was late. Chicago is a dangerous city late at night, Henry, did you know that?"

"I've heard. Look, Leonard, is there a point to this story?"

"Patience, Henry. I was not a happy man. I had just made a fortune in the commodities market. Winter wheat and sorghum. [Lies, by the way; Gent didn't know sorghum from Juicy Fruit.] I was rich. I could do whatever I wanted. What was it I did? I walked through the darkness, filled with need, desire. It's not my desire that I regret; desire after all is merely a consequence of being a man. My shame was the outlet I sought; the humiliation and pain that haunted me. What I wanted was a blowjob performed by a child in a fetid toilet stall in the heart of a ruined city. Something happened, Henry."

Just wait, I thought, just wait until I tell Birdwhistle this. Things happen all right, Birdwhistle.

"Something happened to change my life."

Why me? Milton is approached by sweet little Girl Scouts dressed in little green uniforms asking him to buy cookies. I get nutball blowjob buffs demanding that I listen to their oral-sex/salvation sermons. I wanted him to wrap this up, ask for money, and find someone else to torture. But blowjob did not seem quite the point. He was leading me up to a higher summit. Some sort of K2 of the soul.

"A young black man stepped out of the darkness and grabbed me by the shoulder. I thought he was a mugger. I had money, an expensive watch. I was terrified of him. I was sure he was going to kill me. I fell to my knees and begged him not to hurt me. But he helped me to my feet instead and held me close. It was a tender embrace. He had a kind face, radiant with love and understanding. 'Leonard,' he said to me, 'this life you are leading is villainous, evil. It is a one-way street. You have to find a way out of it. Look for a house on the hill, and you'll find the love of Christ.' That's all he said. But I was filled with an unbelievable joy. My life had meaning."

"Look, Mr. Gent, I have to go."

"You don't believe me, do you?"

"Well, Leonard, here's the thing: as epiphanies go this one is a little ambiguous. I thought maybe you'd see the baby Jesus or maybe you'd have a tumor suddenly go zap and disappear. Something with a little punch."

"I see. Well, that is what happened. I was touched by something holy, something divine. In the park, in the darkness, Jesus sent a messenger to me and saved me from a life of terror and destruction. I was destroying lives and would have destroyed more. No kidding."

Did I suspect, even for an instant, he was kidding? I though Gent was a genuine psychopath, a dangerous guy. He was sweating now and squeezing his hands together and the rough skin of his palms grated like sandpaper. He was truly loony. I believed him; a lot of people would believe him. Unless he was carted off, I had the feeling he was about to become famous, even if locally.

"I really have to go," I said.

"I've been on the road for a long time," he said. He pointed to what had to be his vehicle, a '60 Chevrolet Impala, hand-painted a

Passion purple (the color of a grape-juice stain on a beige carpet) and decorated with golden crosses. *"Seek the Love of Jesus"* was painted in a slanting script beginning at the rear tire and traveling across the passenger-side front door, finally scrunching itself tortuously between the wheel well and the hood.

"Do you know what I've discovered?"

"No, and this is the last question, okay, Leonard?"

"I've found that the search is at least as important as the discovery. I searched until I was terribly weary, and now I've found my house. I'm going to stop and rest for a while."

"Fantastic."

"Don't patronize me. You're searching after something as well; in fact, your search is just the same as mine."

"What would that be?"

"You know. Peace or something like it."

"Are you crazy? Lay off the cheap wine. Take some nourishment."

"Mock me. You know I'm right."

"I'm not mocking you, pal. I'm just saying something that should be self-evident: you're fucking out of your mind. House on the hill, messengers from Jesus in fellatio parlors. Look at that car of yours: is that the work of a stable personality?"

I was getting a little worked up. Peace! Why, I had about all the peace I could stand. What I needed was a little action. You dog that walks like a man, I thought, go howl at the moon. I stormed out.

The son of a bitch smiled at me with unnerving serenity.

"I'm right about you, Henry, and you know it. We'll meet again."

Correct. We would meet again. Outside I took a deep breath. I would have liked to have taken a belt sander to get that conversation off my brain. I felt like my pocket had been picked. The warmth of the sun cheered me up a bit. Airy, I guessed, had gone to the library to spend some time with a difficult translation. Classical languages are her second love; I'm vain enough to think I'm her first. I decided to walk down State Street toward the library, hoping she was on her way.

I felt badly shaken by the events of the day. After a somnolent winter, during which I had barely budged from my cave, suddenly, my life was filled with complexity and controversy. (I'm not really complaining. I'm a complexity and controversy aficionado.) I saw Airy weaving through a middle ground of shoulders and heads, solemn and thoughtful, coming from the library. She was wrapped up in her Mexican sweater, walking slowly, mesmerized by the beauty of an ancient, dead language. I was never happier to see her.

7

The Sorrows of Claire

SO I DECIDED to behave myself. Weeks passed and I didn't see Claire. I stayed away from our rendezvous. No more sniffing around Claire's tree, I promised myself. What was the percentage in groping with C. Cohen in broad daylight on a busy street? Zero. Claire was obviously in a bit of turmoil about things, and turmoil, as Milton has so generously pointed out, is something I don't need. I like it; I just don't need it.

I have had a shaky romantical history, that's the consensus. Who hasn't? Still with all this Claire squeezing at various venues, I was having serious tertiary worries about my affianced. The fact is Airy was beginning to bore me. An unpleasant admission, but who likes to be threatened with demotion to the deep minors because, for example, his feet smell? It's genetic anyway. All right, maybe I should change my socks every day, but sometimes I sleep with my shoes on.

Most critically, it seemed that I had an Outlook Problem. The Outlook Problem was a major motif in arguments with Airy. In short, I wasn't serious enough. I felt bad about that; I did. I tried to get serious. I failed. I was sternly reprimanded. Then, totally dispirited by my lumpishness, I would have to go out and try to cheer up: mostly with B. Birdwhistle and not infrequently by slipping cash money into the G strings of Bambi or Loralei, girls who danced semi-naked at the Dangle Lounge.

However, I decided to put all that behind me, strap myself into the Cockpit of Sobriety. I was going to impress on Airy, who was about to leave for Greece, that I was a serious guy, to be taken seriously. She didn't have to dump me for some fey grad student in English Literature. The kind of guy who had an Irish setter named Leobloom and who flew to New York once a month to have his hair styled by a French lesbian. (Oh yeah, I'd seen that sleazoid Barry Boyarski making nice-nice with Airy while he thought my back was turned. I don't miss much. The son of a bitch splashed on cologne like he was the Polo Correspondent for *Town and Country*.) And there was an additional inducement for getting my mind right re Airy: Claire had disappeared. Okay, maybe once or twice I *had* sought her out in all the old romantic places, but she was hiding from Henry. What alarmed me was how much I missed her.

I was feeling well pleased with my progress as I walked away from a little birthday celebration at my brother's house (20 May 1972: my twenty-third year to heaven). My brother was blue, but I felt great, so we swilled champagne (the drink of choice for the Fitzgerald boys) hoping that our moods would meet in the middle. It was just Milton and me hitting five irons off his front lawn into an adjoining corn-field, sucking the bubbly right out of the bottle. (If they ever built a Five Iron Golf Course, Milton would have the low handicap. The man is a genius with a five iron.) Milton went to bed after we finished the last jeroboam. I marched homeward, no longer a lonesome trav-eler but a happy man on a steamy spring night.

Walking through James Madison Park, I often run into people I know. That's how I found Claire, or vice versa. Anyway, I heard my name called out of the darkness.

"Henry," said the voice, "I've been looking for you."

Perched at the apex of a steel playground apparatus, the dome of a jungle gym, a polar presence, was Claire; also alone, looking east, faced away from the lake, she must have seen me coming for a long time, as I walked down the long Gorham Street hill and angled across the grassless, dusty plain of the park.

"Why are you walking so slowly?" she asked.

"Strong drink."

"Are you drunk?"

"I was almost drunk, but I sweated myself sober. What are you doing out here? It's past twelve."

The night was steamy in the midwestern fashion. Sweat trickled into my crotch; my T-shirt was yoked with perspiration.

"Fresh air," she said. "Too hot."

"Can I come up?"

"Of course. It's nice up here. Great view."

I climbed the apparatus quickly. I was in that interesting twilight between being a little drunk and virtually (though not totally) sober. I climbed carefully, like an amateur Alpinist, toward Claire. I didn't want to fall for many reasons. She had on a white T-shirt and a pair of khaki shorts. They were tight across the behind and very short. Her legs were slender and muscular, and when she walked the muscles rippled in her thighs. This is the kind of stuff I notice. She was a healthy girl, an athlete. I hadn't seen her in what seemed like a long time, probably ten days. It was finals time, maybe she had been busy. She was sunburned, and her nose was peeling. Her hair was pulled back into a thick Claireish ponytail.

Having achieved the summit, I was forced to share a tiny perch with Claire. I had to reach past her—my arm angled like a support strut—past the small of her back and her rear end. To our right, a local motorcycle gang—the Williamson Street Marauders—was having a weenie roast, mid-night barbecue. Spaced erratically throughout the park (or according to a pattern I was never able to decipher) were picnic tables and grills—55-gallon barrels split vertically, welded onto a steel tripod, and covered with a grate. Fire burst out of two of these barrels—the site of the cookout—dramatically. The silhouettes of the bikers moved in front of the flames.

The bikers had long hair, baby-fine blond hair—perhaps such mock warriorhood is a Nordic atavism—which hung down their backs. In the heat of the fires, their hair fluffed around their faces; the effect was fetching. Each of them wore his "colors"—the sleeveless denim jacket which can be read like a barometer—geography, typography, the myths and symbols of their particular clan had meaning, indicated how seriously these boys should be taken.

Middle-aged, they were sad to watch in their decline from ferocity. Their wives and girlfriends were with them, and they sat in a frumpy knot near the beer, talking about TV dinners and television starlets. The fire did not relent; it seems as if they had tapped a direct line to hell.

"Maybe they used napalm," Claire said, staring at the fire. (All that flame and smoke to char a few hamburgers seemed excessive.)

"Don't talk so loud," I said, "you'd be just another morsel."

"They're all right," she said, "they keep offering me beer."

And, in fact, the biggest of them—you'd have to measure a man as large as this in cubic yards—walked over to us, two cans of beer held in his hand and a barbiturate smile on his face.

"Hey," he said, "I'm Lynn Ludlow. Hope we're not bothering you kids. We're having our anniversary picnic. Ten years. I came to give you guys a beer if you want one. Join the celebration."

He climbed up two tiers on the dome and reached up. The beers were wet on the outside—they had been sitting in a garbage can full of ice water—and the water ran down his hand, trickling into the cuff of his jacket. "Ludlow" was stitched on the breast of his jacket. I thought he might be a good match for my landlady, who was as fierce as Attila's wife in her post-Vatican II way.

"Thanks," I said.

I took the beers, smiling.

"Hey, buddy," Ludlow said, "you know anything about abandoned Mayan cities? The boys and I were attempting to isolate the causes for the evacuation of Machu Picchu. I've been saying there must have been an epidemical insult to the general health. My pal Anthony, he's the one with the wooden leg, says we shouldn't overlook the possibility the inhabitants were kidnapped by humanoids from elsewhere in the galaxy to revivify a depleted gene pool. What do you think?"

"Epidemic. No question. Typhus or something."

"Exactly. Good man. Machu Picchu and all that," Lynn Ludlow said, "I always wanted to go there. Mysteries, mysteries."

He threw himself against the tubes of the jungle gym, stretched out in a posture of utter defeat. He stared at the ground for many moments in absolute silence.

"Christ," he said, "mysterious things are so fucking beautiful."

He climbed down, smiled at us like a man with a broken heart, and went back to the party. He stood with his arms folded watching his steak cook, a sad figure indeed. Mysterious things seemed to move him out of his ordinary orbit. Perhaps this is as it should be.

"I've been looking for you today, Henry, you weren't in your usual spots."

My usual spots: a certain table in the corner in the Union Cafeteria, a table in the graduate reading room, a booth in an Italian restaurant. I have a tendency to be habitual and predictable. I can be found in those spots, often expect to be found there. Not a good thing. Claire has found me many times, and each time we pretend it is an accident. Tonight was the first time she made her searching me out explicit.

"I spent the day with Milton. He made dinner for me. He lost a case on appeal today, and he was feeling sort of blue."

"How is he now?"

"Oh, he's fine. He got drunk, and I had to put him to bed. I'm afraid he's entering a period of obsessive behavior."

"Henry, can I tell you something?"

"Please."

"I like you."

"I like you, too, Claire. I thought we had gotten beyond that stage."

She looked up over the lake. She was pensive, that old-fashioned word for an old-fashioned girl. Her face was turned away: I could see only the smooth, sculpted line of her cheek and jaw. Her skin was perfect: dewy and fresh. Looking at her with utter concentration, I thought she was becoming more womanly. I found that not a little daunting. Hey, Lynn Ludlow, here is a mystery for you: this is a process that will make Machu Picchu seem tidy, explicable, as limpid as the Caribbean at dusk.

"Did I say something stupid?" I asked. With dispiriting regularity in the past the answer has been yes.

"No."

"What's wrong?"

"I'm pregnant again."

My throat constricted, and my pulse raced. Who knows why? It wasn't my child. But I couldn't listen to Claire without strong emotion, and this set of circumstances intensified and prolonged whatever I was feeling.

"Again?"

"Yeah. I seem to be as fertile as hell. I'm on the pill, but it doesn't seem to matter. I keep getting knocked up."

"You were pregnant before?"

I was slow to absorb this megadose of fact. Claire, preggers, one more time.

"This October. I had an abortion. Obviously."

"Nicky?"

"No, Gordie Howe."

"Claire, I don't like Nicky."

"He doesn't like you either."

Claire moved closer to me. After a shower she dusts herself luxuriantly with baby powder, and that was what I smelled. I was going to say something but decided a reference to children in diapers, at this moment, was inappropriate. I moved my head close to hers and kissed her neck. Give me an opportunity to nibble on a neck and I'll take it, regardless of the circumstances. It's hard to imagine a less appropriate moment to slobber on Claire's shoulder blade.

Our beer cans fell to the ground. She didn't resist much, but her heart wasn't in it. She grabbed her ponytail and pulled it aside, then pushed me gently away. Because of the precariousness of our perch, serious grappling was out of the question. I kissed her a few more times, suddenly very aware of gravity. We teetered passionately, holding onto the bars with one hand and our toes.

"We can't do this," she said, "it's stupid."

"Do you mean, it's stupid where we're doing it or it's stupid in general?"

"In general."

"Thanks."

"It's not personal, Henry. I really like you. Under normal conditions I would forget about Nicky and neck with you up here all night. I have this serious problem: I'm pregnant."

Timing is everything, I told myself. Patience, pal.

"Okay," I said. "What are you going to do?"

"I'm going to have another abortion, I guess. What choices do I have?"

"The obvious one. What does Nicky say?"

"Not a thing because he doesn't know, and he's not going to know. He's an absolute shit."

"I agree."

"He was unbelievably obnoxious this fall. He said it was my fault. He practically accused me of getting pregnant on purpose. For Christ sake, what does he think he was doing, fucking the mattress? He's got to share some of the responsibility. I don't have any money, Henry, and I'll be damned if I'll ask him for another dime."

Claire raised her hands to her face and placed them, like parentheses, on her temples. She was untouchable, alone. She was intent on not breaking down, on being strong and willful. It occupied her complete attention. Henry was elsewhere, in the world of colors, of warm breezes, of droplets of sweat at the back of one's neck. Claire was inside herself, in a little room with no windows and the exit blocked by fishing tackle and cardboard boxes. Trees moved in the wind, and little ground-bound currents of air carried along candy wrappers and shards of the day's news. The smell of burning animal flesh was greatly in evidence. I felt the polished solidity of the steel bar. It was paintless, except for small white scabs. Claire was unsupported as she sat on the bar, only the friction of our hips held her in place. I put my hand, gently, on her waist because I was alarmed at the tentativeness of her perch.

"I feel real bad, Henry. This is almost too much."

"Hey," I said, "things have to get better."

"They don't have to. I've found that out, Henry. I have a favor to ask. I am embarrassed because it's not your responsibility. You don't deserve this."

Suddenly, I knew why Claire had been looking for me. I was neither angry nor sad: I had plenty of money and was happy to give her some. Borrowing money from an acquaintance—albeit a favorably disposed one, me, that is—did not seem to be a good idea, but she was pregnant and not I. Now neither of us was aroused; a wild understatement. The flaccidity I was experiencing can only be a rare thing. Claire wanted badly to cry: her lower lip trembled, but she remained dry-eyed. (I felt a little like crying, too.) I had never gotten anyone pregnant. I was saddened by the choices she was forced to make. For a woman in her youth to make this decision—not to carry her child to term—seemed to me to be an awesome thing. Her two pregnancies and her abortion seemed to resonate through her life like vibrations from a broken radio.

We were two souls out of place among the jolly-making. Morose Lynn Ludlow had recovered and was dancing by the barbecue pits with gentle, preoccupied steps. He was back in familiar territory, I guess, having shaken off the mysterious.

"I can lend you the money, Claire."

My voice was full of affection.

"I need two hundred and forty dollars. I have only twenty-four. It would only be a loan, and probably only for a few days. I'm expecting money for graduation."

"I can give you a check. Or would you rather have cash?" I was trying to make this as easy as possible.

"Cash. It would be simpler."

"Is Monday soon enough?"

"I have an appointment Thursday. Just give me the money then."

"How do you feel?"

"Stupid."

"You shouldn't, Claire. Things happen."

That was in the nature of a totally fatuous remark. Claire, wisely, didn't respond to it. I'm sure she thought I was a genial idiot, though.

She placed her hand on my forearm.

"Thanks, Henry."

It occurred to me that this was the first time I had ever been seriously called upon to help someone. True, I didn't actually *do* that much. Still, I was pleased. I thought that I was kind. The park was jumping, now early on a Saturday a.m. Claire yawned and leaned sideways, putting her forehead against my shoulder. You know, I really don't know my ass from my elbow about women. What the hell was I doing? I was getting in way over my head, funding abortions and necking with someone else's girlfriend.

We climbed down and walked through the park. Our shoes raised dust on the baseball infield. I made another grab for Claire near second base. (She slid underneath the tag.) We walked up the Gilman Street hill which led to our homes. We were silent. And we said goodnight in the shadow of an elm tree across the street from her apartment building. She kissed me, chastely, on the cheek. Her cheek was uncommonly cool and smooth. She was an altogether womanly creature, and I was tempted to pull her into my arms. I resisted but only because the heel of her hand was planted in my chest.

"Goodnight, Henry," she said. "I'll call you."

I didn't bother to tell her it would probably be pointless to call me because I was hardly ever home.

"You can find me in my usual spots," I said, "if you want."

She walked down the bush-bordered path that led to her entry—to the basement apartment she shared with Waller. (He was away in New Jersey concocting toxic wastes, which he dumped on village playgrounds and Little League fields.)

I was very happy Claire had looked for me; happier still I was found. Maybe this being serious was a feasible proposition. I watched her as she walked away. In a dark world, and I have learned it is a very dark place indeed, Claire's white T-shirt was the whitest thing. If I live a long life, so filled with extraordinary circumstances, improbable coincidences, great adventure, amusing happenstance that I will require an amanuensis to record them properly—and I intend to—this image will linger: Claire in darkness, walking slowly away from me. The sorrows of Claire.

8

Birdwhistle Burdened

LONELY AS A cloud I walked home. I really had no reason to be unhappy, and I wasn't. What I was was worse: agitated. I sat on my steps for a few minutes, wondering whether or not I should call Airy (who was home soundly asleep) or Noburu (who was upstairs soundly asleep)—they are both early-to-rise and early-to-bed types. It must have been two a.m. Many apartment lights were still on; a loud party was percolating up the street. A multi-speakered stereo system—the expensive kind that comes from trust-fund money or drug-sales profits—was playing a gloomy jazz album. Too dirgelike and downbeat for a party, I thought; hey, let's have a good time up there. The music was very loud—all the sadder because it was so—and seemed trapped between two moderate-rise apartment buildings, bouncing back and forth off their cinder-block sides like an image caught between two mirrors.

Manfred Grace's lights were on (he lives across the hall from me), but I wasn't in the mood for a tendentious lecture on Thomas Mann or post-Marxist thought in pre-Nazi Germany. He was a former Franciscan priest (he and Sister Lawrence were a scandalous combo in Fort Wayne, Indiana). He inherited some money and bought a liquor store. He deserted the church for, in addition to the fleshly attractions of his lover, old-fashioned entrepreneurship. No contradiction there, of course. He had clearly abandoned all his vows except the one of alleged poverty; he lived like a rat. I knew he would be at his desk, an unfiltered cigarette burning in his right hand, listening to early Beethoven and reading Walter Benjamin. No, I won't be speaking to Manfred Grace tonight; I am too distracted to talk about the work of art in the age of mechanical reproduction. I would much rather talk about women and my problems with them; those problems being consistent and embarrassing. I needed advice.

I tapped my feet to the music, listlessly. I felt energyless. A galvometer attached to my tootsies would have registered virtually nil. I tapped and tapped, my chin in my hand, deep in thought. Gradually, a plan formed; gradually, I revived. Shortly, I was as ready as a shortstop for anything hit in my direction. I was thinking about Claire and about the odd set of circumstances into which she had fallen and into which I was being tugged, bitter inch by bitter inch. I had this feeling in my heart of hearts that there was going to be a couple of fourth-and-fifteens before I gave my pads back to the equipment manager. It's nights like this that I felt most like an orphan.

I went inside, a modern Magellan, navigating in the dark. I swept around the Mission-style rocking chair (Airy had bought it for $19 in a thrift shop in Black Earth), nudged aside an Ottoman (a footstool, not a citizen of a defeated empire). I was going on a midnight ramble, and I needed some American money.

The phone rang.

"Henry?"

It was Milton, in a deep funk.

"Hi, Milton."

"Did I say anything about my ex-wife?"

"Nothing you haven't said before." Milton has not yet accepted the fact his wife left him for another and, to his way of thinking, inferior man. Occasionally, he indulges his deep unhappiness.

"I just want you to know I'm not as pitiful as I sound."

"Milton, you're drunk. Go back to sleep."

"I just wanted you to know that."

"I know that."

"Good. Because I'm completely over her."

"I know you are."

"I'm going out with someone very nice now."

"Who's that?"

"I can't remember her name. I have to throw up, Henry. Good-night."

I was even readier to hit the bricks, and I still needed money.

In a ceramic pot on my desk (glazed white with a narrow blue line near its shoulder) is about three thousand dollars. The lid has a crack in it which I have repaired with some sort of magic adhesive and duct tape, enhancing the beauty and restoring the functionality of the entire assemblage. I bought this pot at a craft fair held in the parking lot of the Crocker National Bank in Santa Cruz, California. I spent a summer in Santa Cruz, a period of my life that is now only a spasm of miserable memory: a white roller coaster against an overcast sky; a rocky beach against which green-foamed waves fell monotonously; a bookstore filled with works about wholistic medicine and organic farming; willowly blond-haired hippies living in the Santa Cruz Mountains. I was there with my uncle, who was overseeing the construction of his last commission: a mountain aerie for a Chicago liquor-store mogul. (The mogul was retiring to San Jose, in the foothills just on the western outskirts of town.)

I turned on the desk light, a crane-necked architect's lamp that usually evades my grasp, dodging away cleverly at the last vital instant. I slapped at it in the darkness, and it leaped back and hit the wall, vibrating with a springy twang. Captured and snapped on, the light shone on the center of my desk, the lump of correspondence, the lawyer's crisp letters, and the ugly clot of torn-out notebook pages. I sat down. My records are confused: offers to subscribe to magazines, inquiries from the university (library books: where are they?), old letters from Airy, Airy's notes from a history class, and a perky missive she had written in the first days of our love affair on a sheet of legal paper which began "Henry, you sweet thing" and closed almost lasciviously. These papers seethed in a state of incompleteness. They were largely unresponded to; they would very likely never be responded to. The cash is in the jar as an emergency fund, designed to keep creditors off my trail. I am a bad bill payer, waiting for the very last moment. (This is an adolescent form of rebellion, I suppose.) My landlady usually has to fetch the rent herself, three days after it's due. She is nasty about it, and so I wave a thick wad of bills in her face and peel off tens and plop them into a ragged-edged pile.

Money, money, money. Currently I have $3040 in my jug: 102 twenties and 100 tens. Claire needs $240, leaving me with $2800. Enough money to get me to Paris, London, Nairobi, anywhere. Graduate students in stinking graduate-student housing with tiny babies to feed and tearful wives to comfort with the promise of a mock Tudor in some distant Professor's Park could live like sheikhs on the amount of money I've dropped behind my sofa. Some earnest and harried soul poring over a statistics text in a cramped library carrel can't afford the price of sirloin steak, and here I am with cash to burn. I could afford to buy a bunch of abortions with this dough. I could buy ten more and still have enough left over for a plane ticket to the Caribbean and three nights in a seaside hotel. The sad fact is this money means very little to me. I would trade it all for one hour with my parents; for one long walk through the countryside with my old man. I can hear a mosquito buzzing in a dark corner, patiently. Sister Larry's toilet flushes; she's suffering from another urinary tract infection. The antibiotics she's taking, she told me last night in her cups (she swills South African sherry), have turned her urine a bright orange.

I stuck Claire's twelve twenties in an old telephone-company envelope (the one that held the threateningly ugly final disconnection notice). I felt bad for Claire; I felt her loneliness. How is it a woman of such intelligence, spirit, and beauty can be so sad? I know I don't have any answers, which perplexes me, who is anxious for answers.

When I fall into this state, up against the wall, on a hot spring night bursting with rare blooms, I turn my face and direct my feet toward Birdwhistle: not found on any map, unlisted in the phone book, can't find him by looking but only by happy accident. Birdwhistle makes doughnuts. He works at night making doughnuts in splendid isolation, dusted with flour and spices, churning huge bowls of dough mix into huge slabs of dough, which in turn becomes the delicate edibles on thousands of breakfast tables. After a period of desperation (one failed marriage and a suicide attempt) he has found and married the woman of his dreams, Crescent Laverno (some complications exist). They have a young son, Harry.

By training and true talent he's an artist, a bookbinder, a fine one specializing in ancient volumes and irreplaceable knowledge (he corresponds with the chief bookbinder in the Vatican, Monsignor Capeeci). There is no money in irreplaceable knowledge (not enough anyway) so he supports himself in the doughnut trade. He has become a king of doughnuts. He finds this mystifying in the abstract, but happy is the man who deposits handfuls of cash every Thursday morning. Birdwhistle is a boon companion on a hot night.

I changed my clothes (a rain-filled breeze out of the southeast had commenced blowing), stashed my cash, and slipped out into the darkness. I am ready to ramble. Lately, I have developed odd habits: night walking or hiding away in the basements of research libraries (a current favorite is level four of the Federal Document Depository). A person could conceivably spend a lifetime doing these things, but I don't want to. I think it's okay for a short time to be spooky and move through night landscapes, feeling unattached. I'm getting near the end of that epoch, however; too much more of this stuff and even I'll begin to worry about myself. I definitely don't aspire to geekdom, to being a weirdo, some psycho soldier pacified by Thorazine staring out the window of a YMCA coffee shop.

The wind brought a drizzle, and the drizzle shut down the city. Momentarily, the drizzle put me off. I was inclined to go back to my apartment and go to bed. The rain added a pretty sound: the beguiling swish of car tires through water-covered streets. No, by God, a little rain was not going to discourage me. If you set a course, you shouldn't waver. The night has had a somber aspect (how often is one asked to fund an abortion?). I set off for Birdwhistle's like a man about to steal home, dancing forward on the balls of my feet. Lord, I was becoming strange. I was a strange boy, full of secrets, silent for days, easily hurt. My brother calls me Old Weird Henry. Most people assume he is joking. He isn't. Well, I am weird. I have odd concerns and obsessions. And I did go out in the middle of the night wearing an old baseball cap to meet a whole-wheat doughnut maker because I felt both aroused and touched by a sad, pretty girl. Along that conifer-bordered path—the darkest part of the woods—trouble was poised in a deadly crouch.

I felt fine once I began to move: loose-limbed, limber, joints lubricated with graphite. Birdwhistle's operation occupies a defunct diner. He uses the kitchen only. The rest of the joint is still more or less intact, but ghostly: stools still spin, booths are ripped along the line where hip and fabric meet, napkin holders yawn rusted open, a coffee pot sits on its steel pad, utterly empty (Birdwhistle has found the bottom of the bottomless cup). He has remodeled the kitchen to high-tech functionality: the paradigm, the acme of doughnut creativity. Every surface that could possibly be skinned with stainless steel has been. It is polished to perfection; the place is a doughnut maker's Versailles with its own Hall of Mirrors.

"I just hose the joint down in the morning, Henry," Birdwhistle said, "and buff it with this electric gizmo. It looks like a sheepskin thing fastened to a rubber disk and mounted on an electric drill. I buff and buff. I buff the hell out of it. Shines like the beach, like the sun coming up over the mountains."

His operation is on Monroe Street, east of the football stadium, wedged between a laundromat and a shoe repair shop. The glass front of his diner has been plywooded over (Monroe Street somehow got trashed during one of the Days of Rage knockoff demonstrations), and the plywood painted red. (Birdwhistle, I am reluctant to admit, is tight with his money. He didn't plan to replace the glass until the war was over, although that decision also smacked of domestic politics as well, his wife being a well-known hippie communist. The plywood became a place to post bills, mostly notices about upcoming meetings of the Young Trotsky League. The YTL was not an organization for baseball-playing lefties, but the brainchild of Mrs. Birdwhistle, and dedicated to eliminating any remnants of Stalinism from radical thought.) Over the red, in bright white letters, towering capitals, he had painted this slogan: BIRDWHISTLE! It was a mysterious exclamation, soaring out through politics-stricken streets, through the dinginess of a midwestern spring cityscape (salt-whitened blacktop, cracked concrete, parking lots full of rusty Ford station wagons, aged widows carrying home one pork chop and one can of tuna fish from the market). Birdwhistle, *Birdwhistleisme*, is vivid and violent.

My trip was uneventful; I passed through the empty streets like the rain, close to the curbs, clinging to the gutter. Bob has been held up twice, both times by the same codeine addict, and so he has installed security devices. The exterior door is a sheet-steel monster, with a lock impossible to penetrate with anything but an anti-tank missile. You have to buzz to alert him to your presence and then identify yourself into an intercom. Should his elaborate security be breached he keeps a Browning shotgun, loaded with one shell, within easy reach behind a bag of raisins. If provoked, he will use this weapon. Unfortunately, little enough will provoke him. So, the moment or two between my sounding the buzzer, the throwing open of the door, and the flashing of his famous grin is tinctured with dread. Bob is tethered with only the slenderest of strings to normal and well-socialized behavior. This is why I love him so.

Moody, unpredictable, and violent is Birdwhistle at his worst; brave, intelligent, and wise is Birdwhistle at his best.

But before I can buzz, a voice blurts out of a new black box inserted, like a pacemaker, into the heart of his steel door. He has retrofitted his security system; he has taken his technology one step farther.

"Henry"—Birdwhistle's voice is easily recognized—"you're on fucking TV, Bubba." But he doesn't sound chipper at all; he sounds downright glum.

A camera has been installed over the door, captured in a steel mesh box with a camera-lens aperture.

"Don't bother punching that black button, you're wired. Microphone is built into the camera. Say something. This is a test. You're my first intruder."

"Bob?"

"That's it. Keep talking."

"Where are you?"

"I'm in Nepal."

"I mean really."

"I'm in the kitchen, Henry. Where else would I be? I just had my closed-circuit television installed today and I'm checking it out. I'm looking at you in the monitor over my countertop. You look great on TV. Except you look shorter than real life, if that's possible."

"Can you let me in?"

"Monday."

"It's raining out here, Bob. Let me in."

"The electric switch that'll open the door is going to be installed Monday. The electrician had some sort of family emergency. His son swallowed a peach pit or something."

"Can you open it now?"

"Sure, by hand."

"Okay, then, will you open it? I'm getting wet."

"Sorry, Hank."

His voice sounded tinny and far away. Maybe he was in Nepal. The rain was falling quite heavily now, thank you, and I was soggy.

"Bob, the door."

"I'm on the way. Hold tight."

Birdwhistle is built like a tributary of the Upper Mississippi: thin, elastic, irregular. His face seems unfinished, a confusion of converging planes. Many women find this rough-hewn quality (he looks like he could be a cowboy, a Badlands buckeroo) attractive. He's hideously tall (at least six foot four) but bulging in the belly, beginning to outgrow his wardrobe (it pops out in a half moon from beneath his T-shirts).

Birdwhistle was a Buddhist or is still a Buddhist. I have never been clear about his religion. He shaves his head, leaving only a velvety stubble. He said he was a Buddhist anyway, but do Buddhists eat spareribs? Birdwhistle does. A large, sinuous, blue artery snakes its way from the front of his head to the back (most obviously after a haircut), pulsing (throbbing and wobbling when he is in an extreme state) like a turn indicator in a sleek sedan. Unlike all other bakers—whose floury calling makes it good sense to dress in white—Birdwhistle dresses in black: black shoes, black socks (winter wear), black pants, black sweatshirt. By morning, he is white, however, and pleased with his transformation.

"Neat little metaphor for the soul in transition, don't you think, Hank? Black to white; darkness to light; ignorance to knowledge. If one examines the day-to-day procedural sort of things in his or her life, that person will discover they live ritualistically and metaphorically, having drifted away from the center of being. The point of which is fleeing from the real and the actual; hiding ourselves in the dung heap of socially acceptable ritual. Sadly, Hank, most people obey the rules without knowing who made the rules. Bitter and hopeless is the life consumed with that fucking mumbo-jumbo, you'll pardon the vulgarity."

Birdwhistle could talk; no question he was chatty. He beat you over the head with his analysis, which was derived from extensive reading in left-wing psychological journals, most of which were published in West Germany. Many people found him to be an insufferable bore. Milton wouldn't stay in the same room with him, and Airy refused to allow him in the apartment. He had had an odd life, born and raised in northern Wisconsin (Iron River). He went to art school in Chicago, and then spent ten years on the Gulf of Siam creating a fish farm for the government of Thailand. He had also become a leading expert on Thai whores, whom he frequently sought out. His Thailand experience made him the man he is today.

He was pumped up tonight, having discovered his wife—the formidable Crescent Laverno—was planning to go to Italy to organize cloth cutters. He had other, bleaker, suspicions (all untrue) as well.

"You, for example, Henry, live from day to day the way a toddler climbs stairs: haltingly, holding on, making sure you have a firm foothold and a firm handhold. Fine, Bubba, as far it goes. But you're always clinging to a preceding mode: let go, I say, little buddy, let go. You're not daring enough, old campaigner, not daring enough by half. Hey, what's the worse that can happen?"

"I could fall, break my skull, and die."

"Exactly. And you're going to do that anyway. Do you see what I mean? Don't hold yourself back so much you sad son of a bitch. Let's go into the back and talk about it. Chez Birdwhistle is kaput, Hank. Old Mr. Bob has brewed up his last batch of tasties. I'm finished; broken; on the rocks; I feel wonderfully clear about it though. Crescent is taking little Harry, the fucking light of my life, the star against which all my courses are set, the sap in my branches, and going to Italy to prove just how committed she is. She's breaking my heart, the sweet thing is making me into a sad sack of shit. I know it's unseemly to appear so bereft and blue, Henry, but I'm back to square one. I'm history, Hank. I'm more obsolescent than the vacuum tube. I hate my life. But Birdwhistle refuses to be a victim."

We walked back into the kitchen, through the dark dining-room part of the space, following an ancient path worn in the linoleum by waitresses. Bursting into the bright light of the kitchen (the light had an odd bluish tinge of moonlight in it), it was as if we had passed into the future from a particularly shopworn past. The walls and the countertops were clad in bright steel and gleamed. Also gleaming was Birdwhistle's apparatus: the craterlike mixing bowls, the dough mixer (which had a short, friendly, humanoid shape), the cooling racks, the deep fryer, the whetted knives, and the battered spoons. These things were the fruit of singular labor. Tonight, however, a solemn silence and emptiness had descended. No doughnuts sang in their bath of hot vegetable oil, no globs of greasy flour slipped rapturously across brightly polished surfaces. Operations had been suspended.

Birdwhistle sat on a stool, his arms thrown out across a countertop, suddenly silent and defeated. His manic mood had ended. Birdwhistle was gloomy. Birdwhistle gloomy is a threat to even his dearest friends. He passed his hand across his skull, the bristles bristled; he was a sad guy. I had come for a little cheering up, a tiny chunk of good fellowship and advice and had run into a firestorm of depression.

"Old Birdwhistle's life is on the rocks, Henry. I'm shipwrecked."

Crescent Laverno is quite extraordinary. She is a communist, a radical feminist, and a poet. She is a large woman, with the body of a perfectly conditioned lady wrestler. At the beach (the Birdwhistles love to skinnydip), she is awesome. No other word is adequate. She is also kind, gracious, and funny. However, she writes longish poems which, frankly, are not much fun to read. (See the "Sing in me, Karl" sequence.) Try wading through the 872 lines of "November 1917: A Poem" or the 1242 lines of "Rosa Triumphant" and you'll see what I mean. Crescent, in pursuit of her political vision, periodically goes off to someplace like East St. Louis, Oshkosh, or Oakland to organize communist/feminist food coops or radicalize ideologically unformed mill hands. Her politics can be contrary and unpleasant, and we've argued bitterly. (For a long time the only thing she called me was "that mini-fascist"; I called her, purely in self-defense, a "communist cow.") But many times, mostly when I'm feeling a little low, Crescent has hugged me (in her exuberant but sisterly way) to her impressive bosom, holding back nothing.

"Bob," I said, "I don't think Crescent would go away if you asked her to stay. I think she loves you more than the Party." I hoped she did, anyway.

"You think so?"

"Yes."

"You're right. She's not taking any more orders from the Kremlin. That was part of our prenuptial agreement. But I wish she didn't feel she had to go to Italy. Christ, it's not even in our hemisphere. Why not Costa Rica or Guatemala, Henry? I'd even go with her. I'd get a super tan. I can see myself stretched out on a beach, white sand and blue water. Surf streaming across the beach, me running down to the water to cool off. Dark-skinned native girls; wealthy Germans running away from their husbands. Costa Rica is the place."

"Why don't you suggest Costa Rica?"

"Because of the oppressed Italian laboring class, Bubba. I am speaking of our laboring brothers and sisters in some fucking Italian sweatshop cutting cloth, and if we don't help them, who will? I mean, don't you understand to be committed is to dodge the old capitalist comfort trip? We are taking about setting suffering working people free from their, what do you call them, their chains."

"Okay, I take your point."

"She's home packing now, Henry, this is it. She's taking Harry and going on down the road. The big bugout. Goodbye, Birdwhistle and all the homey virtues you personify. Goodbye marginally bourgeoise existence. Goodbye three squares and a big hug at bedtime. Hello existential nausea, anomie, an unhappy end to an unhappy life."

"Bob, even if she does go, it's not the end of your life. There are other fish in the sea."

"Barracudas, Henry," he said sorrowfully, "sharks and bottom feeders. There are few sleek dolphins like my Crescent."

He blushed. I smiled wickedly. It was pressing things a bit to think of as solid a woman as Crescent in just those terms. Sleek dolphin missed by a wide margin conveying her pleasing solidity. She could smother even a large man with her chest. And the wonderful thing was she didn't jiggle or sag; she was as taut as a strung bow.

Birdwhistle was in distress. His breathing was harsh and irregular. Not good signs.

"I can't kid myself, Henry, it may be another man. It may be that smirking fiend, that lower than no other thing is this thing, Tommy Tucker. I'll rip off his lips."

"No."

"Yes. Let's be adult about this. It happens. People develop unpretty sexual obsessions about one another. Okay, I'm going to deal with it. I'll murder Tommy Tucker and then I'll go to Costa Rica."

"Bob, forget Tommy Tucker. You're not going to murder him."

"Maybe not."

"She's not having an affair."

"I know that. Rationally, I know that."

"Don't you feel better? Just ask her to stay."

"Right. Good. She won't. She'll be furious that I even asked. Well, that's that. Henry, my buddy, right this instant I've had an epiphany. Just as you stood there trying to comfort me. Crescent is gone, out to lunch, over, ended, finito, so long, and so on. She's in the archives. Birdwhistle is going to have to live his life alone."

I was beginning to lose my patience. But a big tear trickled down his cheek and fell on the stainless steel counter. Then another.

"Now," he said, brushing aside his tears, "about the reason you came. You came to ask me, although you might not want to formulate the question quite this simply, about the existence of evil. Does it, in fact, exist? Evil we're talking about now. Do you follow me? As opposed to mere bad luck or the randomness of tragic occurrences. Evil. Sad to say, Henry, I've been forced to conclude that it does exist. It sits in the living room playing canasta, buries itself in the sand at the beach, complains about stomach cramps." He wiped another tear off his cheek. "What is the solution? What would Birdwhistle do? Henry, life is simple. You love a women according to all the rules, even the new ones, and then she dumps you. I could get nutty thinking about that. Oh, pal, I'll be out there beneath a streetlight, in the wintery darkness, looking for a bridge to jump off of. I'm waiting. I'm waiting for the resolution. The problem of evil: you have to be very careful. Don't overestimate your capacities. Work from your strengths. Don't do anything hasty or rash. Patience, Henry, patience. Do you see the big picture? Simplify, Henry, simplify."

I didn't have the faintest idea what he was talking about. I had never asked him anything about the existence of evil; had no opinion about it myself. Maybe it exists. Maybe.

No doughnuts would be made this night. I had a sour stomach from not sleeping and a headache from Birdwhistle's distress. The rain beat against the screens and splashed onto the black-and-white tile floor. It was very welcome in a dry and winter-crusty world. The silence deepened. Birdwhistle rippled his fingers along the counter-top, and his fingernails clickety-clacked like dogs' feet on marble.

"My ultimate word on the matter, Henry: it is sheer perverseness to regard life as complicated. Perverseness in the extreme. Life is simple. Really, believe Birdwhistle, simple."

It was four in the morning or so, and frankly I was sick of Bird-whistle's philosophical home brew. I wished him a fond goodnight. Once in the rain, I tugged down my baseball cap and began to run.

The streets were adorned with puddles, flat glimmering ovals full of the detritus of city life, a scum of antifreeze and beer-bottle caps on the bottom like coins in the fountain. Suddenly, I realized that I was not alone. A loud clomping of boots resounded in the night, direction of the feet from me unknown because of the ricocheting of the clomps along empty streets. I was being chased. Birdwhistle appeared in the distance behind me, a white head bobbing up and down.

"Henry, wait," he shouted.

Bob was greatly agitated.

I stopped and stood beneath a streetlight, waiting for him. He was like a rapid messenger from Hell, Mr. Blackness himself. He runs in an odd way, with his arms held awkwardly in front of him, turning them back and forth like an agitator in an old-fashioned washing machine.

At last, at rest, hands on hips, gasping for breath, Birdwhistle was beside me.

"One thing I meant to say, Henry, is that I know the reason for your visit. I suspect it's about Claire Cohen, isn't it? You have a problem." I had indicated to Bob over the months a deepening interest in Claire.

"A slight one."

"I know all about you, Henry. You are as clear to me as midnight in the mountains. Learn the lesson that old Birdwhistle has learned."

Buddhist or no, dressed in black, he was the last bare tree of spring. We looked at each other a long and revealingly painful moment.

"Sexual obsession, Henry, in a young man is a very ugly thing. You are becoming obsessed. I can see it in your beady eyes."

"Obsessed? Christ, I hope not."

"North, Hank, that's my advice. Remember Birdwhistle's counsel: North. Iron River. Get the stink off."

9

Odd Conjunctions;
Ominous Coincidences

SOMETHING EXTRAORDINARY HAPPENED. Leonard Gent
(an immaculately groomed Gent) began to preach, like Savonarola,
extemporaneously, ecstatically standing on the new stone benches of
the Library Mall. (It is their configuration as benches and not the
stone part that is new.) The Library Mall is an odd site for such
ranting: a rectangle perhaps two football fields long and one wide
occupying the space between the State Historical Society and the
Memorial Library. Two sidewalks form a large X on this rectangle,
and at the center sits a fountain, rather a weak effort compared to a
serious fountain. In the winter, the fountain is covered with a sheet-
metal top, yurtlike, indestructible. It looks like a bunker occupied by
Wehrmacht coast watchers prior to D-Day. Abandoned in winter, in
the spring and fall the Library Mall is a place to study, ogle women,
drink beer, throw the Frisbee, and so on. It is an area of much
activity but no focus. Transience is what it is designed for; nothing is
sufficiently comfortable or interesting to want to make you stop.

Gent, however, was clearly undaunted by all that. He was not
interested in architectural disadvantages or traffic patterns. He
wanted to make a splash. He attracted crowds. First only the derisive
and contemptuous; then the curious; then the ones who are willing

to be convinced. Gent was a vulgarian, and his addresses were full of venom and bitterness.

In another time a man might stand on a stone bench and admit to performing sexually perverse acts with children and expect to be judged harshly. Gent expected to be loved. Now that is a mystery that cries for explanation.

I notice things. My skill as an observer is one of my strengths. My eye is drawn to the margins, boundaries, extremities, borders: seams of confusion and ambiguity. I didn't pay too much attention to the concentrated heart of the crowd, the contentious cluster of hecklers and their antithesis, the rapt believers. I scoped the solitaries, standing in anxious attention, listening and alone. You can calculate the angle of entry of the assassin's bullet by plotting the topography of alienation. That's how I spotted the man in the blue sweatshirt.

Now *he* was in a perfect spot to kill Gent.

He stood to the left of Gent, on the Student Union side of the Mall, well away from the center of the crowd. He stood with his arms crossed over his chest, cocked on one hip, like the men who stand at the rear of the church during Sunday evening Mass in a small town: ready to duck out after Communion. This odd creature was, I will tell you now, Norman O'Keefe. He could have walked forward four strides (quickly, like a man in transit from his car to the post office on a bitterly cold day), pulled a chrome pistol from his sweatshirt pouch, put the gun beneath Gent's head, and pumped three or four bullets into his skull. Then, stepping over Gent's body, sprinted to a waiting car—parked on State Street—and sped away in an enfilade of gutter gravel and rubber-tire smoke.

The way he stood, the intensity of his concentration, his separation from normal midwestern campus everydayness made him a man to be wondered about. He caught Gent's eye once, in a moment of especially arcing demagoguery. Gent stopped, a fishbone of fear in his throat, dead silent. He had been talking about the poor man's cathedral he was going to build where the carwash attendant and the night janitor might "pray to the real Christ, not the one of Episcopal social climbers, indulgence merchants, sacrament salesmen"—he really was a hillbilly Savonarola—"who peddle salvation for cashier's checks in oak-paneled boardrooms." (Gent was eloquent today; sunshine seemed to enhance his verbal capacities.) Then he saw Blue Sweatshirt, and he grasped his throat in surprise. Gent spun away from that troubling vision—the way you'd turn away from an imminent act of violence—and stumbled forward with his sermon, greatly distracted.

"Jesus," he said, "was a workingman. If Jesus were alive today, he'd be bolting fenders onto pickup trucks."

But Leonard was throttled out of glibness. He peeked at Norman, but Norman had turned away and was walking up Langdon Street toward Bascom Hill. He walked slowly, with his head down, as if he had no direction in mind and had all the time in the world to get there. I would have followed him, secretly, but I had to meet Claire.

Gent covertly followed the blue back of Norman O'Keefe. He had lost the thread and momentum of his message and was driftingly repetitious. "Or he would be hanging Sheetrock. Sheetrock . . . someplace . . . like a shopping center in Omaha. You know what I'm saying. . . ."

Then Claire appeared at my side, exactly on time, looking wholesome and springy in a blue skirt decorated with little yellow flowers. She had a yellow T-shirt on with the sleeves rolled up past her biceps. She was tan and fresh-looking; the sort of indisputably tidy look women can have wearing bright clothes on a sunny day.

She squeezed my hand affectionately.

Claire watched Gent carefully. He was finding his pace again, and the spit was flying from his mouth. (He was a heavy drool producer.) She seemed fascinated by him. His message did have power, especially if you momentarily lacked personal clarity. The world, Gent said, was full of evil. Wealth and power were the creations of the devil, and the only way to salvation was to reject outward and excessive forms. His religious principles (Gent's First Church of the Hillbilly Blue-Collar Jesus) provided a cut-to-the-bone no-frills path to heaven.

"Who is he?" Claire asked.

"Leonard Gent. That's his name. He's had a vision, and he's become a preacher. I met him the other day in a restaurant. I think he's a borderline schizophrenic. But he's very bright. He's acutely intelligent."

"He's good at this."

"Brilliant."

"I suppose he asks for money?"

"No. He just comes here to the Library Mall and starts wailing away about the children of darkness—we probably fall into that category, you and I—and the children of light. He wants to build some sort of shelter for street kids. His mission is to the motherless child."

"Is that bad? You sound so cynical."

"I don't mean to be. I guess it's okay if he's for real. He's strange. He asked me if I knew what a blowjob was as a preface to a tale of personal redemption. He used to indulge his idiosyncratic sexual tastes with underage boys. Hardly seems like the right kind of credentials for what he wants to do."

"He's reformed. I think that's touching."

"He seems to be. It's awfully odd to hear him confess to the bestial cravings of his former life in front of three hundred people."

"Bestial cravings?"

"His words. Getting his chain yanked by a little boy seems to fit into that category."

"He's sort of good-looking."

"If you like rat-faced scuzzballs."

She let that pass. The main man in her life, Nicky Waller, fit that description rather closely.

"I'm going to come back and listen to him sometime. When is he here?"

"Two performances daily: twelve o'clock and seven o'clock. The evening performance is usually a little heavier on the personal-confession material. It can get pretty vivid. Yesterday's was full of tough poetry: 'semen-slick concrete walls.' He was talking about a highway comfort station near Baraboo."

It was too nice a day to worry about murder and sin. Plenty of bad weather coming for those kinds of musings. I had the money for Claire. It was Thursday, and she had an appointment to terminate her pregnancy.

"How are you, Claire?"

"Fine. Nervous."

I handed her the telephone-company envelope.

"You should count it. I always make mistakes."

"I trust you."

"I think it's all there. Two hundred and forty."

She stuck the money in her bag (a beat-up drab olive haversack).

"Thanks, Henry. You're a life saver."

She spoke without a trace of irony.

"You know what I mean, Henry. Sometimes I feel like we barely know each other, yet you've always been really kind to me. Milton, too. You're both very sweet. I'm going to have you both over for dinner after all this is over. When I feel in better spirits."

"Where do you go? I mean, now?"

"Just down Park Street a little. To one of those new professional buildings."

"How are you getting home? Do you stay there overnight?"

"You don't know much about this stuff, do you, Henry?"

"Not much."

"They let you recover a little while, to make sure you're not bleeding or something, then they call a cab and I go home."

"To Nicky."

"No, Nicky's still in New Jersey. He'll be back tonight or tomorrow. It was his dog's birthday or something really urgent."

Stalwart fellow, I thought to myself.

Claire reached out and shook my hand, formally, as if we were Freemasons or Elks. (My uncle is an Elk, and he taught me the secret handshake.)

"I won't forget this, Henry," she said, "you've been a good friend. I didn't mean it when I said I barely knew you. I'm glad we've become pals. I'll pay you back as soon as I can."

"Can I walk you there?" I asked.

Usually, in circumstances of emotional intimacy, I feel like running away in a lung-bursting sprint. This time I felt like hanging in there.

"Okay, but not too far," she said. "I'm a little nervous, and I need some time to get myself together."

We walked down State Street to Park Street. Above us, Bascom Hill was corduroyed with bodies. The tangy smell of sun-warmed flesh was intense. Warm spring days, in the last sunny hours before the exam period, made the juices flow. The smell off the hill was one of exuberant randiness. Sex was on everyone's mind. It was certainly on my mind. At University Avenue, a disappointingly short trip from my point of view, and even though the light was green, Claire stopped.

"I think this is where you should go back."

I was reluctant, but she pushed me away with a firm hand on my breastbone.

"Go away now," Claire said. "I'll find you in a couple of days."

"If you need anything, let me know."

She smiled and stepped off the curb. The light was red now, and she waited for a hole in the traffic, and ran across the street. She didn't look back although I remained at curbside waiting for—and expecting—a rearward glance. A pattern was forming: Claire leaving Henry in an unsettled, yearning state of mind.

I was uneasy. Claire had me backpedaling. What does one do when he is confronted with the gritty details of life as it is led here in the middle of the midwest? I decided to go play basketball in the Old Red Gym. Milton has suggested that my need for mindless activity, especially basketball—which he considers the apogee of mindlessness—is a form of escapism. I don't want to face confusion or controversy, so I run off to the locker room. At least, I remind him, I don't look for solace from drugs, alcohol, or whores. Not yet, anyway.

I needed a good sweat to get the accumulated poisons out. (I accumulate an unseemly amount and density of poisons.) Afterwards, I might go for a beer (more poison) and watch the evening news (poison again). Claire was walking off alone to change things. We seemed to be synchronized—a fact we were both reluctantly recognizing—on the sine curve of confusion. I liked her a great deal, an emotion that was hopelessly inappropriate.

I walked back up Park Street toward Lake Mendota. I could see the lake in front of me; and I could see the bright white sails of sailboats. They billowed taut with wind, propelling their boats on a reaching course, outbound.

I ambled along back beneath Bascom Hill, thinking of reverse layups, anticipating the pleasure of sweat dripping down my nose and splatting onto the hardwood, the urgent resistance of a dribbled ball. Then I saw him again, Norman O'Keefe. (Of course, I didn't know his name then. I just thought of him as a potentially violent head case with an interesting face. You see a lot of faces like that in America, especially on college campuses, mostly belonging to morally and intellectually defeated graduate students.) He was stretched out on the grass on Bascom Hill, near the Music Hall, staring into the milky blue sky. He had his shirt off, and his skin was unhealthily white. His feet waved back and forth, matching the beat of a song coming from a nearby radio.

He seemed indifferent to what was around him, including astonishing coeds in see-through blouses and a pair of wildly barking Dobermans. He was formulating a plan. Without panic or an obvious sense of urgency, he was mapping out his future. Somewhere in the blue sky was written a message. I looked up and saw nothing, naturally. But levers were being thrown and large gears groaned as they engaged. Motors began to chug and then whine, a horrible turbine screech. What was happening? Claire's spirits had begun a gradual but irresistible decline; Norman's had begun to rise—gradually, irresistibly.

10

What Happened to Claire

JESUS CHRIST, THE things that happened then. After that Thursday in May, nothing was ever the same. Who could have predicted that Norman O'Keefe would have held a pistol to Fletcher Lint's forehead and said, "Tell me, pisshead, or they'll be making Bolognese sauce in your brainpan." Strange stuff, sacred-mushroom stuff, Mexican desert visions.

But we were talking about Claire's fate. What happened to Claire was this: Claire didn't have her abortion.

Imagine that we are chatting quietly, sitting on the broad veranda of the Northern Lights, in autumn, a surprisingly late Indian summer. The air is warm, it is very pleasant in the sun, and the trees are almost bare. The air is clear and sweet. Yes, it is amazing weather for November. I resist making judgments, I say, although we are both aware I am dissembling. Henry makes judgments all the time, and many of them are hopelessly incorrect. Why did she decide to have a baby? I don't know. I've never been able to figure it out. It seemed stupid, really dumb. She had no money, no job, the father was a moron, and her parents didn't like her much either. Her decision seemed to be willfully self-destructive. I was angry when I heard the news; angrier than I should have been given the tentativeness of our connection.

So, listen to this: she left me standing on the corner of Park Street and University Avenue, heading off to her abortionist. She never made it. What she did was sit down on an aluminum bench in a bus shelter in front of the First Wisconsin Bank. Claire sat there and thought about her life, I suppose, and the direction it was taking. Tough job, if you ask me. She didn't weep or cry aloud. She sat in the shade and made a decision. Her left leg was crossed over her right, and her chin rested in the upturned palm of her left hand. (I know these details because Bob Birdwhistle walked past her on his way to make a large deposit into Crescent's checking account.) I'm sure she made a pretty, pensive picture. I like the way Claire looks when she is thoughtful and self-absorbed (which turns out to be most of the time).

On his way out of the bank, having made his deposit, he found her still on the bench, not even looking at the bus that was loading passengers at the curb. He thought she didn't look well (she was probably a little nauseous), and by now it was the heat of the day.

"Claire," Birdwhistle said, "how are you?"

Small talk, small talk. People can't get enough of it, especially Birdwhistle.

Oh, fine, Claire would have said. Actually, only fair. Fair, that's my current status.

"What's wrong?"

Birdwhistle realized Claire was not observing street-conversation protocol. "Only fair" was a troubled admission.

"I'm going to have a baby," Claire is reported to have said.

"You're going to have a baby," Bob repeated, utterly unsurprised. He thought I was the responsible agent.

Birdwhistle attended Claire carefully, examining the determined expression on her face. She isn't joking, he thought, a girl like Claire doesn't joke about something as serious as this. Have I told you Birdwhistle is clairvoyant? He sees things, he says, in the seams between states of consciousness. He had one of his Tinkerbell flashes just then. What did he see? Henry Fitzgerald in a snowstorm, snow-covered, in an icily dangerous spot; a lost and harried wanderer. Not the kind of vision I was going to be comforted by.

"Congratulations," Birdwhistle said, without ambiguity. "I'd like to be a father again myself."

Claire smiled.

"Or maybe congratulations are not in order."

"I'm not sure what's in order, Bob."

There was nothing left to say, so they smiled and parted, vibrating like crystals.

Something began in that May sunshine: the first flake of the avalanche. In quiet moments, in the intervals between hammer blows or oar strokes, I think of Claire, decisive Claire, defiant Claire, and I am touched. Of course, I am a notorious sentimentalist. Milton thought she was being self-indulgent. Not everyone liked Claire as well as I.

I probably should have been able to derive some meaning from the triangle we three sun-drenched souls—Claire, Norman, and I—created. That I did not should not disqualify me as a geometrician, for who ever understands the complicated mathematics of his life? Norman O'Keefe—the man in the blue sweatshirt, potential assassin—sat one hundred yards directly south of me thinking about the tragic circumstances of the recent past, falling into reveries about the violent end he wished to bring to the evil architect of his undoing (Leonard Gent, of course). Claire Cohen, as deeply thoughtful as she had ever been or likely would ever be, sat a block to the east and decided not to pull the plug; to have her baby after all. I, Henry Fitzgerald, true son of the quotidian, was thinking about jock itch (I was badly infected). Oddly enough, on a cold winter's night, this triangle, now sufficiently reduced to fit into a very noisy room, was replicated. Go figure it out.

Boy, it was hot in the sunshine. Perspiration dripped into the corners of my eyes making me squinty. I wiped my face off with the bottom of my shirt. I decided not to exercise. Beer was the word that popped into my head. Henry, you dumb bastard, you sorry shit, wake up! A man is planning murder, there, just up the hill from you. A personal pal of yours has decided to dislocate her life from the course everyone intends her to take, just one block away! People are doing things! Get with the program: jock itch and beer seem sadly out of step with the spirit of the moment.

Of course, you don't know what you don't know, and I didn't have an inkling all this world-shaking stuff was going on. I thought that Claire was being strapped into one of those machines that vacuum fetuses out of wombs. I thought that Norman O'Keefe was just another hanger-on in a university town, a weirdo among other weirdos. And I thought, properly as it turns out, a beer would take my mind off my problems (I wonder how many times I have come to that conclusion). Still, in my defense, I can't help but feel that beneath the surface a certain resoluteness was developing. Hey, cut me some slack, I was the one who risked everything trying to get to Claire. I was the one who was ferocious and determined. Probably, you have to resolve the small problems before you can get to the big ones. And sweating out my warm-weather crotch problems was just one step, albeit seemingly indirect, down the road to Claire's rescue.

In short, don't rush me.

11

Henry Is Happy
When He's Dancing

IT WAS MILTON who told me she didn't have her abortion. We were in my apartment a couple days after I gave the money to Claire (a steamy Saturday, the day the blacktop melted on Gorham Street), still talking about buying a piece of property on or near Lake Superior. A summer house in the piney woods is what we were after. In a relaxed moment, he began to tell me a joke that Gene Clifford, the quadriplegic bailbondsman, told him, the one about the three fat ladies, the cowboy, and the trampoline: "See," he said, with a wicked grin, "there were these three sisters . . ." And suddenly he looked up, and his smile was gone. I see Claire Cohen is knocked up, he said, and didn't I tell you things would get complicated? And then he tried to tell me the rest of the joke.

It took me a little while to absorb what he had said.

"What do you mean?" I asked.

"What do I mean? I'm telling a joke."

"Claire isn't pregnant. I have special information. I know she isn't. Who told you?"

"She did. I ran into her on State Street this morning. She seemed a little uptight. I thought it was really weird that she would just blurt it out like that. Maybe she will marry Waller. That's probably what she wants."

I'll tell you honestly, I felt very low. Very low indeed. I felt like storming up to Claire's apartment and demanding my money back. Cheated, deceived, and abused, that's what I felt.

"What's the matter, Henry?"

"I feel cheated, deceived, and abused."

"Pretty normal, in other words."

"Milton . . ."

"Just a joke, Henry. What happened? Why are you so upset? Tell me, I'm your brother."

"It's so stupid. Claire asked me for money so she could have an abortion. I gave it to her. I mean I gave her the money. Two hundred and forty dollars. I'm an asshole, Milton. I really am."

"Henry, I'm sure there's a reasonable explanation. Look, maybe she tried to call or maybe she stopped by. You're hardly ever around. Probably one in ten times when I've called you you've actually been here. You're out playing basketball or off getting weirdness indoctrination from your friend Bathwater."

Bathwater is what he called Birdwhistle.

"Maybe. That's possible."

"But look, pal, giving money to women for something as serious as what we are talking about is dicey business. Unless you're the father presumptive, which you're not, right? Henry, please tell me that you're not the daddy bear. I see your fortune melting away in an ugly paternity suit. Tell me you're not the father."

"I'm not the father."

"Don't lie, Henry. We are talking about some very serious American dollars."

"Milton, the only thing I ever stuck in Claire was my tongue in her ear. What did she do with the money?"

"How do I know? What do you expect, anyway, Henry? The last thing you should expect from Claire Cohen is consistency. When I met her she was taking so many hallucinogens, she didn't know whether she was in Madison or Minsk. Maybe she had an acid flashback. Look, I told you about her. She's so nutty she could be Mr. Peanuts' mate. All she needs is her own top hat and you could see the resemblance. At least with Waller, to his ultimate credit, she stopped taking every pill she could lay her hands on.

"I wasn't going to tell you this, but I bumped into Claire, by herself. No Waller. She was looking for the Consensus All-American, Nature's Nobleman himself, the estimable Henry Fitzgerald. Her eyes were red with weeping, et cetera. The bitter truth is that Claire and Nicky are yesterday's newspaper. She dropped him like a sash weight. He's a beaten dog, Henry. Nicky is a flower petal in Claire's book of memories. That make you feel better?"

"Milton, why didn't you tell me this before?"

"Forgot. You think all I have on my mind is your little crazy psychosexual dramas? I think the whole thing with Claire is nuts anyway. Number one, you have a girlfriend. Number two, what do you see in Claire anyway? She's cute, Henry, but not more than cute. She's no great beauty. And she has real problems. Take my word for it. But, in her defense, I know she's been trying to get in touch with you. You can be like Houdini's spirit on Halloween: impossible to reach."

"I don't know, Milton, I still feel a little betrayed."

"Henry, this is not a Russian novel. People aren't betrayed anymore. And this is hardly a betrayal. I wish you'd get out of this *Anna Karenina* mode. It's boring."

"I'd like to hear what she has to say."

"And I'm sure you will hear it."

I think I may have skimmed the smooth surface of things too readily; maybe I've developed a pattern of observing too much and actually doing too little. I'll accept that possibility. But I feel things deeply, and I did feel betrayed. I felt abandoned. My hands were trembling. Milton noticed.

"Don't get too worked up. Everything will make sense."

But now I didn't care to listen. A mood that is close to madness comes over me at these times: a kind of profound distractedness. I can't stay still, I have to move around, burn off some energy. If I am a midnight walker, a wanderer, a budding insomniac, these unsettled moods are the cause. I began to pace.

"Oh, oh," Milton said, "hide the cat."

"I'm all right. Really, I'm okay."

"Sure."

"I'm just thinking. I'm trying to figure it out."

"Forget it. Call Claire in the morning and ask her. You won't know until she tells you."

"She probably had to buy her boyfriend drugs. Amphetamines. Beady-eyed bastard is a speed freak. I don't like the way I feel right now, Milton. I feel like I have to extract myself from this situation."

Milton made a gurgling noise in this throat, throttling a chuckle. He knew about my resolutions, and how irresolute I could be.

"Let's go grab a Plazaburger. You'll feel better. You'll lighten up."

Milton had his feet up on the redwood-burl coffee table, and he sat beneath the bright circle of light from my architect's lamp.

"The money, Milton. I'm still annoyed about the money."

"Henry, it was a simple transaction. She borrowed, you lent. She pays back, and you're even-steven. Not good business, but nothing to pace the floor about and scowl menacingly at your closest relative. Remember, Henry: after I'm gone, you're on your own. Think about it."

"It's the principle."

"Maybe she gave the money to charity. Did you think of that?"

I was silent.

"Henry, I could sit here and give you dozens of good reasons—perfectly honorable and touching reasons—why Claire is doing what she's doing, whatever that is. Don't take this so personally. You're only in a very small chunk of it. This is not your movie. Not yet anyway."

That made sense. In Claire's solar system, I was probably no nearer the sun than Saturn. I sat down in Airy's rocker. (I hadn't thought about her in quite a long time; she had exiled me while she was writing her seminar papers. Airy worked like a dog because she wanted things. She wanted to have her Ph.D. in Classics and teach, drive a Volvo, have two children, have a fine old house with a fireplace and a house on the seashore for the summertime; she wanted to wear silk blouses and pearl earrings. She wanted bookshelves full of books she had read and a color television that could be hidden away. Momentarily, she wanted Henry. But she was annoyed that I hung back from accepting her version of me. I wondered how she was, but basically I knew: strong-willed, self-sufficient, and self-absorbed.)

I fell into a deeply thoughtful mood: neither depressed nor anxious. Momentarily I was contemplative and serene. I was sitting in darkness and could rock forward into the light. I rocked back and forth, slowly, repeating the dark/light pattern. The weather was changing. A fresh, cool wind was coming out of the north, stirring the curtains. The widow's yellowed lace curtains blew into the room, like a limp wave from an old man.

I had been packing my belongings, a consequence of my eviction. I had recently patted my landlady's rear end while we were standing at the mailboxes, and she didn't take it well. It was not meant to be provocative, just casually friendly. The kind of pat a manager gives to a relief pitcher he's just brought in out of the pen. The last thing I had on my mind was the seduction of an ex-nun.

My things were jammed into duffle bags and boxes. I was practically out of there. I had found another apartment just up the street, closer to Claire's. It was a large one-bedroom on the top floor of a dilapidated mansion, badly maintained over the years, with hints and echoes of its former elegance: stained-glass windows in the bathrooms and oak wainscoting in the common hallways. Airy wanted me to move farther west, closer. I didn't. In this struggle of wills—one of many—I was the surprise winner. What could she say? It was actually a lovely place. It had a large bay window in the living room, which looked out over Gilman Street. From that window I can also look over Lake Mendota.

I rocked, the wind blew, and Milton looked on in amazement. He really does think I'm nuts.

I got up, feigning nonchalance. I yawned as strenuously as I could. It was a real stage yawn, a scenery-chewing performance.

"Gosh," I said, "I'm tired."

"No you're not, asshole. You're in one of those rambling states of mind. You're trying to get rid of me. It's okay, Henry, I'm going."

"Maybe I will take a walk. I'm antsy."

"Henry, you are getting very, very strange. People are beginning to refer to you as the Weird One."

"Only because you do."

"Henry, if you want to move your feet, you should learn how to dance."

Milton got up from the sofa and walked over to where I was standing. He put his arm around me and squeezed my shoulders.

"Women, Henry, are going to be your downfall. They're going to make you crazier than you have to be."

"Not I," I said.

He snickered, cruelly.

"Fuck you, Milton."

"Henry, just look at things: your girlfriend is off to Greece in a few days for the summer. She'll expect a certain reciprocity in the faithfulness area. She's not going to hum 'Semper Fidelis' while you're off porking Claire Cohen. Besides, Claire is pregnant. You are crazy to get yourself in any deeper. Don't kid yourself. This is a very bumpy road."

"I might walk up the street, or I might not. I might talk to Claire. You have nothing to worry about. Airy is wonderful, and I intend to be reasonably faithful to her. I have a little teensy crush on Claire Cohen. She's as cute as a bumblebee. Milton, she has these perfectly firm little breasts. They're . . . perfect. But, really, I can shrug her off like a cold. I'm not going to do anything rash, embarrassing, or illegal. I'm as solid as a boulder on this one. Can't shake me. Don't even try."

"Okay, if you say so. But you've gotten detached from righteousness before. Just don't be impetuous. But whenever you start to talk about how perfect a girl's breasts are, I know you're in trouble. You got it bad. Don't kid yourself."

He left, and I felt very uncomfortable and very young. The wind made the leaves of the trees outside my front windows crackle like static in the darkness. Here was a problem. Problems don't go away without effort. Fortune favors the bold. You can quote me.

I was ready to roll. I pulled on a sweater (the night suddenly seemed coolish), ducked out the door, and turned sharply left toward Claire's apartment house, up the Gilman Street hill. Nothing, now, between me and her but deep darkness and fuzzy pools of street-lamp light. I walked on my toes, gurgling in the gut. I was nervous. But I didn't care what happened. Damn all fainthearted warnings. I wanted to see quiet Claire Cohen. My new motto: forward.

Of course, I could have turned back. I could have been tickled by my goofy seriousness, slapped my head, relishing my youthful impetuosity, and gone off to bed, chuckling. At many places and at many times, I could have stifled my Claire Cohen yearning. I repeat, I could have turned back, gone home, gone to sleep. I didn't. It's that simple. I stopped for a think at the corner of Wisconsin Avenue and Gilman Street and sat on the curb (a high curb built on the hillside). I was wearing a green sweater (the elbows were rubbed away), blue jeans, and black sneakers. I sniffed my sweater and the T-shirt beneath. I smelled like an ox. My back itched intensely (later diagnosed as shingles). I sat between a brown Rambler station wagon and a metallic silver Cadillac El Dorado. I was hidden from traffic, vehicular and pedestrian. I drew my name in the dried mud scum of the gutter. I drew Claire's name as well. What the hell was I doing? Get up, I told myself. All you can be is scorned and humiliated.

I took tiny steps up to the top of the hill and tinier steps down the downslope. (I could have anchored pitons and rappelled more quickly.)

Claire lived in a house owned by Mrs. Pappas, a widow and a woman of property: 120 East Gilman Street. Mrs. Pappas's husband, Nikolas, had been firetender at a university power plant. (Firetender: I'd like to see that on my resume. Firetender Fitzgerald has a nice ring to it.) He brought his wages home, and Mrs. P invested the cash in real estate: apartment buildings and parking lots. Mr. Pappas was run over by a garbage truck in the summer of 1956. And since his death the widow has lived quietly, collecting rents and investing in Treasury Bills. Sitting in her screen porch on pleasant evenings and monitoring the neighborhood, she has grown rich, gray, and a little overweight. The problem with Mrs. Pappas (who is really very nice) and the reason I mention her at all is that she is a client of my brother's. I didn't want to get into a lengthy discussion with her about her legal problems, which were real, complicated, and hopeless (income-tax evasion). To get to Claire's door I was going to have to get past Mrs. Pappas.

I stood in the darkness across the street from Claire's house, looking down the bushy corridor toward her entry. A light was on in what I knew to be her living room (a glimmer from the basement), and my resolve was strengthened. I took a deep breath and crept across the

street, a part of the still night. I walked down the sidewalk immediately below the widow's roost. Mrs. Pappas must have turned in for
the night; her spot was vacant. Silent as a shadow, I didn't make a
scratch, scuffle, or sigh. I eased my way to the corner of the building
and crouched down to look in Claire's windows. I was on one knee,
squishing into the soft black dirt next to the foundation. My knee
sank into the mud, and a branch of a lilac bush scratched my cheek.
But I was undetected. (I'm good at breaking and entering, I've discovered. Sneakiness seems to be part of my essential being. I also
noticed other footprints. Someone had been here before me. A peep-
ing Tom perhaps, hoping to catch a glimpse of Claire.)

Peering into Claire's windows, I was surprised. I had expected to
see, I suppose, a beatup couch, a dirty off-white rug, a television with
a broken aerial, a lamp with a torn shade. I did not expect to see a
void, a spotless empty apartment lacking even the odd scraps and
under-the-couch debris you find in places recently vacated. The
apartment had been cleared out and meticulously cleaned: hands and
knees scrubbed, scoured so well that there would be no question of
the return of the security deposit (which she was notorious for keeping). It was not totally empty (what is?). A sleeping bag sat on the
floor, rolled up and bound together with a beaded Indian reservation
belt (I had one when I was a kid that said "Davey Crockett" in purple
and white beads). The bag was red and looked like a sea creature, a
mollusk escaped from its shell. Her record player—the one I had so
ably managed—sat on a suitcase. A record was playing a Nat King
Cole fiftyish/early-sixtyish ballad ("There was a boy/ A dum de dum
dum boy"). I forget the words.

I did not expect to see Claire sitting against the wall next to a
tinned-over fireplace, a black sweater draped over her shoulders. Her
arms were wrapped around her legs, and she leaned forward, synchronized with Nat's singing, and banged her chin on her left knee-
cap (she was very lithe and stretchable). She had a shy smile on her
face and was talking, animatedly, to my brother. Milton (ice breaker,
rough-edge smoother, palm greaser) was standing with one arm
leaned across the mantelpiece, gesturing madly with the other. He
laughed, and then Claire laughed. And then he paced furiously back
and forth, shaking his fist at the ceiling. I realized with some pain that

he was imitating me; imitating me quite well. Claire buried her head in her hands, so amused was she with Milton's performance.

Damn Milton, I thought. He's in there explaining my state of mind. I didn't even know what my state of mind was except tangled, confused, and extreme. I rapped on the screen.

"Hello," I said.

"Hello," they answered.

"It's me, Henry."

"Of course it's you. What took you so long?"

"Milton, what are you doing here?"

He didn't answer. I was getting muddier all the time under the bushes. It's a drag to live in a basement.

"Come around to the side, Henry," Claire said. "Go stand by the red door. I'll let you in."

Milton came out of the red door followed by Claire. He had a cheery smile on his face.

"I just stopped in for a minute to say hello. She'd rather talk to you anyway."

"You don't have to leave on my account, Milton. Please stay."

My words said stay, but my icy expression said take a hike. I was still feeling the sting of his coarse lampooning.

"I have to walk the dog." He dashed away, slapping my shoulder and giving me a conspiratorial wink. Milton doesn't have a dog. He stopped midway down the path and made an abrupt return. He kissed Claire on the cheek and patted her head.

"Remember what I told you, Claire," he said.

"I will."

I was curious to know what he had told her, but I wasn't going to ask. Not ever. It's always painful to discover what flaws people I love the most can detect in my character. Airy, for example, has an agonizingly long list.

"I have something to tell you," Claire said.

"It's not necessary." I was being disingenuous since, if I thought it weren't necessary, I wouldn't have been squatting in the dirt peeking into her window.

"Don't stand out there. Come in."

Claire's apartment (about to become in a matter of a few hours her former apartment) was the cleanest I had ever seen. The living room floor was polished slick and satiny. Her red sleeping bag looked even more mollusk-like up close: a complicated organism turned inward and inward. The walls and ceilings were white in a wide range of tones from Arctic blizzard to tropical meridian. Except for the fact that sunlight was always absent, it was very pleasant.

She walked to the middle of the empty living room. She had pulled on the sweater, which must have been Nicky's because she was engulfed in it. She stood directly beneath the overhead light, dimmed by two-thirds, with only one functioning bulb out of three. She took a deep breath and smiled at me. Why do men do strange, dangerous, or otherwise inexplicable things for or to women? Sexual obsession. Birdwhistle was right on the button.

"My life is changing," she said.

I am not a cynic, but the one statement I distrust above all others is the one Claire just uttered. I was quiet.

"First, Nicky and I broke up. As of about four this afternoon, he's left Madison permanently and gone back to New Jersey. He's not my boyfriend anymore."

It was not a true statement to say Nicky was back in New Jersey. In fact, he was occupying the same muddy spot I had just left. He was crouched by the window looking in. He was listening as well. Most amazingly, he had a bayonet in his hand. Nicky, it seems, had been stalking me (his was the eerie presence I felt behind me on the way to Claire's). He wanted to hurt me.

"Second"—she seemed to have prepared this speech—"I didn't have an abortion. I guess you know that. I have been trying to find you. Milton told me to say you're harder to contact than Houdini's ghost. I think I'm going to stay pregnant. I think I'll be having a baby. I've not made many decisions for myself, Henry, except this one. It feels good to me."

Okay, I was touched. I admit it. Momentarily she had a deep serenity. One could look a long time, I thought, and not find a woman finer than Claire.

"And I have your money," she said. It was still in the envelope I gave her. "I spent forty dollars of it, but I managed to replace it all."

She was pleased with herself.

I took the envelope and stuck it in my pocket. I tried to think of something to say, but I had fallen into a deep and wordless well.

Finally, after an awkwardly long shared glance, I popped the inevitable question: "May I use your bathroom?"

"Don't you have anything to say?"

"I do, Claire, a lot. But if I don't pee I'll burst."

I had not foreseen any of this and was thrown back on my least favorite terrain, undefendable raw emotion. I like a bit of order, and the momentum of Claire's changes had displaced me from my usual orbit.

"It's the door to the left of the kitchen. Jiggle the handle after you flush," she said huffily, "or the tank won't fill."

Claire was irritated.

In the bathroom, a roach was climbing the wall above the bathtub. I startled it when I turned on the light. I guess you can startle a roach, or maybe that's a pathetic fallacy. I didn't kill it. While I peed, I thought about Claire. I was greatly tempted to abandon all other connections, affiliations, and relationships for a desperate lifeboat fling with her and see where that led. I had just finished and was zipping up when I heard the bathroom door burst open and a wild scream reverberate against the tiles. A figure rushed at me out of the semidarkness and leaped on my back: Nicky Waller with a knife. I twisted my upper body sharply to the left and down, banging his head against the wall and dropping him into the bathtub. He was stunned but unhurt, and my ear was throbbing where he had clubbed me with his scabbarded weapon.

"What's the matter with you? Are you fucking insane?"

He didn't have to answer because it was obvious. Claire stood in the living room, staring in at us. She was horrified at what was happening.

"You bastard, Fitzgerald," Nicky said, "you've ruined my life."

He was a bit woozy (he'd knocked his head going down) but still held the bayonet. He kept it in front of his face, as if he were reminding himself what he was supposed to do. The bayonet itself, up close, was not much of a weapon. The scabbard was a dull olive green and was pitted with rust. The haft was black rubber. Under the conditions (I was happy that I had had time to stuff my pecker back into my pants) it was a bit daunting. Nicky smelled strongly of whiskey; he seemed to be drunk or at least enlivened with drink.

"Wait a minute, Nicky," I said, "let's talk about this."

Claire had begun to cry (it had been a rough day for her too), and Nat King Cole was still warbling in the living room. It was a real Fifties love-and-marriage tune, which was somehow weirdly appropriate. I had gotten into Claire's movie after all.

"I'm going to slice you up with this blade," he said.

Now that stuff I wasn't going to take seriously. He was from Teaneck, New Jersey, not the toughest town on the eastern seaboard.

He tried to yank the blade out of its scabbard, but the haft snapped off in his hand. He was left with an ugly stump of a bayonet in his right hand and a greasy smear on his left arm.

"Shit," he said.

I could tell he didn't have a backup plan. He was sitting in the bathtub, a really pathetic picture, staring at the two pieces of the weapon in his hands. Claire stepped into the bright light of the bathroom, and she looked at him pityingly. That's what sent him over the edge.

"I'm really embarrassed, Nicky, I thought we had all this settled. Henry hasn't done anything." (This was not exactly true. I had been bad just a little.)

His chin trembled. He began to cry; Claire was still crying, too. Ah, but I felt quite well, just having dodged a bullet. It's possible, had blade and handle been a unit, he could have done some serious damage.

He climbed out of the tub; his pants and the back of his shirt were wet. Nicky tossed the pieces down—they skittered across the floor like waterbugs—and headed for the exit.

"Have a nice life, Claire." His sarcasm was not very convincing. And then he was gone. I walked to the door and shut it.

I felt bad for him.

"The little rat-faced shit," Claire said.

The little rat-faced shit indeed: it seemed that once Claire dropped you, you were unlikely to be welcomed back.

She went over to the record player and lifted the arm off the vinyl.

It had been riding along the innermost curve, bumping along silently. She leaned against the mantelpiece, resting her head on her forearms. She seemed tired.

"Is he gone?"

"He seems to be," I said.

"That's always a bad moment, when they storm out. All my boyfriends seem to end up screaming at me and slamming the door as they leave. You won't do that will you, Henry?"

"Probably not, Claire. I usually slip out unnoticed."

"Quite a lot of men have gotten furious at me. I seem to drive them to extremes. I don't mean to."

"Who does?"

"Do women get angry at you?"

"Most of them."

I was having a hard time hearing her.

"Turn around will you, Claire? I can't hear when you mutter into your elbow."

"No. I want you to come over here."

Oh oh, I thought, finally, the distinguished thing. This was really the very last moment I could have pushed the terminate button. Right then I could have turned on my heel and walked out. But, of course, I didn't. I went over to where she was standing. I put my hands on her shoulders and felt the strong muscles of her back. One large muscle group led to another—this is simple anatomy we are speaking of now—which in turn led to other places. She returned my attention, caress for caress, kiss for kiss.

We edged over to the sleeping bag, unbuckled the belt that held it together, and rolled it out flat. It smelled of mothballs. We slipped out of our clothes (ripped them off might be more accurate) and crawled into the interior. We slid and slithered on its smoothness, and we clawed at the floor for a toehold or a finger jam. It was perilous business, but we were intent and inventive. Claire's skin was delightfully cool and smooth. I could tell you quite a bit about our lovemaking, but I won't. At the end, at the exhausted finish, after the smooching and the slurping, the grunting and giggling, the oohing and ahing, we made a pleasant discovery: our bodies fit together perfectly; we were exactly the right size for each other. (And if I had only remembered my calipers and a calculator, I could have proved it mathematically.)

Claire fell instantly asleep. I couldn't. First, I thought I heard Nicky in the bushes. It was only the wind. I lay there for a long time in the dark wide awake. My hip and shoulder hurt. When the pain became intolerable I went into the bathroom and sat on the edge of the tub. Nicky's bayonet was on the floor, and I kicked the pieces behind the toilet. Something for Mrs. Pappas to think about. It was pleasant to be alone in the dark, forearms on thighs, head leaning forward into the darkness. It was an odd moment for scruples.

I felt very well, though, and not greatly burdened. I was happy in a dumb postcoital way, feeling the solemn joy that results from pleasurable sex. And sex was pleasurable with Claire. The light came on in the living room, and I heard her go to the door. She made sure it was locked. Claire called my name, but I didn't answer. She came to the bathroom door and knocked.

"Henry."

"Yes."

"What are you doing?"

"Sitting here."

"Are you all right?"

She opened the door and a triangle of light entered. She was shivering and goosefleshy.

"I'm thinking."

"Can't you come out here and think with me? It's three in the morning, and I have to catch a plane in a few hours."

"Where are you going?"

"To see my family. To Brooklyn."

"Are you coming back?"

"Probably. Is that bad?" she asked.

"Of course not, Claire. I don't want you to go away."

"If I came back, I'd like to see you."

"I'd like to see you, too," I said, taking another turn in the labyrinth.

"Don't feel like just because we had sex you have to. I know there's Pixie."

"Airy."

"What?"

"Her name is Airy. Nickname actually. Elizabeth is her real name."

"Pixie, Airy, whatever. I think it's a dumb name. I'm sorry if that offends you, Henry, but one of the Three Stooges should be named Airy. Come out of there. It won't help to sit in the dark," Claire said.

We both stood in the living room bare-ass.

"I have to put something on," she said.

She grabbed my T-shirt but wisely sniffed it first. She dropped it on the floor and kicked it next to the record player. She put on her black sweater.

"Here's your chance to be loyal to Airy and nice to me. We can shake hands and no hard feelings, Henry. Here's your chance to make a clean break."

"I'll stay, I guess."

"I have this problem. I'm pregnant, and the chances are I'll decide to remain pregnant."

"I know."

"Sort of sticks in your throat, doesn't it? Mine too."

What could I say? Sexual obsession in a young man is a complicated thing. I shrugged my shoulders and walked over to the record player. I turned on the power—red light, low hum, wobbling turntable—and dropped the needle randomly: "Mona Lisa."

"Let's dance," I said. "My brother said it would calm me down, cure my happy feet."

Considering our recent intimacy and our state of undress, we began quite decorously. I held her at arm's length. For a few moments, we actually danced a gentle and uneventful box step. I was so smooth I didn't even count out the measures. Gradually, things got a bit thicker, and we tugged each other closer. Our movement disintegrated gradually until, at last, we merely stood in place and held each other tightly, swaying to the music. I could feel her heart beat. It was really pounding.

Suddenly, I was gripped with an astonishing thought. I grabbed Claire's shoulders and pushed her away from me so I could say something and look into her face.

"Claire," I said, "I'm very happy right now."

She looked at me and shook her head. Claire placed her cheek against my collar bone, exactly where it had been. The music ended, and we stood silently, clinging to each other like survivors of a shipwreck.

"Of course, you're happy, Henry," she said. "So am I. Everyone is happy when they're dancing."

12

Apologia pro vita mea

MEA CULPA, GUILT buffs. Here's where I jumped in with both feet. No more dawdling at faithlessness's foothills, I commenced the climb. After Claire and I became lovers, I fell into a strange mood. Strange even by my heroic standards. Moments of euphoria alternated in a wild drumbeat, a regular Gene Krupa festival, with moments of panic. As usual, things were out of control.

Too much free time: that's it. Airy had put me on the back burner while she was cranking out her luminous scholarship, bristling with footnotes, many of which, for Christ's sake, were in *German*. About a week after I commenced congregating with Claire, Airy finished her seminar papers and summoned me to her side. In the late spring, she had moved back in with her parents, subletting her apartment, in preparation for her digging in Greece (Mycenae, rich in gold) to do field research.

We hadn't seen each other for almost three weeks (her idea, not mine). And we'd talked on the phone only sporadically since she hated disturbances when she was writing. (She wrote very slowly.) At last, finished with her academic work, she was ready to turn her attention to me; she was ready to set my life on its proper course.

"Henry, you have to promise me you'll think about what you want

to do with your life this summer. You can only be an undergraduate
so long."

She sat on the couch with me, staring into my face. She reached
out and squeezed my hand. She does this when she's trying to be
very, very sincere. Airy had cut her hair, and it was charmingly short,
fuzzy like the crewcuts professional athletes wore in the Sixties. Boog
Powell, for example. It was blonde and bristly, and I ran my hand
over it gently. I'm a fool for sleeping with Claire Cohen, I thought,
a real idiot. Men would sail the seas for a woman like Elizabeth. Airy
had written her seminar papers sitting on her parents' patio, surrounded by note cards, dusty library books, and glasses of iced tea.
She was deeply tanned. She looked a different woman from the one
I had last seen. Not being around me agreed with her.

I had some exciting news to tell her.

"I'm graduating."

After five years and 135 credits, much against my will, the university was going to award me a B.A. in history. I didn't like it.

"Congratulations. Why didn't you tell me?"

"I didn't find out about it until yesterday. I got a congratulatory
note from Miriam Mackendrick."

Miriam Mackendrick was my academic adviser and friend. She
looked exactly like Debbie Reynolds, except she was a lot heavier.
She took an avid interest in my undergraduate career because of the
odd circumstances of my personal life. I was one of those students
who had been singled out as a potential numb nuts. She actually
saved me once from a terrible mistake (joining the Marine Corps
because of a broken heart). She was writing notes (congratulatory,
encouraging, scolding) to her favorites (I was included in that happy
group) because she was dying of breast cancer and knew she wouldn't
live through the summer. She didn't, and when I read her obituary
in the paper, I cried like a baby.

Airy and I were sitting in the Florida room, which was packed with
plants. The place was corrupt with knickknacks, Airy's mother being
an avid collector of ceramic birds and Wedgwood doodads. The
plants made me sneeze.

"Do you want to have sex?" she asked.

We were alone in the house. Her mother was out shopping for

tonight's festive farewell dinner, and the old man was at Blackhawk Country Club playing golf with his real estate syndicate.

The truth was that since Saturday night—this was Friday morning—Claire and I had been doing it a lot. (She had moved in for a week with her friend Franny. Claire was going back to New York any day, except the day kept getting postponed.) I was rubbed raw, and I think I had an inflammation of the prostate because I was in excruciating pain when I peed. (Nature's way of short-circuiting sexual profligacy?) But what could I say? Airy was leaving the next morning, so some sort of intimacy was required. And I loved Airy and wanted to be intimate. I did. I really did.

I was also hoping that her mother would come home.

So we went into Airy's room and crawled between the sheets. She liked to have sex in her room. It was full of stuffed animals and crayon drawings she had made as a toddler. Her diaries were here; little teenage fantasies had been concocted in this very bed. The entire effect was inflammatorily erotic on Airy. One montagelike combination of images—Henry without clothes and Jerry the Giraffe—sent her over the edge. I found it all very weird. Once my trousers were down, my chaffed state was observed. (Airy has always, casually but thoroughly, inspected me for symptoms of disease or infidelity.)

"What's wrong with your thing?" she asked. "Why is it all red?"

The ball was in my court. Clearly, I should have made a clean breast. I should have told Airy about my assignations with Claire Cohen. But what did it amount to, after all? Just a little good-natured copulation between two acquaintances. These kinds of friendly couplings happen every night of the week, every hour of the night. It was ordinary, part of the general program. Don't rock the boat needlessly, I told myself.

I told a lie, quite a complicated one.

"Remember when I smashed the bathroom wall with my work-boot?"

Airy and I had had an argument, and I lost my temper. I created a boot-heel-sized hole in the bathroom wall with my Redwing boot.

"Yes. You were horrid."

"Well, to get my security deposit back, I had to plaster and paint.

I had to use oil paint, and when I was going to the bathroom I got some on my penis. I used benzine to get the paint off but forgot to wash myself with soap and water. The redness is irritation from the benzine. I have to put hand lotion on it until the soreness goes away."

"Does it hurt?"

"A little."

"Well, come here then, and I'll make you feel better."

She pulled back the covers. Her body had a bathing-suit tan; her breasts were banded with a scallop of white skin. Her chest was freckled and very brown against the white of the bottom sheet.

Slime that I am, I jumped into the cool sheets next to Airy, for a lengthy farewell cuddle. If Lippy the Lion had real teeth, he would have ripped my throat open.

Airy and I, according to her phrase, "had sex," showered, and dressed, a little nicer than normal, preparing for the party. It was festive. We all got a little tipsy, and, in a radical departure from the norm, I was allowed to spend the night with Airy, back to back and belly to belly: a concession to modern mores the Elders were usually unwilling to make.

The next morning Airy's mother and I drove her down to O'Hare. We said almost nothing to one another, except harmless chitchat about the quality of last night's standing rib roast (better than good) and the weather (suffocatingly hot). At the gate, standing clinging to each other, we made such promises lovers make at these moments. I'll think about you; I'll miss you; I'll write. Blah, blah.

On the ride back with Helen Elder, who, after a period of relative indifference, was beginning to actively dislike me (but not the stocks, bonds, and other financial instruments in my portfolio). I felt blue. I didn't say much, so stricken was I with remorse.

"You'll see how fast the summer will go, Henry," Helen Elder said to me, mistaking my anxiety. "Airy will be back before you know it."

That's what I was afraid of.

Within hours of Airy's departure—perhaps just as she was sipping a midflight cocktail, wondering what I was up to—what I was up to was kissing the fragrant skin behind Claire Cohen's right ear. Claire and I were sitting on the floor in my new apartment making out. Claire's housewarming present, a chilled bottle of Italian sparkling wine, sat on the floor next to me. I had just finished emptying boxes and bags, putting away clothes and books. The sun was going down, but the temperature still was 95 degrees and I was sweat soaked and exhausted. I had found this fragrant spot on Claire's neck, and I was devoting my attention to it. She pushed me away.

"Henry, it's too hot to be nibbled on. Let's take a break."

It was as if Airy had fallen off the face of the earth.

"You have a pretty body, Claire."

"I know, Henry. I wish my boobs were a little bigger."

Me, too, I suppose. Not much bigger though.

I sat in silence sipping my wine. I poured another glass, enjoying the cool sliminess of the bottle as I rested it against my belly. I sulked, feeling drearily unfaithful.

Claire was smiling at me. We sat close together, our shoulders barely touched. She tried to look serious but couldn't. The lights were not on in the apartment, and we sat in the twilighty semidarkness. Claire pulled her hair away from her neck, gathering it in her right hand.

I wondered what time it was in Athens, early in the a.m. probably.

"Henry?"

"Yes?"

"What's going to happen to me if I have a baby?"

"You'll be a mother."

"I mean seriously. I think sometimes that I'm being stupid. I should go ahead and have the abortion. What am I going to do for money?"

"Get married."

"I'd shoot myself before I married Nicky. Henry, I think it's you or nobody."

She was joking, I think. At any rate, she started to laugh. Claire slapped me on the shoulder, a real pal.

"Make an honest woman out of me?"

"Okay. You've got it. But Milton is going to insist on some sort of prenuptial agreement."

Claire's smile disappeared.

The fact is I probably was willing to marry Claire. Even more oddly, I think, she would have been willing to marry me. And, most preposterous of all, we would have been happy together. So what that, according to Claire, her father was a kosher butcher in Brooklyn? So what that her mother's ulcer-making fear was that Claire wouldn't marry a Jew? What difference did that make to a couple of crazy kids in love? My, the shit would hit the fan if I married Claire. A large drop of sweat ran down my nose and plummeted onto my belly. Then another. This was thunderstorm weather, and it was possible that the rumbling we heard was not from trucks laboring up Gorham Street, but a storm off in the west.

How quiet we became. We were aware of the distance we had gone. Had we been a little older, or a little stronger, or a little more willful, we might actually have gone through with it. But in that silence, thick-throated, heavy-tongued silence, we let the moment slip away. Seize the day; *carpe diem*: that's the lesson to be learned. I sipped my wine, and Claire hummed ("Mona Lisa, Mona Lisa, dum de dum dum"). Of such awkward, paralyzing silences is a disappointed life composed. The thunder was no metaphor: the literal rain moved in quickly, dampening (but not cooling) the shabby literal world. Claire and I went into the kitchen, deciding salads would be the perfect meal for such a hot evening.

It seems to me that, in the beginning, in the first week Claire stayed with me, it rained constantly. It was the summer of monsoons, full of dramatic lightning bolts and window-shivering thunder. Whenever Claire and I were in bed together, I would lie awake while she slept (Claire could sleep through a fire drill) listening to the rain on the window screens. I had pangs of guilt, shafts of guilt, actually. I felt like a scummy lowlife: foul, unclean, untrustworthy, friendless, and alone. Thank God that mood passed!

One night, in a content after-dinner lull, Claire decided that I should come to New York for a weekend. She was leaving in a few days for her much-postponed visit, and I would follow hot on her heels. I could stay in the Plaza, as she'd always wanted to sleep in the Plaza. We could explore the city, and maybe she'd take me home to dinner with her family.

"Why don't you come?" she asked.

"No. I can't afford it."

"Bullshit, Henry. You have to come. It'll be great."

It didn't sound great to me. Although I was at what are called loose ends, the last place I wanted to hunker down was Claire's house. I imagined Claire's father as intensely intellectual, terribly learned, and resentful of me, a Gentile, disconnected from the traditions he was struggling to preserve. I saw him as a small man with a powerful handshake, bowed slightly beneath his burdens. No earlocks or frock coats, I knew that, of course; still, a serious and even sad man. Little did I know that Blanche and Howard—Mom and Pop Cohen— aspired to be the First Family of Woodstock Nation. They were looking for fun and feeling groovy: macrobiotic rice and meditation with a weaselly-looking dude in a saffron robe. Mondo Cohen was a queer set of contradictions.

Claire had done some major dissembling. Kosher butcher. Ha! The old man was the veal king of the Washington Street Market; the Baron of First-Class Baby Beef. Blanche had been a lingerie model; her specialty was push-up bras. At the moment, they were into caftans, Lebanese hash, and trying to get Claire to have an abortion. Of this stuff I was then utterly ignorant.

"Have you told them you're pregnant?"

"Yes. They're upset about it."

I didn't realize it then, but Claire's suggestion that I visit Chez Cohen was probably not completely spontaneous. I was Claire's ace in the hole. I had been promoted in her regard—field commission, just like Audie Murphy—from agreeable acquaintance to occasional lover, to temporary cohabitor, to the man who might derail the abortion juggernaut. I think that was her personal and private judgment. To her parents, I was to be represented (actually, misrepresented) as a pal and clearly a candidate for buddy status. (Using Milton's well-known definition: pals are friends, buddies sleep together.) Somehow my persona—orphan and millionaire—was going to help Claire in establishing her decision to be pregnant and remain so. I was the twerp who was going to make things okey-dokey.

But I was adamant, and Claire was resigned to leaving without me, exactly a week after Airy's departure. Burma couldn't have been any more fetid than that June in Madison. Sex had become a slippery ordeal, and the slithery sheets were crusted with sweat and other mysterious bodily fluids. (I actually sort of liked the smell: a salty,

seaweedish aroma.) We exchanged phone numbers and fond embraces. I stood with her on the front stoop while we waited for the
airport limousine. Her hands were clammy, and her lips were dry.

"I'll miss you, Henry."

"I'll miss you, too," I said, perhaps a bit too perfunctorily. Maybe
I'd miss her. On the other hand, it would be nice to have a short
vacation from the colon-clenching insomnia I was experiencing. I'm
really cut out for monogamy. This is a true fact.

"I'll be back in a week or so. I think we should have a serious talk."

"It's confusing," I said, more mournfully than I had intended.

"What's the matter?"

"I feel like a zombie."

"I see. I'm glad I have such a beneficial effect on you."

"Nothing personal, Claire."

"Thanks."

"It sounded worse than I meant it. Everything is going awfully
fast."

"Looking for the lifeboat, Fitzgerald?"

Illucid, lonely, dehydrated (a shark could swim in the volume of
salty stuff that had dripped down my nose in June), I felt a tiny touch
of panic creeping up my thighs, past my groin, into my gut. I was
horribly socialized, I see now. I had not really learned to do anything
except the hard way: bloody nose, smashed knuckles. I refused to
accept advice. It was as if I had been raised by Arctic wolves. And
now, as a result of my imperfect socialization, I was in one of those
midnight-rambling happy-feet states of mind. The reason? I suspected that what I wanted out of my odd life was to get comfy and
settled with this dark-haired beauty. I wanted things to be simple; to
delete the complications. I was pleased by Claire Cohen but lacked
the vital gram of will to make that pleasure permanent. So I withdrew
into goofy Henryness. Is it any wonder I ended up in jail?

Of course, I believed I was perfectly fine. No different, at least,
than I had always been. I was rich as Onassis. If I wanted, I could get
on The Empire Builder and go flyfishing in Montana. In short, I
knew perfectly well that I needed Claire like a dog needs a leash,
which is not at all. But dumb desire prevailed.

"No."

"I want you to stand by me. My mother is making my life hell. She's trying to force me to have an abortion. She's made appointments with a clinic and a psychiatrist. I need your support, Henry. It may not be fair to you, but you had a chance to bug out. You didn't. So please help me now. I need you."

Put it that way, and I'll charge through the gates of hell.

"Okay. But I'm not sure I'm very good at this stuff."

"You'll be fine."

"I don't want to feel like I'm in over my head. I don't want to feel responsible for you. In fact, you wouldn't want me to be responsible for you because I am not at all trustworthy. I fuck up a lot, Claire. I really do. I'm disgustingly weak. I treat my friends badly. Eventually everyone is disappointed in me. I'm not reliable."

"I don't really believe that. I hope that's not true. But I do have a feeling it will get very strange before long."

She strained to look up and down Gilman Street, and she checked her watch.

"Where's the limo, Henry? I'll miss my flight."

Claire was sweating and silent. She had undone her braid, and her hair was hanging across her back. Claire walked toward the street with her hands clasped behind her, downlooking and pensive.

The question that was in both of our minds at this moment was: How did I get into this mess, and how am I going to get out of it? That's two questions, I guess.

The answer to the first was "by accident"; the answer to the second was up in the air.

The airport limo, empty except for the Sikh driver in a blue turban, rolled to the curb. She climbed in without a look, or a word, or even a wink for Henry, who had just pledged something, however ambiguous. The limo lumbered away, air-conditioned, sealed as tight as a tomb. At the last second, just as she was about to disappear down the steep Gilman Street hill, Claire turned and waved, shyly, as shy as a schoolgirl.

13

Right Thought; Right Action

THINK ABOUT IT. If you stand outside your home—say, a three-story wood frame house, one of those three-layered three-family apartment houses so often found in the heart of old midwestern cities—in the gray of the false dawn and see your wife and children carried out of smoky ruins dead, what can be the result? For Norman O'Keefe, my great friend, the answer is simple: a wildly murderous channel was gouged into his soul. Retribution was always on his mind. Revenge—the bloodier the better—was what he wanted. He looked for allies, even if only subconsciously, for kindred, ferocious, spiteful spirits. Me, in certain close-to-the-bone moments, in other words. I am a spiteful shit, no doubt about that. Grudges are my specialty (see my attitude *viz* Nicky). Old-fashioned and deep-seated anger has dogged me like an afternoon shadow most of my life, putting me into some difficult spots. Grudge holding and bitterness underscored the circumstances surrounding my startling decline into criminality. I'm not happy about it, but you have to play the hand you're dealt. Just don't forget I'm an orphan.

A week had passed since Claire left for New York, and it had been two weeks since Airy left Madison for Greece. In the interim, I had not received a word from either of them: not a phone call, no telegrams, postcards, or greetings through third parties. Is this any way to treat the light of one's life? Excluding the awkward circumstances that infidelity creates, I felt badly used. So badly used, in fact, that I was tempted to call Lily Campbell, who wanted to make up with Henry anyway. Still, I know I'm down to the last slice of bread in the loaf when I get the yen to call Lily. On the other hand, and I admit this without a trace of reluctance, Lily Campbell could screw like a dry-wall gun.

Bereft of female companionship, I was sitting on my sofa, as worn as a first baseman's mitt, picking dead skin off the bottom of my feet. I had just come in from a twilight run. I had stripped off my soggy running duds and was wrapped in a towel. My shirt and shorts were hanging from the faucets of the bathtub, drip, drip, dripping, as the sweat wicked out of the cotton and ran in a grayish stream down the drain. My shoes—which smelled abominably (something I always denied when *Airy* said it)—were propped up in the window with the laces undone and the tongues pulled out.

This was the way I had passed my Airyless, Claireless June days: as a solitary celibate. I was bored. I felt I was missing something; that I had lost my way. Mostly, without the diversion of women (fragrant hair, smooth skin, tender embraces, etc.), I was restless and discontented. I wondered why my women friends hadn't been in touch. But, in keeping with the surliness of my mood, I thought, who needs them? Unfortunately, I knew the answer: Henry.

I was terrifically bored, and boredom is worse for me than heroin. At least if you're shooting a narcotic, you can slump against a brick wall and drool down your chin and more or less feel okay. When I get bored, I get all nerved up and I get happy feet. Then I have to take one of my midnight walks and end up watching Birdwhistle making doughnuts while he babbles on about cosmic topics. The bitter truth is what I really longed for was snuggling up with Claire Cohen, playing hide the salami three times a day.

A circular saw was whining outside even though it was late in the working day, overtime. Someone was fixing up one of the old dingy mansions on Bug Hill, the one essentially catty-corner from me, although I wasn't on a corner: up the street, anyway, on the southwest corner of Gilman and Pinckney, a big old brick house with a mansard roof and a cast-iron widow's walk.

All I had on was a towel, and I wrapped it more snugly around me. I threw my running shoes off the sill onto the floor and stuck my head out the window to con the situation. Bug Hill was swarming with tradesmen. Pickup trucks with plywood tool boxes bolted behind the cab were pulled up on the lawn of the brick house—the Peabody House, all these places took the name of the original owner, a 19th-century entrepreneur (land swindler or sweat-shop owner). Except, now, someone (that person being almost immediately recognizable and notorious) had erected a large white sign on the lawn.

On the sidewalk in front of his property, the soul of proprietorship, a magnate, a prince surveying his fiefdom was that syrupy minister to baby birds with broken wings, Leonard Gent, my new neighbor. This was to be his halfway house for underage hoodlums. The hairs on my neck rose. My toes curled; my testicles retracted. I stood in my bay window—my perch, my crow's nest—which overlooked Gilman Street and looked down on Leonard and his enterprise. The sign said, in black letters against a white field: SAFE HAVEN: NO ONE TURNED AWAY. A workman with a roll of plans in his fist stood with Gent, probably conferring about Gent's preferences: where did he want the secret, soundproof chamber? Where did he want the pillory installed? Where should he mount the manacles on the wall? Where the slots for the bread and water?

Gent engaged in animated conversation with a jockey-size man with red hair. Gent pointed to a two-by-four, and the little guy picked it up and threw it on a trash pile; he pointed to a beer can, and the midget scurried to dispose of it. Gent's flunky, of course, the ersatz orphan Mickey Monahan was out there scratching Gent's itches. Gent and Monahan: weasels major and minor.

And somehow I wasn't surprised to catch a glimpse of the embryonic assassin, the blue-sweatshirted psychopath who gave Gent such a chicken-bone-in-the-throat start on the Library Mall. He sat, hunkered down on a high curb, stolidly observing Gent and his minuscule minion. His appearance had changed greatly. His hair was pulled back into a tight ponytail, and he had shucked off layers of clothing. The beer bloat was gone, and now he was skinny as a paper clip. Obviously, he had spent some time in exaggerated exercise, in serious training, pumping the heavy weights, running up stadium steps. This was a man with a plan: a new man; a dangerous man, because Lenny wouldn't even look at him. Norman had been getting his ducks in a row, preparing for the Ultimate Conflagration Itself: the end of the bombastic child-fancier Lenny Gent.

I know now this was the future laid bare. I glimpsed à la Birdwhistle into an ugly and incendiary future with Gent on my block, corroding my view. Enlightenment, as Bob says, isn't like a bomb exploding. Before enlightenment, he quotes his master, I worked; after enlightenment, ditto. Partially enlightened, I see it is possible to write an epic poem based on the scurrility of Leonard Gent. Except for the part about Norman's anger (I like that part), it would not be a savory thing to read or a very savory thing to write. The conclusion— Leonard Gent floating face down in the Chicago River on St. Patrick's Day, 1974, tinged green, bloated, feasted upon by river beasties, deader than any doornail—would be necessarily ambiguous. No hero ever proclaimed the deed his doing, and suicide seems rather beyond Gent's capacities. Maybe he slipped.

Late afternoon in the city, and the carpenters were in their time-and-a-half mode. My ends were looser than normal. The one man I could really count on for consolation, Milton, was out of town, taking depositions in St. Paul. My feet felt very happy indeed. I decided if I could only talk to Claire Cohen, find out when she was coming back, hear her husky voice, have her coo into my ear sweet lascivious little mutterings about what I could do to her and she to me, I would calm down.

I found her number and dialed. It rang a long time, and then Claire answered, a quiet "Hello." Then there was the unmistakable click of an extension being picked up (maybe Claire was only allowed to speak while being monitored, with a steel-blue revolver held to her temple).

"Hello," Blanche, the Ava Gardner of push-up bras, butted in, or bosomed in, as the case may be.

Claire said hello again. (Was that a hopeful—is that you, Henry— note in her voice?)

"I've got it, dear," old Blanche said.

And Claire hung up.

Hello, that creature said again. Then she slammed the receiver down with a whump.

If only Blanche had been at Bendel's buying lingerie, my life might have followed a profoundly different course. Now I knew I was going to go out and march around about midnight. Hey, but who really knows, karma-cally speaking, which path is the right one? As a result of that night's midnight ramble, I discovered some crucially important things. For example, that Norman O'Keefe can talk to elephants. He insists (and who am I to say he is wrong?) that an elephant possesses an acute intelligence and, if given a chance, can offer very valuable insights into knotty dilemmas, celebrated conundrums, seemingly unresolvable contradictions. Elephants, as a result of their reduction to mere spectacle, offer wisdom tinged with melancholy. I can understand that. If you were to see him, as I did, sitting cross-legged between mother and daughter elephant (Tiny and Crystal), you might sense an odd mutual comprehension. I am no judge and have been wrong—embarrassingly wrong—about men and dumb animals both. Yet, with Tiny's trunk draped around Norman's shoulder—and Norman's spirits raised by this seeming gesture of comfort—you might believe that a man could address one of these great beasts and be understood.

After my aborted call to Cohen, I vowed to stay inside. But I was never good at solemn vows, and I called Lily Campbell. She was thrilled, thrilled to hear from me. (Sincerity is not one of her strengths.) We made a date to have a couple of beers at Bob and Gene's, the launching pad of all my Lily-related endeavors. I actually admired Lily (except for her inverted nipples, which even she described as a "bummer"). She was a great innovator in her affairs, creating a kind of platoon system for her lovers. Five of us, six of us: we were like the Chinese Bandits for Christ's sake. Finally, Lily's hygiene got to be a problem: I caught the crabs from her. Embittered by infestation, I fell out of Lily's favor completely and was replaced in the lineup by a Syrian medical student (whom I commenced referring to, with customary equanimity, as "that goat-fucking rag-head").

I took a shower and a nap, preparing myself for grappling with Lily.

When I woke up it was almost dark, and I was late. I left my apartment, seething with frustration, thinking I was going to do the boda-bing boda-bang with Lily Campbell. And worse: revenge boda-bing boda-bang. I tried to decide how long I had to chat her up before I suggested we come back to my place for a little of the old horizontal mumbo-jumbo. (Fifteen minutes would be enough, I decided.) My pockets were full of twenty-dollar bills; my head was full of blistering lust. Lily could do it until dawn, I remembered.

But when I got downstairs, wouldn't you know it, but the dreaded mid-twentieth-century *Weltschmerz* overcame me, and I realized I didn't want to see Lily. I realized I didn't even like her. I sat down on the curb and stared at my grommeted sneakers, overladen with anger and regret. Oh, no, I didn't want to pork Lily Campbell. I wanted to hear Claire Cohen laugh at one of my moronic jokes. I wanted to stroke her thick black hair. What were the chances Claire was weaving a complicated tapestry in my absence? Not good.

"Kid," a voice erupted out of a bush behind me, a voice clotted with rage, "you're blocking my view."

"Up yours, pal," I answered, "whose sidewalk is it?"

"Mine," he said, "mine and Leonard Gent's."

Norman O'Keefe, dazzled, I suspect, by Gent's hubris was maintaining some sort of solitary vigil. The bows of our ships, Norman's and mine, were beginning to sheer the same bright Gentward course.

"I've seen you before."

"I've seen you," I said.

"Norman O'Keefe."

"Henry Fitzgerald," I said.

"I know that," he answered, "your brother is a lawyer."

"That's right," I said. Everybody knows me once removed.

"I might need a lawyer," Norman said, "I might need one soon."

I had also come to that conclusion. To say the least, Norman was skirting the Cataract of Diminished Responsibility.

"Norman," I said, the *Weltschmerz* easing a bit, "can I buy you a beer?" The old musical question.

"Maybe. Maybe. Hey, I got something to do first, you want to come for a walk with me?"

Sure. What could I lose? Was I not a lonesome traveler? I had found a kindred spirit. We both had happy feet.

"You know what, pal? I think you're all right," he said. "You might just be the one."

The one what, I was momentarily inclined to ask but did not. I had a feeling the answer would involve throwing myself on a live grenade; something to do with being cannon fodder, anyway. We ambled westward, unhurriedly. We stopped once so Norman could buy bread—three day-old loaves. I figured he was carbo loading. When we got to the Vilas Park Zoo, he leaned against the hurricane fence that surrounds the zoo, as pensive as Pascal.

"Come on," he said, "you can meet the girls."

We climbed the outer fence of Vilas Park Zoo just before ten. It's a pleasant place. I come here often to read. The animals are well cared for and not cage crazy. The Elephant House sat in the center of the compound. It was new, angular, squatish, like a garage in an expensive neighborhood of Santa Fe, New Mexico. It was circled by a concrete ditch, a moat, which keeps elephants in and paying customers out. The ditch was dry most of the time; occasionally it was flooded. Tonight it was empty. Norman waved at me from the enclosure, telling me I had to slip into the ditch and scramble up the inner lip. It wasn't hard, just requiring one to slide carefully down one side and thrash back up the other. My hands were skinned up, but in a few moments Norman was hauling me up into the dusty, elephant-smelling circle.

The first of many coincidences became clear: Norman and I had exactly the same sort of outfit on. Blue jeans, black T-shirt, black tennis shoes. The right knee of both our jeans was ripped and ragged, and a wedge of whitish knee skin showed through, scratched and a little bloody from our exertions. Many such coincidences were to hover over Norman and me, like mosquitoes over a fat baby.

Norman peered back into the darkness.

"Do you think anybody followed us?" he asked.

It's possible, I thought, but just barely so, tangible reasons exist that might justify this question. Under normal circumstances, Norman might seem merely paranoid, unpleasantly so. But these were not normal circumstances.

"I don't think so. But tell me, why do we have to come to the zoo?"

"I like it here." To his credit, Norman didn't say because he wanted his pals, elephant mother and daughter, Tiny and Crystal (Crystal was the daughter), to check me out. They—Norman and the elephants, he stood between them—faced me and were grim. Christ, it all seemed so natural. What could I have been thinking of?

"Norman," I said, "why are you here with these elephants? What if they got mad or something?"

"Mad?" He laughed and then smiled cheerily, the first time I had ever seen him other than burdened. "I'm here because they're excellent company."

He opened the loaves of day-old bread—19 cents said a brilliant orange sticker on the cellophane. He threw the cellophane wrappers on the ground. He grabbed a huge handful of slices, pounded them into a lopsided ball, and motioned to Tiny to lift up her trunk.

"That's a good old girl," he said. He pitched the ball into her mouth. (Her mouth looked just like my running shoes with the laces undone and the tongue pulled up.) He repeated the process, with a smaller ball of bread, with Crystal. They had dainty tongues, which they used to lever the bread back into their mouths. They chewed and swallowed with amazing delicacy.

"Is this how you usually spend your evenings?"

"Only once a week. I don't want to push things."

He picked up the bread wrappers, and stuffed them into his back pocket. They made a goiterish lump on his hip.

"What would happen if I climbed in here without you?"

"I'm not sure. But Tiny would probably crush you if you got too close to Crystal. She'd drop you in the moat like a half-smoked cigar."

The Elephant House itself occupied about a third of the moated area. The stark concrete building and the fan-shaped elephant yard created the appearance of an abandoned bandshell in a 19th-century park. I suppose they went in there—a huge doorway permitted elephant entry and exit—in bad weather or to get some shade. There was a watering tub in there (water trickled in and out constantly); thick red hoses were suspended from the ceiling, tightly coiled; blond long-handled brushes leaned together in a corner.

"Sit down, Henry," Norman said.

I took a position against the cement wall of the Elephant House, which was the color of a dirty elephant: light gray, overcast sunrise gray, mottled by whitish powder. Crystal rubbed herself against this wall daily, satisfying a mammoth itch. The zoo was unlighted except for floodlights on the administration building. These lights created a dead zone of acetelyne brightness—a disincentive to burglars—circling the offices. The remainder of the compound sat, undisturbed, in darkness. Norman sat down next to me. His elephant pals wandered over to us, ambling amiably with decidedly pleased expressions on their faces, and took up a position between us and the prying eyes of any late-night watchmen. They stood above us, as massive and as colorless as a headwall.

"Leonard Gent," he said, "is my enemy."

"I know Leonard Gent," I said. "I've heard his Lincoln Park routine. I know all about his perversions and his fortune. I know," I said with some smugness, "everything."

Norman laughed. "You don't know your ass from a hole in the wall. You don't know anything."

He sounded angry. I suppose I had been impertinent; in fact, my ignorance was abysmal. Of the poisoned waters of the Sea of Gent, I had twiddled my toes in only the tiniest tidal pool. There was a great deal more to know than the fortune in commodities, the sordid liaisons in Lincoln Park, the remarkable transformation to near priestly status. More than that?

Oh, yes, much more: stolen cigarettes distributed in Michigan and northern Wisconsin with forged tax stamps; tuna boats berthed in San Diego used to smuggle Russian assault rifles to drug syndicates in Mexico; suitcases crammed with banknotes delivered to politicians sitting in the backrooms of expensive steakhouses on Michigan Avenue. That and worse.

"You see, Henry, I have a complicated family history. My father was involved with Gent a little, and to be involved with Gent a little is to be sucked down the drain. He did two things. Number one, he owned a small trucking company, four trucks, strictly nickel-and-dime stuff. He was also a shylock; they called him Six-for-Five O'Keefe. His real name was Ed. When Gent was real hard up—he lost a lot of money on a trifecta scheme at Hawthorne Park—he borrowed some money from my father. They got to be friendly, Gent sent him some customers, and my father kept an eye open for business possibilities for his pal Lenny."

His voice was calm.

"I didn't have anything to do with it. I was a happy man. That's a dangerous thing to be, I guess. I rarely saw my father; my mother was dead by then. I thought the old man was an absolute shit. I had a wife and two kids. I was busy. I owned three houses; I was a landlord. I had some money in the bank, in fact, I had quite a bit of it. You know, Henry, I've forgotten what my little girls looked like. I've sort of had to forget a lot of things. That's not right. Anyway, this is what happened.

"My father's business was doing lousy. You can't make any money with four trucks, and he loaned money to a lot of deadbeats. He ended up holding fifty thousand in worthless paper. But he couldn't collect because he wasn't a tough guy. He tried to be, but his heart wasn't in it. Then he met this punk—Fletcher Lint—in a bar in Eagle River, Wisconsin. They talk and drink. Ed's playing the big shot from Chicago. I saw that act so often I had it memorized. After a lot of drinks, Lint has this proposition for my old man. He has some connections who can deliver counterfeit tax stamps on stolen cigarettes on demand. His idea is to dump them up in the sticks: northern Wisconsin and the UP. They need trucks and drivers. He's also looking for a little investment capital. Some money to underwrite expenses. Lint used to run a whorehouse up in Hurley, and he has a lot of contacts but no cash. My father brings Leonard Gent in on the deal, who has cash and is excessively greedy. The three of them get together, they make this deal, and start the operation. They do well, real well, and since the old man is set up for business and can hide a lot of cash in his bank accounts, they let him be the bookkeeper. Big mistake. He's desperate to pay off his bookmaker, a guy named Butterball Buscarelli. The fattest man in Cicero, which is saying something. He borrows—without telling Lint and Gent—fifteen thousand dollars to pay off his bookie. Embezzles it. You follow me?

"He gets the fifteen thousand and decides to make one last bet.

Naturally, he loses. What else? The dumb bastard bet on the Bears and gave the points. Naturally, some Mexican beanhead for the Cowboys kicks a field goal in a gale, and the Bears don't cover. Now he owes Buscarelli thirty thousand and the boys fifteen thousand, and he doesn't have a pot to pee in. He asks me for the money, but I say no way. That's my good money after your bad. His trucks are being used to deliver bogus cigarettes, he owes a lot of money to persons who are suddenly very interested in being paid back. He's got no money and no hope. My father has the good sense to have a massive heart attack and die. He leaves me all his worldly possessions: four trucks, one with a bad transmission. I signed over the operation to Butterball, who was not a bad guy, by the way, and who was in his own way the only legitimate businessman of the bunch. My father was practically penniless when he died. Come to think of it, he was less than penniless, and I had to pay for his funeral. But Gent thinks my father has a lot of cash hidden away from when he was a shylock and I know where it is. He came after me."

Crystal, that paragon of sympathy, shifted her feet anxiously. She inched toward Norman. I swear—maybe the midnight moon encouraged this particular pathetic fallacy—but she gave me a swift, encouraging look: don't let Norman go too far down this road.

"He came to see me and demanded his money. They also can't locate the account my father used for their partnership. He had that little retard Mickey Monahan with him. Monahan had a baseball bat, and he pulled back his overcoat to show it to me. I guess he thought that would scare me. I said I didn't have his money, and get off my property. Period the end, I told him that standing in my front yard. It was snowing, and I remember we were both very cold. Get out, I said, just get out.

"Then I began to get threatening phone calls. Someone threw a rock through my living room window. I didn't think much about it. I thought I could weather the storm. I called the cops, but Gent must have called them too. He's like a cockroach. He can crawl into places you wouldn't think it possible to penetrate. I realized that I was going to be absolutely alone in dealing with this threat to my life. I suppose that's everyone's realization sooner or later. I was one of the unlucky ones who learned sooner. There was a small fire on the porch of one of my buildings. I want my money, he said. I bought myself a shotgun, and I held it up in the window as he and Monahan drove by. I figured as long as I could I would defend myself. Then it seemed to end. For months I didn't hear anything from him, and I began to relax.

"I thought I had won. I was a little arrogant about it. I tempted the gods, I guess, because they squashed me like a bug. I was fixing up the second floor of my apartment. I was plastering and painting, basic stuff. I stored my paints and brushes—turpentine and buckets—on the landing outside my apartment door. I'm very careful about that stuff. There was plenty of ventilation, no open flames or sparks. Nothing except human agency could have ignited a blaze. So, one night when I was at work—I was a mechanic for the Transit Authority—someone set a fire among those cans. I had to work a little overtime that morning. I was about an hour late. If I had been home at the right time, I would have caught it before it got out of control. I'm sure Gent didn't want to kill anyone. He just wanted to scare the hell out of me. The fire exploded. It was incredible. My family was trapped inside. They all died. My wife and daughters died. The investigators said the fire started in some rags, rags that were soaked in paint thinner. Spontaneous combustion. Basically, they said my negligence in disposing of my painting supplies was the cause of the fire: that I had killed my own family. But none of that was true. I was scrupulous about that sort of clean-up. All the cans were clean and tightly sealed. All the brushes were dry. I put all my rags in the garbage can in the alley."

"What happened to Gent?"

"Nothing. He had a nervous breakdown. Spent a month in the Caribbean studying offshore tax laws. He came back to town with a suntan."

"Was he ever charged with anything?"

"No."

"Has he ever spoken to you again?"

"Not a word. I sent him a letter. I said I was going to kill him. The next thing I knew he had seen the light and was delivering sermons in public parks. I followed him to Madison. That's all I know."

"And that was last year?"

"February of 1971."

"What have you been doing?"

"Traveling around from town to town. Keeping an eye on Gent. Waiting, my friend, waiting for just the right moment. I feel like a ghost. I'm searching for the right spot, the right moment. Then, bango, I'm going to split Gent open like a watermelon. I'm tired of the process; I need to have the conclusion. Nothing worse than that."

So this was how we commenced our adventure together. Alone and in the dark, we had climbed into a forbidden zone in violation of our civic responsibilities.

"What are you going to do?" I asked.

"I'm not sure. I'm looking for Fletcher Lint. I need confirmation before I do the deed to Gent. He and Gent had an argument about their little enterprise, and I heard it got ugly. Lint left Chicago and went up north again. Lenny beat him out of some of the profits. I've looked in every whorehouse and barroom north of Wausau. You ever been to Bessemer, Ironwood, or Wakefield? Don't go. I've been there, in every dark tavern, in every collapsing town. I got callouses on my elbows from leaning on sticky bars, making small talk with the local alcoholic underclass. I've been looking for Lint the way the wind looks for a mountaintop. I'm just about beat. Have any ideas?"

I didn't, but I knew who might. Bob B. knows all the secrets along Highway 2.

"Ah," I said, "Birdwhistle will help."

We clambered down into and back out of the moat. He boosted me up to the top, and I reached down and pulled him up. We did the same at the fence. Our climbing was well coordinated. We were a good team. I led him away from the Zoo toward that inflammatory declaration in red: BIRDWHISTLE!

This was the first of many, many midnight strolls that summer and autumn, punctuated by chilly beers in Jingles or the Amber Grid. We formed some sort of odd, searchers' cabal. I had started off the evening ready for action, turbulent in my groinal area, tingling with Lily-lust, and I ended up hearing a story so sad it changed my life. Things seemed to be crowding in on me, weighing me down. My inattentiveness to details, my infatuations with smooth-skinned women, my directionlessness, my spendthriftness, my bizarre friends, my bleeding-heart brother: they all danced around me like tipsy ballerinas. Unsettling phantasms. They jostled me, shoved me aside, led me down dark and savage paths. The essence of the problem came to me while I was out walking in silence with Norman O'Keefe, in our stately lonesome way: I lived too close to sea level. If I lived in the mountains, where the seasons are richer and more intense, the small heartaches would fall away, disappearing in eastern slope sunlight. I should take Claire to Montana.

"I've seen the sign," Norman said, referring to BIRDWHISTLE! in red.

"It's hard to miss."

"I don't like the doughnuts, though. Taste like sawdust. I like the gooey glazed kind with the jelly filling. Now, that's a doughnut."

Somehow I knew, down deep, that I was going to be at or near sea level for the foreseeable future. Norman was going to be fighting through those marshes as well. Mountain living—the sweet smell of early fall, snow in October, evenings cuddling one's sweetie near a hardwood fire, the kind of clarity you get near the tree line—would have to wait, maybe for a long time.

"I wouldn't want you to say anything to anyone about my family or Gent, Henry. That's pretty much a confidence between the two of us."

"Norman, I'll be frank, I'm not a hundred percent sure about you. It's a story that stretches credulity. But I'll not say anything."

"You can read about it in the *Sun-Times* if you want. 'Family Perishes in Inferno.' Page one, 21 February 1971."

"It's not that I don't believe you. But I hardly know you. I don't really understand why you told me all this stuff."

"I'm not completely sure either. It was a leap of faith. Besides, and this is not meant to be an insult, you looked harmless."

Now that made sense. Henry *was* harmless.

Norman walked slowly, evading circles of light, sticking to dark areas, lacunae impenetrable without a nightscope. Dignity is what he had. I could imagine him very well following four caskets out of a crowded church, one bronze casket and three white. He would have been as erect as an obelisk, in control, and self-contained. He would have walked out, the black-mantled priest behind him, past the faces of friends and family, past funeral ghouls and a line of photographers. His life would have been narrowed to a knife's edge. No one seemed more solitary than Norman O'Keefe; no one more ripe for violence. So he stayed out of the light.

Birdwhistle, busy with his batter, buzzed us in, but only after a thoughtful pause. He sometimes doesn't want company. He was working hard, black to white, etc., a soul in transformation.

"Bob," I said, "this is a friend of mine, Norman O'Keefe." Introductions are always a problem for me.

"Norman, Bob Birdwhistle."

Bob smiled and nodded. His hands and arms were floury, and he held them up to suggest the futility of a handshake.

Bob nodded again and was silent. He sometimes decides not to speak or use electrical appliances. I find it annoying.

"So," he said to my relief, "you don't look very interested in doughnuts."

Nobody knows more about the phenomenal world than Bob Birdwhistle. He can tell you what the winter will be like from the smell of a squirrel's urine. (This winter will be Arctic in its fierceness. Plan carefully, don't take anything for granted, stay out of South Dakota: Bob's advice for February.)

"No. You're here for something quite different from your typical undergraduate course of study. I got you scoped. Quite different."

"What would that be?"

"I know who you are, don't you see, Norman? I read the papers. I've seen you around, and so have the cops. The weird thing is that even though you can't find a cop when you need one, nothing really escapes their attention. But they exert remarkable restraint. My wife wouldn't agree with that, but the fact is the repressive potential of the police is enormous. Viz the Black Panther Party. You see, I have this theory that police power is under the direct psychic control of the middle class. What I'm saying is that a person can do anything—treason, rape, arson—if his P.R. is good enough. Your first step will be to uncover the cyst in the flesh, the tumor in the brain, the pederast in the pediatrics ward. You get my drift? Henry, you follow?"

"No."

Birdwhistle had trimmed his scalp, and he looked particularly intense. He was sweating, and his face (his entire head) was flushed. I was out of my depth now; I knew that. Norman had a skeptical look on his face.

"You don't have to understand, Henry. You have your own problems to solve. I got a call tonight from Claire Cohen. Wants to know where you've been. Has to speak to you. She's coming into town on Sunday. Call her."

Birdwhistle does know everything.

"Now, Norman, my advice is this: use every means available except self-sacrifice."

"What in the hell are you talking about, Bob?" I asked.

I felt like a dog paddler in a world of Australian crawlers.

"Henry," Bob said impatiently, scooping doughnuts out of frothy vegetable oil, "what I'm talking about is getting away with murder. Perhaps not literal murder, but a figurative kind of destruction. He's here to deal with Leonard J. Gent, the evangelical felon. Every carwash attendant in town knows that. I'm just advising patience."

"Oh."

"You're in over your head right now, Henry. You've got to be a little more focused. You've got pussy on the brain. You're grappling with too many coeds. No, not too many, the wrong ones. Clear your head if you're in for the long pull. Am I right or am I right, Norm?"

"Who knows?" Norman said.

"By the way, Henry," Birdwhistle said, "that's Republic Flight 515. Arrives 10:20 p.m. She'll have had breakfast. Her appetite is back. She had a slight problem with morning sickness, but it's passed. She's been in Quogue with her parents."

"Where?"

"Quogue, pal, rhymes with dog, near the south fork at the eastern end of Long Island. Sand and money. Parents wanted her to jump on a coat hanger, but she fended them off. She spent some time on the beach, probably thinking about you. She has some serious illusions about your capacities, Henry. No offense, old campaigner, but you're going to have to rise to the challenge this one time. I'm irritated with you, Henry, because you initiate but never finish.

Blanche has put some sort of evil eye on you. She holds you responsible for Claire's delicate condition. Very dicey spot you've got yourself into."

"Why did she call you?"

"Because she couldn't get a hold of you. I told her you were probably in some barroom watching a baseball game. Where have you been, anyway? She sounded worried. She said to say that she misses you. Henry, you've got a problem."

Doughnuts filled Birdwhistle's kitchen. Dozens were spread out on stainless steel trays cooling; dozens of dozens were in plastic bags, and the bags were in boxes, and the boxes were piled near the back door. He was making a fortune. Whole-wheat doughnuts were like manna to the nut-and-fruit crowd: Cuisinart liberals on the west side, vegetarian geeks in Miffland, organic-truck-gardening hippies in Black Earth and Spring Green. It didn't hurt that Birdwhistle was a Buddhist oddball; didn't hurt that he was a genius at self-promotion. He made so much money that he was embarrassed to tell Crescent, who would have tried to send it to Freedom Fighters in one Third World battlefield or another.

Birdwhistle said, "Boys, I have a few more doughnuts to bag, and then I grab an hour of sleep. A little nap to get the circuits cooled off. You're welcome to stay, grab some shuteye with old Birdwhistle, and then help with the deliveries. Plenty of room on the floor, and the van is right out back."

"I don't know, Bob," I said. "I'm pretty tired."

"No problem, Henry. I know hard work is not your cup of tea."

"Would you pay anything?" Norman asked.

"Not a cent. You'll accumulate wisdom. Can you drive a stick shift?"

"Sure," said Norman. "Like I was born to do it."

"Great. You are now the wheel man in this outfit. If I like what you do, I may offer you a permanent position, remunerated of course."

I was feeling sort of excluded.

"What did I do wrong, Bob?" I asked. "I feel like a fifth wheel tonight."

"Henry, I love you. I'm just trying to toughen you up. Birdwhistle predicts a full moon means trouble. I am talking about high-grade agitation here. I don't want to scare you, Henry, but I would lay in a supply of fresh water and plenty of canned goods; get one of those top-of-the-line Swiss Army knives. You are going to be out in the wilderness, sleeping under a cotton blanket listening to coyotes howl. You are going to be squeezed like a tube of anchovy paste. But look, don't be a stranger; you can always hide out here. Birdwhistle intends to help you when he can and feel real bad when he can't. But, Henry, my advice is to get a good map of Shit Creek because I have this feeling that that's where you're headed."

He opened the back door and pointed a slender finger out. He slapped me on the back as I passed.

"Henry," Norman called from behind me, "I'll call you. Thanks for everything."

"Okay," I said, "be careful."

I looked up at Birdwhistle and started to complain.

"Not a word, Henry. The time for talking ended about an hour ago," Birdwhistle said. "Reflect upon your past mistakes. Vow not to repeat them. Patience, old friend, and courage. For the moment, taking no action at all is the proper path. Think about it and get out. Norman and I have to load the van. These onerous chores don't do themselves."

I retreated, whistling in the dark.

I was sweating. The night was hot, the way it must be in Subic Bay. The stars were hidden by heaving clots of clouds, and the air was saturated with moisture. You couldn't be more exhausted than I. I staggered up the stairs, opened the door, and felt my way through the black living room, too tired to find the lights. I undressed in transit, peeling off my clothes on my way to the bedroom. At last, I climbed between the frosty sheets (the air conditioner had been on all day).

Here, a notation to myself: Henry, N.B., Birdwhistle is not always right.

I found Claire Cohen asleep in my bed. She had a pillow over her eyes, and she was wrapped in a corner of the sheet like a larva in a cocoon. Her smooth right leg stuck out. I ran my fingers up it, gently. I kissed her on the shoulder and tasted her salty, seawater taste.

"Don't," she said blurrily. "Just don't."

Then she rolled over and plopped her head on my shoulder and went back to sleep. Who was she discouraging? Not Henry, I surmised, her firm breasts against my chest, at least not yet.

14

Summer Light

MY FIRST LETTER from Airy arrived simultaneously with Claire. (Look me in the eye and tell me that isn't ominous.) Yesterday's mail, which I had dug out of my box and thrown unopened on the sofa, also included—communications coming in desperately delayed bunches—two postcards from Airy of the "Hi, I'm here. Miss you." variety. The letter was a fat one, dated much after the postcards, and encrusted with postage stamps. It had a greasy stain in the corner by the return address, and that greasy stain smelled like the expensive coconut/avocado-pit suntan lotion Airy uses at the beach. Airy is a serious correspondent. Many more letters were to come over the next few months, not all as fat, but their tone was consistent: affirmations of love mingled with subtle exhortations to get moving.

Her first letter: she was a bit blue; a heavy-limbed anxiety crept into her sentences. Gloominess—in utter contradistinction to me, Mr. Chicken Little, who was always falling into spastic funks—was a condition she didn't often permit herself. She displayed the tiniest bit of homesickness and self-pity.

Basically, she said, "Henry, I miss you, I love you. You're a wonderful guy. Absence makes the heart grow fonder, and from this great distance, I am able to better see your strengths and flaws"—this is a rough transcription—"but I wish you'd put a little lead in your pencil and get a job." What would make her happy? A job for Henry. And not a job cleaning boilers either. A job that required a tweed suit, a regimental tie, and shoes with little tiny holes in them. And, she added archly, there are a lot of sandy-haired classicists in training—whose predecessors were on interlocking boards of directors; the heirs of robber barons, in other words—and these lanky fellows (decked out completely in khaki) were lining up to take a run at her. Some real hotshots—in a few years they'd be Fellows at the American Academy in Rome and well on their way to Tenure—would like to get (and keep for a long time) Airy horizontal. But, no, she wasn't having any of it. She was pining for H.F., and that was that. She had had a bout of diarrhea and, one night after dinner, collapsed in tears and cried herself to sleep.

I read Airy's letter in the kitchen, cooking coffee. The shades were still pulled. The sun was very bright and shone through the parchment-colored, dingy shades. The light was almost amber. I was beginning to find this light very comforting. I read the letter twice—there was a lot of stuff about the colorful local residents and the turbulent nighttime taverna scene—and put it away. I was reading *Tom Jones*, and I stuck it in there.

Claire was asleep in her birthday suit, in my bed, and the coffee I was making was for her. I had burst outdoors early, restless from overstimulation, to buy some orange juice, English muffins, and raspberry jam (a particular favorite of Claire's). It was now that Claire was back that I realized how much I had missed her.

I sat in the kitchen, in my T-shirt and shorts, my legs stretched out on an adjoining chair, reading the sports pages and waiting for Claire. To a casual observer, I was a picture of ease, of well-rested placidity. Who could have guessed at my pulsating desire for Claire Cohen, who had become, to me, as desirable as any woman alive? (I'm thinking about having a brass plaque, engraved with Birdwhistle's admonition about the perils of sexual obsession, mounted beneath my bathroom mirror.) Scuzzball, creep, human horror story, jerk of jerks, chief asshole, shit for brains, cheesebrains, pissface, spitface, smegmaface, deadbeat, ratlips, twerp, twit, nerd. Call me those things, and I won't fly into a murderous rage. I won't even wince.

Call me those things, and I'll answer limply, believing them all to be true: "Here."

Presently, I heard Claire stirring in the bedroom, zipping open her bag, digging through the neatly layered clothes for panties, shorts, and a shirt (khaki shorts—from the Army-Navy Store—a white T-shirt, and a bra, I predicted silently).

She walked in with a sweet smile on her face. She looked very tan and very tense, the way a girl would look after resisting brainwashing at the beach.

She was dressed exactly as I had foreseen. She was barefooted, and her hair was piled and pinned on the top of her head carelessly.

"I knew you were going to come out dressed like that. I even guessed you'd be wearing a bra."

"How did you know that?"

"Nipple anxiety," I said. "Afraid of being too visible in a white T-shirt."

"Henry, do you always have to say the first thing that pops into your pea brain?"

"More often than not."

She sat down on the chair next to mine and put her elbows on the table. She leaned against me, bumping against my shoulder with hers, again and again. Her hair was fastened with a silver barrette, and her hair brushed against my cheek and ear as she banged against me. She seemed like she was about to cry.

"Henry, am I stupid? I've been accused of that a lot lately. Sometimes I feel like I don't know anything."

Maybe she had been crying, and this was the delicately oversensitive aftermath. Maybe she'd been in bed with the pillow over her head to muffle her sobs. I got up and went behind her chair and put my hands on the powerful muscles of her shoulders. She was tight as an overwound spring. I rubbed her neck and ran my hand down her spine, gently touching each vertebra as if I were playing my way down a piano keyboard one key at a time.

"Claire," I said, "you're not stupid or ignorant. Believe me, I've known some people so dumb that you wonder why they haven't drowned in the bathtub."

"I almost drowned in the bathtub once, Henry. Doesn't that prove it?"

But she was smiling as she said that—her head was bowed beneath the probing of my hands—and I had to bend low to see her expression. She was making a tiny joke.

"Maybe I'm not exactly stupid, Henry, but I'm not as smart as you. I'm not as smart as Nicky. I'm not as smart as Blanche."

"Claire's feeling a little sorry for herself this morning, isn't she?"

"Fuck you, Fitzgerald."

"That's the Claire I know and love. Dumb and dirty."

"You like me now, Henry, and you think I'm intelligent. I appreciate that, but I don't think it will last. You'll see. Pretty soon you'll say I'm too stupid to be trusted with a serious decision or too stupid to do something important. Too stupid to be loved by an intelligent man. I'll bore you. I don't read very much. You'll see."

There seemed to be no arguing with Claire's opinion of herself. I was a little surprised by it. Among my many flaws of character, I am happy to say, brow-beating vulnerable young women into submission had no place. It had never occurred to me that Claire wasn't intelligent. She surely seemed so. Perhaps she didn't know what happened at the Battle of Midway or the proximate causes of the English Revolution, but not many people do anymore. She was a gifted mathematician (she explained trigonometry to me in bed, for example, tracing out complicated equations with her forefinger on my belly). And she was brilliant at chess.

"Claire, I'll say this once and then we can move on to other topics. I'm not going to be able to convince you. I think you're as sharp as a Marine's bayonet. And I'll stick my finger in the eye of anyone— old boyfriend, close relative, casual acquaintance, stranger, anyone—who says differently. That's all I have to say."

"You will? Go stick your finger in Blanche's eye, then."

"You got it, darlin'. The next time you see your old lady they'll be calling her Squinty."

"We had a terrible fight the night before I left. They are completely opposed to what I'm doing. They threatened a lot of ugly stuff, Henry."

I grunted a sympathetic grunt.

"I promised them I'd think about aborting. That's why they let me leave."

"So what are you going to do?"

"I'm not sure."

A meaningful pause ensued. Claire was about to say something serious. She squinched her face into a sober expression. Looking back, I understand that this next stage was necessary and inevitable.

Ahem, ahem: Claire cleared her throat.

"Blanche asked me what our relationship was, you know, in what direction it was headed. I didn't know what to tell her. I said I was your assistant girlfriend. I remembered what you said."

"I was being nasty. I didn't mean it."

"I know, but it's true. I realized that on the plane. I don't want to be that, Henry. And I don't want you to look at me as your second-string sex partner."

"Claire. Come on."

"It's the truth. Let's face it. This is not a productive situation for either of us."

"I've never thought of you as a second-string sex recipient."

"Partner."

"Right, partner. You're. . . ."

I started to say something amusing.

"Do not make a joke, pal. I'm serious."

"Okay. I don't think of you as anything other than a woman I love—in a complicated way, in a complicated situation."

"Would you leave Pixie for me?"

"Claire, you're pregnant. Everything happened between us really quickly. I don't know what to think about it. I don't know what to say." I felt like a weasel caught in the bright glare of day.

"Say yes or no. I'm not angry, Henry, and I understand how complex things seem. But my question still stands."

"The way things are now, no."

"Henry?"

"Yes, Claire."

"Can I stay here?"

"Of course you can."

"Thanks. But I don't want to have sex with you."

"You join a vast number of women who don't want me to punch their tickets."

"What I mean is: I would like to have sex with you, but I don't think it's appropriate given my condition and your situation. I'm going to look for an apartment and a job. I'll sleep on the couch. Okay?"

"You're really going through with it, aren't you? I mean, you know that." The stuff about reconsidering her abortion was so much honey for the bears. She was going to stay knocked up.

"Yes, I think so. Don't you want me to?"

"I don't know. It would be simpler if you didn't."

"It would be simpler for you, Henry. I don't think it would be for me. I've made this decision, and should I unmake it because you might ditch Trixie for me if I did? Christ, I'd hate myself."

"I know."

"If you resent my staying here without sleeping with you, just tell me. I can stay with Franny."

"If you can keep your hands off me, I can keep mine off you."

She unfastened the barrette and pulled it out of her hair. She ran her fingers through it, trying to undo the tangles and curls. Her hair was sun-lightened and wonderfully tangled. I raised the shades, which were as fragile as an ancient manuscript, and the amber light was transformed into silver.

July, the weatherman said over the radio, will be as sulfurously hot as the seventh circle of hell. (That was his implication, at least.) Claire looked at me with her cow-brown eyes, pleading to be understood. She was right. Tell me, how could I not have understood her?

"Everything you've said is true, Claire. You can have the bed, and I'll sleep on the couch. I don't know what this means, but I was miserably lonely when you were away. But there is this chasm that I can't cross. Your circumstances"—she was going to be a mother in a few months, but I couldn't say that—"make things impossible."

It will be cooler in the north, the weatherman said, with a band of showers near Lake Superior. In the north no roads buckled from the heat, rivers were full to their banks, birds found sufficient breath to sing. I realized that if one's destiny obstructed happiness in every other spot—Brooklyn, Chicago, Madison—one would have a chance, in those empty regions, to be content. The pines are vivid and green against a summer sky so pale blue it is almost silver. It is hard to be mean or sullen there. If you are, friend, accept that mean-spiritedness and sullenness are your ugly fate.

Claire was flipping through the paper; her English muffin was in the toaster. (I had just cleaned the last roach carcass out of it the other day, shaking the coppery crumbs and the coppery dead roaches into the garbage. Claire wouldn't want to see roaches dart out of the toaster as the coils began to glow. It might affect even my appetite.)

I brought the coffee pot to the table and placed it on a trivet. Birdwhistle had been encouraging me to explore those mysterious precincts he called, simply and ominously, North. North, Bubba, he told me again and again: go get the stink off. "Getting the stink off" was an expression meant to indicate a liberation from the daily grind, the quotidian humdrum. I decided the time had come to go to Iron River.

"Do you have any plans?"

"A big wedding and a honeymoon in Monaco."

"Does that mean yes or no?"

"It means no, I suppose."

"Do you want to go get the stink off?" That's a phrase that gets a little getting use to.

"What?"

"Take a trip up north."

Claire looked at me the way a frog looks at a snake, the way a snake looks at a pig: scrutinizing my face for signs of aggression.

"I can't afford it."

"Minimal expenditures on your part will be required. Food money."

"For how long?"

"I don't know. A week? We can rent a cabin or something. Birdwhistle told me about a place up there. We'll be as chaste as the Bumsteads. I swear I'll behave myself."

"I like sex with you, Henry, I really do. I just can't get any more attached to you than I already am. If you promise to behave yourself, I'll go. But the first time you put your hand on my ass, I'll punch out your lights. No kidding, Henry."

North, Bubba, that's where we were headed. Inevitably, of course, the summer monsoons commenced and ruined our plans. We had two weeks of rain that washed babies in their carriages into storm sewers and out to sea. Mildew raged through the city like a fever. And Claire had another priority as well: finding a job and an apartment in preparation for the blessed event. Unbelievably, she was hired as a dance instructor at a middle school on the west side of Madison. It didn't pay very much, but in September she would be employed, full-time and long-term. (Milton gave her a recommendation profusely laudatory. If a Nobel Prize were awarded for dance instruction, Claire, based on the evidence of Milton's praise, would have won it. I've only recently realized that, since she was preggers, unexperienced, and would soon need maternity leave, Milton must have called in a few favors to get Claire a job. He's okay, my brother. I love the guy.) Then she found an apartment, on Gorham Street, near James Madison Park and very close to me. She could move in on 1 September.

So we settled in to wait out the bad weather, in the process becoming a very cozy couple. Her hair found its way to my brush, her stains on my towels, her happy wailing filled the kitchen as she sang along with Top Forty-type radio stations (she was disastrously tone deaf). I grew used to her being around, accustomed to her voice calling from the fire escape to bring out the bottle opener, used to her standing behind me brushing her thick hair while I, grumpily, shaved with a dull blade. In short, I did as stupid a thing as I have ever done: I graduated from desire; I actually finished falling in love with Claire.

From her own testimony, Claire was happier than she had ever been. (So was I, although I didn't say so.) She talked about her former anguish and confusion (I've never quite understood why or how she got so turned upside down emotionally; Blanche and Howard couldn't have been *that* bad). She was fierce in her determination to lead a happy and independent life. After dinner, in luxurious twilight, she soaked in the bathtub (her flat belly was beginning to bulge). I sat on the toilet and read to her. I don't know how this started (maybe she asked me to get her a towel and wanted to know about the book I had in my hand), but it became a habit. She sat in the hot water as I read—sweating a little, droplets sliding down her forehead, and her cheeks rosy—with her eyes closed.

I explained baseball to her that summer as well. (What odd, sweet, celibate weeks we had together.) Claire and I curled up on the floor in front of the television (Claire in front and I wrapped around her like a shadow), my face close to her smooth sweet-smelling neck. We'd flip on the game, and I muttered away, narrating, with such patience and good humor I surprised myself, the difference between a suicide squeeze and a safety squeeze.

Inevitably, this moment passed: no more watching baseball games in the dark, no more cookouts on the fire escape, no more scrubbing Claire's broad back, no more cockroach hunts after doing the dishes, no more tedious foreign films at the Majestic, no more waiting out rainstorms beneath elm trees. Something very bad happened later that summer; something much worse happened in the next winter.

Momentarily, Claire and I were tilted toward the sun, sleeping separately, of course, and not unhappy. Milton was very doubtful about our living situation, but he was too preoccupied with his own woes—he'd heard a rumor his ex-wife was coming back to town—to say much. He was keeping late hours in his office, not answering the phone.

A lot of people and things slipped past without notice. Leonard Gent's house was finished but empty, awaiting certification as a group home by the state. We often saw each other in the street and nodded pleasantly. Claire and I even had a street-corner conversation with him one morning in front of his spooky house. He was sleazily charming and jolly, coaxing overloud laughter from Claire. I had an insane flash of jealousy when he complimented her, admiring her hair and deep tan.

Finally, with a stretch of good weather before us, we were ready to go north. I borrowed Crescent Laverno's car, a boxy Volvo, squat as a big toe. If speed and comfort were our number-one priorities, we would have been epically disappointed. But the engine hummed along cheerfully, and it gripped the road the way a circus flyer grabs her catcher's arms.

At last, Claire and I found ourselves in that most pleasing of states:

on the road. I drove, and Claire kept a road map of Wisconsin on her lap. We roared up East Washington Avenue, with a tankful of Shell gas, toward I-90. Watch out, I thought. Just get out of the way. Her finger touched a blue dot, traced a path among blue dots.

"Henry, I like the sound of this place. Iron River. You have to go through Blueberry to get there." She studied the map. "We can go to Lake Muskelunge." She called it Musky Lungy. "Sounds like the king of Finland."

I pronounced it properly for her.

"We're going to lovely Lake LaPointe, right?"

"Correct," I said, "lovely Lake LaPointe."

"Oulu, Blueberry, Iron River. Sounds nice, doesn't it, Henry? It sounds far away from everything."

It was. Claire and I drove north. It's a tough trip once you get past Eau Claire and the Interstate turns due west toward Minneapolis. You have to take Highway 53, as funky a road as I have ever been on: a narrow, frost-heaved corridor of friable blacktop. Claire read while I drove. (She got into the habit of reading while she stayed with me, picking up books I had left lying about half read. She was reading *War and Peace*, a book I had abandoned very early. Claire was a slow reader. She'd read a page and then think about it with the book clasped to her breast. I figured, at the pace she had established, she had about fifteen years of reading in front of her. I couldn't talk to her while she was reading/thinking thinking/reading. For the moment, I didn't mind.)

Highway 53 climbs from the flatlands around Eau Claire—corn-fields are planted according to Euclidean principles, severely geometrical—toward the second-growth forests of the Lake Superior highlands. Northern Wisconsin is so silent and empty it might be controlled by a foreign power. In fact, I learned that it is held by a foreign power, for we were now in the kingdom of winter. It is so cold six months of the year ice alone is sovereign.

The narrowness of the road, the dangers of passing pickup trucks on the downslopes of hills, made Claire anxious. She alternately read her book and, as we passed through tiny road-wide towns, consulted the map. We were headed for Superior, virtually due north on Highway 53, which seemed to me to be an ideal spot, if only it were accurately named. She was an excellent navigator.

She studied the map, following another road with her finger.

"We have to turn east at the junction of Highway Two and Fifty-three. Listen to this: we have to go through Oulu, Maple, Went-worth, and Brule."

I liked the simple sound of those names. None of your mock-Red Indian nomenclature; no corruptions of European backwaters; no Neos, News, Neues, Nouveaus. Maple sounds like a pretty place, with a gas station and a grocery store, with a recluse who lives in a shack by the railroad tracks and collects spent shell casings. Find me a Sunshine or a Marigold or a Blueberry; an Evening Breeze, Autumn Leaves, or White Cap! One day I'll end up there, a cup of raisins in my hand (I'll have to gum them because my teeth will be in a coffee cup in the bathroom): a happy old man at his leisure.

"I don't care where we go. I like the names: Maple, Brule, Iron River. They're beautiful, aren't they?"

"They're nice."

I was gurgling with a powerful Claire-related emotion. What was the point of not admitting it? I loved the sound of her voice; I loved to hear her throaty, reassuring laughter. I was rolling along, grasping the huge steering wheel of the Volvo loosely, feeling that I was north of something and free. By that I meant free of certain long-standing conflicts. It was cool and clear here. The sun was high but not hot, and the road rose and fell through glacier-carved country. If we just went straight, we would be taken to the edge of Lake Superior, vast and icy blue. Hang on, I thought to myself, your direction is the proper one.

"Claire," I said, "no kidding, you're a cute number."

"A what?"

"A cute number."

"Just drive, Henry."

"I am."

"Let's not get goofy, okay? I'm not sure I like you when you get goofy. You have this odd sentimental streak."

"I said you were cute. I didn't say something moronic. Besides, what's one person's sentiment is another's strong emotion. I felt, momentarily, a strong emotion. Excuse me for breathing."

"Okay, okay. I didn't mean to be unpleasant. Thanks. You're cute, too. How's that? I'm cute. Basically, I'm cute."

"Do you want to go directly to Iron River?" I asked, huffily.

"Yes."

I was still feeling very worked up. Where did all this excess emotion come from, and so suddenly? I was ready to crawl out of my skin.

"Claire, Claire," I said, "you sweet thing."

"Yes, Henry." She was exasperated.

"I like you."

"And I like you, too, buddy. I love you."

"Fuck you, Cohen."

"I'm serious, Henry. You know that I love you."

"Really? Me, too, Claire. Whatever happens I hope you don't ever forget that."

"How can I? You tell me every other mile or so."

I reflected momentarily on my mood. I was a happy guy. The immediate cause: the presence of Claire Cohen. Claire loves Henry; Henry loves Claire. Net result: Henry, the amiable dunce, wears a moronic smile, is exuberantly cheerful. Then it all seemed so direct and simple. I didn't want to be a sufferer, one of those ersatz-angst-filled Late Romantics. I am a person who is inclined toward contentment. I'm a pipe-and-slippers kiss-the-kids-goodnight kind of guy.

"I feel real well, Claire."

"It doesn't seem to take much."

"Much? Christ, Claire, most men would walk in their bare feet through a fucking firestorm to be driving with a cute number like you on a sunny day to a lovely lakeside cottage. This is very nearly *everything*."

Claire smiled and rubbed my shoulder.

"How is it we didn't meet before? It would have been so much simpler."

"I have to calm down."

I was beginning to concoct a complicated scenario which involved imminent stepfatherhood. I was well down that road, grinding through the gears, when Claire encouraged me to chill out.

"Good idea. You really do have to calm down. We can't fool around up here, Henry. The rules still apply, regardless of what we might be feeling."

The rules, I thought, will break my heart.

"No smash mouth," I said.

"None."

"No kissy face."

"Zero."

"No hide the salami."

"Out of the question."

"Very little tickle and giggle."

"Very little."

"Chaste and sober?"

"Sober and chaste."

"Okay," I said. "Those are the rules, and I can live with them."

"Good."

"Hey, the fucking rules must be obeyed." That was bitterness in my voice.

"It's not that I don't want to sleep with you, Henry."

"This is the part of the movie I came in on. Say no more: you want to but you can't. Got it. No problem."

So I settled down a bit. We passed through Maple, Oulu, Ino, Blueberry: Iron River-bound. (I was heading there under the mystical imprimatur of native son Bob Birdwhistle.) We passed through an abandoned landscape: empty farmhouses, rusting silos, collapsing barns; an inevitable process of decay seemed to have set in. It wasn't quaint here, merely sad. Claire and I became quiet. We had reestablished certain boundaries, the ones I had tried to blur in my manic moment. My appeal before the Court of Public Opinion would have been: I was intoxicated with the loveliness of the names of Highway 2 towns; the simple, plain, elemental names. They described a geography of astonishing possibility. Forget the cyclic economic depression which had emptied the countryside; that would change. I could be happy here.

The latest letter from Airy was levered into my back pocket, a flimsy air-mail sheet. It described a harsh and beautiful landscape. Her days were windy and sunlighted. Her letter questioned my strained, restless communications. Most of the time I tried not to think about Airy.

After a solid bit of silent motoring, I tried to talk to Claire, but she would have none of it. She was crawling through Tolstoy, punctuating every few pages with a sigh. With her head bent over her book, I noticed her chin had begun to double just a bit. She was losing her well-exercised tautness. Her body was softening, released from its exertions. Over the weeks she had become increasingly quiet, not withdrawn but wonderfully calm. Her laughter—and how I tried to make her laugh—pleased and comforted me.

Iron River, it turned out, was just down the road. The joint was jumping. If you like bars, bustling bait shops, and gas stations crowded with large American-made automobiles pulling mobile homes, Iron River in midsummer is just the place to be. I had followed Birdwhistle's general advice and specific directions in finding a place to stay. His instructions even included a cunning map of the shortest route to the Northern Lights, the resort he had enthusiastically recommended. "More beautiful than any other place on earth except Venice in December" is what he said, for once, without hyperbole.

15

In the Dark Forest

BIRDWHISTLE'S DIRECTIONS WERE precise. I found the way
to the driveway of the Northern Lights Lodge without hesitation.
From the road, you couldn't actually see the lodge, but a sign with
an arrow pointing up the long sandy hill showed the way.

Perhaps it's merely pride of ownership, but I think the lodge itself,
the Fulmonars' home, world headquarters, executive offices, is a
handsome building. Built of local logs, impressively joined, painted
a chocolate brown, with a bright green roof and shutters, it strikes just
the right note of handhewn rusticity. It has a wide, old-fashioned
porch that wraps around the building on three sides. It was filled with
green fanbacked chairs, beaten up but still serviceable (like Fulmonar
himself). Bright white curtains waved out of the second-story windows. The parking lot was behind the house near a sort of service
entrance; actually near the kitchen. Five cars were parked there,
bumped up against stacked railroad ties (slick with sand-encrusted
creosote).

Claire and I got out and walked up to the lodge, hopeful of finding
something to eat, a hot shower, and a comfortable bed. Stretched out
on a white wicker sofa in the shady part of the porch was a bootless
flannel-shirted gentleman, badly in need of a shave. His nose was
sunburned. He was a bearish man but not fat: round, well-formed

belly and round, well-formed face with a black slash of mustache. This was Ernie Fulmonar, the lost heir to the Swedish throne, the baron of Lake LaPointe, the owner of the Northern Lights Lodge: a hard-working guy taking a well-deserved snooze.

We tiptoed inside. No one about: an empty dining room, an empty parlor; no voices, or radios, or footsteps. We went outside again and stood helplessly on the porch. Finally, we took a spot on the steps, sitting close together and wondering in whispers if we should bid the sleeper arise. He was dead to the world. No fitful tosser and turner, he snored loud enough to attract bears.

"Let him sleep," Claire said, "he looks so sweet that way."

"I wouldn't call that sweet," I whispered. "That's the way gorillas sleep, except they sleep in trees."

We waited. The lodge sat on a grassy knoll which fell away from us toward the lake. It ended in a white strip of homemade beach (Wisconsin River sand, powdery stuff used in the sand traps of exclusive golf clubs) and a gray dock that pointed into the lake north and south, like a compass needle. The lake was empty, and it was very quiet, a pleasant period of breezes and birds. A good time to take a nap.

Claire put her arm around me momentarily, buddylike.

"This is really lovely, isn't it, Henry?"

"Yes."

We sat on the porch, keeping our voices just above a whisper. We didn't have to. The sleeper slept, and, as the afternoon lengthened, the light grew simpler and clearer. The shadows of Norway pines elongated on the lawn. We basked like tortoises on the cedar steps. I was pleased just to be here.

Finally, the sleeper roused. He groaned and rolled over and up (the wicker creaked in an excellent imitation of muscles and tendons). Claire and I stood up, smiling awkwardly, glad not to have been the sleep ruiners.

Fulmonar woke up utterly startled. He was rumpled from sleep: the tails of his shirt were sticking out, and his hair, which he combed straight back, had flopped over to the side and was pressed into a juvenile cowlick. He looked underneath the wicker sofa for his shoes and put them on, first carefully pulling up his socks.

"Sorry to wake you," I said. "We just arrived. We have a reservation."

"Fitzgerald, I assume," he said, extending his hand. "We've been expecting you. I'm Ernie Fulmonar. Bobby Birdwhistle called this morning. You're to get the deluxe treatment."

Fulmonar was bent over tying his shoes. His feet were swollen, and they hurt him.

He smiled at me.

"I wouldn't talk too much about Bob, though. Enemies outnumber friends for the whole family. His father used to be a county judge up here. A real hard case. Come on in, you have to register and I can give you our brochure. It describes the meal plans and all that."

Fulmonar was as squat and as powerful as the spring at the bottom of an elevator shaft. He would make a perfect holder-upper in a nine-man pyramid. His hair was dark, but his beard stubble was almost completely gray. He was rooted to his life; dug into Iron County deeply. He played with his moustache and tried to brush his hair with his fingers. Fulmonar held the screen door open for Claire and studied her as she passed. Suddenly, she looked very tired.

"My name is Claire," she said to him.

"Oh, I know your name, dear. I think you'll like it here."

Fulmonar took us in and showed us the dining room and kitchen. His wife Pat was there, she had been upstairs, and she offered us lunch—sandwiches and icy bottles of beer to take down to the cabin. Claire helped make the sandwiches, spreading mustard on the pillars of ruddy beef, and she and Pat talked about me. Pat thought I was Claire's husband. I could overhear them as they stood at a work counter chatting. (I was listening to Fulmonar explain the Northern Lights' terms of engagement: fees, regulations, and meal plans.)

"What does your husband do?" Pat asked. In those days, in that place, couples traveling together, sleeping in the same room, were married or pretended to be.

Claire looked up at me quickly to see if I were listening. I acted as if I were not. She smiled at me, Henry, her putative husband.

"He's just graduated from college. He's going to law school in the fall."

The cabin and meals cost $250 for one week, breakfast and dinner, hot showers and fresh linen. No loud music, no parties, no sneaking extra guests into the rooms, no drugs. Simple rules, easily followed.

Fulmonar grabbed Claire's bag and the sack of sandwiches. I carried the beers in my fist; the bottles clicked together like castanets. His broad back filled the narrow path.

I followed Claire, taking tiny steps so as not to overtake her. Her head was down and her hands were in her jeans pocket. Maybe she was thinking of my promotion to husband. I think she wanted one of those. Sad was Claire. Maybe it was low blood sugar or the voices of her recent past bubbling out of the quiet. Unprincipled dog that I am, I found the casual twitches of Claire's rear end arousing, and I wondered if I could resist her physically. She really did have a lovely body: small firm breasts crowned with bright-red nipples; a broad, freckled back; smooth fresh skin which tasted sweet and salty, like sea air, like the sea itself. After we made love the first time, I tasted her for days; her delicious smell had been all over me. It wasn't going to be easy.

We got to the cabin and found the authorized version of resort living: knotty pine paneling, fieldstone fireplace, wide-planked floor all in a green-shuttered white cabin surrounded by mature pines and juvenile birch. It was uncluttered, cool, and quiet. The sun would set right outside the door, over the placid lake.

Fulmonar opened the windows and tried the shower.

"If you need anything," he said on the way out, "someone's always at the lodge."

These were my first moments at the Northern Lights, my first moments in Cabin 15, far away from the chatter and the unhappy hoopla of my previous life, my life in more southerly latitudes. I wish, now, I had been braver, as brave as Hector, and had taken the direct approach with Claire Cohen. If I had only moved forward rather than meandering.

I opened the beers, and Claire took a long sip from her bottle. She belched, a rippling, satisfying rumble. She put the bottle down and looked at the beds. There were two of them, one for each of us, broad plains of quilted comforters, bright red and blue.

"You can eat my sandwich," she said, "I don't feel very well. I think maybe I should take a nap. Do you mind?"

She flopped on the bed with an ungraceful unswanly collapse. She seemed close to tears; once again I didn't know why. Hormones, I suppose. I sat on the bed next to her, and I stroked her thick hair and offered what awkward comfort I could. She shut her eyes tight and wouldn't speak. Her face was colored her funny Claire pink, and it was full of pain. It was then, I think, I realized how little I knew of her.

"Could I be alone, Henry? I have to think."

I wasn't angry, but I didn't feel great about being sent away either. I grabbed the bag of sandwiches and the bottles of beer and went outside. I sat on a wobbly steel chair by the door (every cabin had two of these fanbacked chairs close by). I looked at the lake and the sun reddening in the sky and listened to the voices of the other guests, erupting in songs, and laughter, and private domestic conversation. Sunburned couples ducked into the other cabins along the path, bathing suited, wrapped in towels, staggering under a load of rubber mattresses and fishing tackle and aluminum beach chairs. End of the day, time to wander down to the lodge for walleye and cottage fries and chilly glasses of iced tea. They were happy. That's what I wanted.

Claire slept in the dark room behind me, wrapped in her own complicated expectations. I, her temporary and occasional husband, her false husband, sat in the failing sunlight and ate my roast beef and drank my Miller's. I felt like a sentinel, patient and watchful.

I sat there contentedly for hours, watching the light thicken, fighting off black flies. I drank my beers and leaned back in my chair, suspecting that nothing was going to work out happily. I felt like one of those irradiated women who paint numbers on watches; it seemed strange to be taking such an active part in my own undoing. I was going to glow in the dark, an object of curiosity. Ernie Fulmonar walked up the path, traveling in a custodial route past each cabin, along the smooth lake-echoing parabola he had created. The cabins were bright and white in the evening sun, rising out of the shadows, gathering the last bit of light. He ambled bearishly along, discreetly peering into cabins, on the lookout for trouble.

My spot was his turnabout point.

"How were your sandwiches?"

"Delicious," I said.

"You and Claire can still eat at the lodge, you know."

"She's beat. I think maybe we'll skip it."

He wasn't in the mood for small talk tonight; nor was I. He was just out making his rounds.

"Not many mosquitoes this year," he said. "Dry spring. You're lucky."

He was a sweet shy man. Reminding us about breakfast, he suggested that we wait until after the first wave, the single-minded Chicago-area muskie-fishermen, were out of the lodge and on the water.

When it was almost dark, and the sun was a blaring red ball in the west, I finally went inside. Claire was throwing up. The last of the sun was bursting through the blinds, and in that clear, magical light I could see her seated on the edge of the tub, holding her hair away from her face, her ancient flannel nightgown pulled up to her thighs and her vividly nippled left breast popping through a ripped seam. She was dry heaving over the toilet, rhythmically, following the sea surge of her guts. Pregnant, poor Claire was a puker.

"Are you okay?" I asked.

"It depends on what you think about projectile vomiting."

"That's all right, Clairissa, it's all part of the package."

She smiled at me.

"You haven't called me that in a long time, Henry. That used to be your little after-sex name for me. I never had one for you, did I?"

"Oh, sure you did: 'Pull Up the Sheet.' Like in 'it's getting cool, Pull Up the Sheet Henry.'"

Claire laughed a little. She stood up and grabbed a towel and wiped off her mouth and wiped the scum of her shivering sweats off her face. Her hair was matted on the back of her neck.

"I feel like shit, Henry. You know, I thought that it would be great not to bleed like a stuck pig three days a month. I didn't realize that would be compensated for by my constantly puking my guts up. You should be glad you're not the father of this kid, or I might shoot you."

"Darlin'," I said, "you might shoot me anyway."

"I have to take a shower," she said.

She pulled off her nightgown, almost believing it wouldn't get my attention. Her breasts and bottom were milky white, and she had a lovely line of freckles across her tanned chest and shoulders. Claire's belly had only lately developed a noticeable bulge. We had an en-lightened attitude about nudity. Actually, the attitude was Claire's invention; one that I happily indulged. Since we were not exactly unfamiliar with each other's bodies, why bother to cover up? Why bother? Insane desire on Henry's part, that's why. She was getting ready to take a shower, and she piled her hair on top of her head, turning from me slightly. She looked like a model in a sketch by Degas: her delicate arms and the womanly line of breast and belly and bottom were deeply touching. A few strands of hair hung loose near her neck. Lord help me but I stared, rapaciously.

"Don't look at me that way. I don't like it."

I knew what she meant. My glance had narrowed itself to a very untender, carnal leer. Truthfully, I wasn't happy at all with the arrangements; I was beginning to be furious with them. Lately, I realized that this period of abstinence was probably my punishment for not showing Airy the door. Claire Cohen usually worked by indirection.

"Sorry, Claire, old habits die hard."

"I don't like this either, Henry. There's nothing I'd like better than to sleep with you tonight. But I can't let myself depend on you."

"Good instinct."

"I'm sorry."

"Me too, Claire."

She grabbed her nightgown and covered herself, thinking that that was somehow less arousing. She was very confused. Jesus Christ, I'm not a terrifically resolute guy. This was making me nutsoid. She stood in front of me, wrapped in her tattered flannels, with a stricken look on her face. She was sorry, I could see that. I was inclined to slam a door on my dick.

"Go take a shower, Clairissa. You need your rest."

"Henry, if you really want to do it, I will. I don't want to hurt your feelings."

"Take a shower."

"I can't get attached to you. I have to make this distinction right now."

"Okey dokey."

"Are you mad at me?"

"No."

"I think of you as my best friend."

"Great."

"I've ruined everything, haven't I?"

"No, for Christ sake, Claire, I'm sorry. Take a shower, it will be fine."

"Just say you don't hate me."

"I don't hate you."

"And don't sneak off with some cocktail waitress. I'd kill her."

"Claire, take a shower."

She went into the bathroom, carefully wrapped in her nightgown. She started puking into the toilet again, sick as a dog, Nicky's revenge. Then there was a knock on the outer door, and Pat Fulmonar was on the other side. My brother, she said, was on the telephone. It was important. I had given Milton the name of the place we were staying, just in case. I thought that maybe his ex-wife had come back to town and was carping at him to raise the alimony again. He's a sensitive guy. I could imagine him in a deep funk. I trotted down the gravelly parabolic path and stood in the Northern Lights' kitchen with the handset pressed to my ear and a finger jammed in the other because of the end-of-the-day cacophony—dirty dishes and pots being scraped, screaming babies, and the dynamo groan of an ancient dishwasher. I had to strain to hear what Milton was saying.

"Henry, I've got some bad news," he said.

"Dora's back?"

"No. I wish that were all it was. I got a call from a guy named Julius Cohen tonight, just as I was leaving the office. That's Claire's uncle. Here's the scoop: Claire's mother is dead, and her father is going gonzo. They want her to call home."

"What?"

"Claire's mother is dead. She had a stroke or something."

"Christ, Milton, I can't believe it. What am I going to say to her?"

"I don't know. You'll think of something. You'll have to get her on a plane tomorrow. Duluth has the closest airport, I think, Henry. Tell her how sorry I am. You all right?"

"This is terrible."

"Just go tell her now."

He hung up, and I stood for a pensive moment in the steamy kitchen wondering how I could bridge this chasm. A salty bead of sweat dripped down my nose. What was I supposed to say: it's a lovely night, Claire darling, and oh, by the way, your mother seems to have dropped stone dead in the garden? I wasn't going to like being an adult.

I walked down to the cabin and told Claire the news. Less was indeed more in these circumstances, and I didn't waste any words. I told her what had happened, directly and gently. She didn't say anything but pulled on her jeans and a sweater and ran down to make her phone call home. I wanted to go with her, but she wouldn't let me come. She slammed the door in my face. Afterwards she cried in Pat Fulmonar's arms, recounting for Pat and Ernie the gruesome details. Blanche had an aneurysm in the brain that exploded like a water balloon at a Legionnaire's convention. Blanche hit the floor a corpse. Ernie walked her back to the cabin, shuffling his way through the darkness—great bearish Fulmonar—with his arm around Claire's slender shoulders.

I was in bed when she got back, and Claire went straight to the shower. It was dark and cool in the cabin, all the lights were off, and she showered and dried herself in the darkness. I pretended to be asleep.

"Henry," she said, standing in front of me, "come to bed, please. I know you're awake."

What?—a tiny, mad voice in my brain screamed—what?

"Come on, Henry, I'm all pink and naked, just the way you like me."

Lord, Lord, I'll be a sad old turd before I forget that invitation. That was *just* the way I liked her.

She pulled back the comforter on her bed—the better of the two— and slid underneath the sheet.

"Come to bed," she said and stuck out a slender bare arm, reaching out to me.

"Do you mean with you? Over there?" I can turn the brain wattage down real low.

"Yes," she said patiently, "over here, Henry, over here with me."

16

Youthful Yearning, Hysterical Exercise, the Invention of a Dog-Bane

IN LATE OCTOBER—I sensed it was autumn because the trees were bare—I had a fierce argument with Airy. At its bitter conclusion she gave me what sounded like an ultimatum: either I get a job or she was going to marshal her resources and find one for me. It was a my-way-or-the-highway proposition. I told her to start looking.

Gent's bedroom window was observable from my living room window. The lights were on late on night, especially since the reluctant machinery of state and local government had licensed his operation (there were some concerns regarding Gent's history, which is sordid, as we know). But in the spirit of the age, it was decided that there could be no better spot to warehouse youthful male wards of the court than with a sexual deviant with an advanced degree in pedophilia. In a way, it makes perfect sense.

Gent had seen me with his blood enemy, Norman O'Keefe, and I suspect had decided to make a project of winning me over. Among other things I harbored strong resentments toward the greasy, supplicating manner he used with Claire. I had seen this past summer, when Claire and I ran into him in front of his house (he and Mickey Monahan landscaped the yard in July), that Cohen had an inflammatory effect on him. (I could smell the musk rising from him when she was close by.)

Quite unexpectedly, he even began to call me on the telephone, late in the evening, if he saw my lights were on. He sent me clippings from newspapers and magazines of an inspirational nature. He invited me to dinner, and once, out of curiosity, I accepted: Chicken à la King in his private, lavish apartment on the top floor; real uptown bachelor digs with marble in the bathrooms and a Matisse drawing in his bedroom. He wore a black suit and a white shirt, tieless, buttoned to the neck. His hair was quite long now, and he combed it straight back, still slimed with hair oil. Mostly he wanted to know how Claire was. He asked me sly questions, trying to piece together the permanence of our connection. He talked at length about the silkiness of her skin and how beautifully it contrasted with the darkness of her hair. He often applied the word "innocent" to Claire. His intentions were fiercely carnal, you couldn't miss that. The thought of Gent touching Claire made me murderously unhappy. He wanted her phone number. He wanted her address. I would cut out my liver before I gave him either. I actually said that to him, and he cackled hysterically, having found a vulnerable point. He was getting me in his cross hairs.

Gent joined the Rotarians and the Chamber of Commerce. He gave a speech at the Optimists Club: "Optimism—The Spirit of Youth." "Optimism," Gent, that cruel man, said, "is indeed the Spirit of Youth. In a larger sense it is the Spirit of All Free Men." Gent was now as well connected as the ductwork in a Turkish bath. It was a measure of my bitterness and confusion, perhaps of my feeling of being abandoned by Claire Cohen, that I had come to see him as evil, purely evil; as a contender for Claire's affection and, therefore, an enemy.

Gradually, whatever pretense of civility existed between Gent and me vanished, and we grunted a snarling greeting to each other on the street. He made it a point to practically laugh in my face, that fellationist, that pervert. And where was Clarissa? Why had Claire taken the proverbial powder? I don't know. The day after she heard about her mother's death, following a series of increasingly hysterical long-distance phone calls, I drove her to Duluth International Airport, the closest airport, to catch a New York-bound flight. Since she didn't have any money, I bought her a ticket and put her on the plane. She was in shock, I guess, just beginning to grieve. She said she'd call when things "settled down a bit." Her father sent a check, wrapped in a sheet of blank paper, reimbursing me for the airplane ticket. A provocation, I thought, and a humiliation. I was going to call and demand an explanation for her silence but was prevented by my overarching pride.

Maybe I was a jerk in Cabin 15 of the Northern Lights Resort; maybe it's my destiny to be bounced around like a beer can in the back of a pickup truck because of my obsessions both sexual and sentimental. Whoa, that's a hell of a thought. Sometime around dawn of the day she left—birds were twittering and fishermen were arguing—neither of us having slept much, I made a dramatic, Henryesque pronouncement. I admit to being overly dramatic and too sensitive, okay? So shoot me.

"Claire," I said, "I'll take whatever steps are necessary for us to be together."

An odd way to put it, I know. But I wasn't kidding or saying it for effect. I was as serious as a man could be. What I was trying to get at was that I would throw Airy over and happily accept the fact, even though I was repulsed by the thought of Nicky, that Claire was going to be a mother. I was willing to share that burden. Not an insignificant admission, I thought. How often do you peel back your hide like that? But I had always assumed, as I have said before, that my fate involved great accomplishment, acts of tenderness and courage. Somehow I had decided that the person for whom I might accomplish these things was Claire Cohen, black-haired Claire Cohen, quiet Claire. I know it seems air-headed, self-indulgently romantic, probably unfair to her, but it was the truth. I waited, vainly, for a response. She just cuddled up a little closer and pretended to go to sleep. A few hours later she left, and that was that. She didn't say yes, she didn't say no: *she didn't say a word.* It was that silence which cut the deepest.

After Claire's departure and being at loose ends, I began to spend a lot of time at the Northern Lights, taking over more or less permanent possession of Cabin 15. Norman and I even spent a week up there, sitting in the sun like lizards, cold-blooded creatures temporarily at a loss for meaningful activity. Airy came back from Greece in late August, brimming with plans and ideas for her education and our money. It was going to be our money because she wanted to get married. Sure, I said, why not? Then I would wander off to my local (either Bob and Gene's or the Hilltop, depending on my venue, Madison or Iron River) and drink a couple of beers. My late nights were spent wandering through abandoned streets, small talking with Bob Birdwhistle or staring out my bay window. I missed Claire Cohen. I was the chief zombie on the Zombie Patrol. In short, I was not a fun guy.

As long as the good weather held I spent Thursday through Sunday afternoon at the Northern Lights. Airy was busy with school but occasionally was willing to go north with me. She read fat leather-bound books sitting on the lodge's porch. Airy looked wonderful sitting in the sunlight, kept warm in a submariner's turtleneck sweater, with her short blond hair bristly as a johnny mop. On the whole she was happy, although annoyed that I hadn't come up with a career path. We stayed in Cabin 13.

Fulmonar and I spent a lot of time together. There were days when I was his only guest, and I began to help him with the two-man chores around the place. We discovered that we could trust each other, and I confessed what had happened vis-à-vis Claire and Airy: the whole sordid truth (only slightly improving my role). He admitted to a serious money crisis, the culmination of a cycle of cash-flow problems and high-interest bank loans. It was actually Milton, not I, who suggested we invest some of our capital in the Northern Lights. The deal was actually made much later, in February, and initially we bought only 49 percent of the Northern Lights, Fulmonar retaining majority interest. It was a long time before Fulmonar sold me the equalizing one percent.

Very gradually, very quietly, I altered my life, anchoring it to an inconsequential spot in the north woods, absenting myself from contention, controversy, and strife. From real life, according to Airy. That was Milton's analysis, too. I was lonely, that was all.

"What the hell is wrong with you, Henry?"

Milton asked me that fifty times a week.

"Nothing," I said fifty times a week.

"What did you do, inject Mazola oil into your brain?"

Milton was always fascinated by pathological behavior. One of his clients had tried to inject salad oil into his head after hearing it was the ultimate high.

"No," I said, "sounds interesting though. Maybe I'll try it."

"Are you depressed?"

"Compared to what?"

"Compared to me, for example."

"Compared to you I'm sailing the vasty Sea of Joie de Vivre."

"I'm not depressed."

"Oh, yeah."

"Okay, I'm depressed. But I'm me, you're you. I rely on you to be in a good mood. So really, what's wrong?"

"You wouldn't like it if I told you."

"Tell me. Except if it's about you know who."

He was tired of hearing my Claire cavil.

"Ah, forget it, Milton, I'm okay."

"Mazola oil, Henry, get your cranium lubricated. It might cheer you up. And this is just for the record, Henry: I warned you many bitter months ago about the consequences of Cohen. You, the dog you are, laughed. To whom, my brother, does the last laugh belong?"

"You, you bastard," I muttered into my fist. "You."

After the Northern Lights closed for the season, and I was squeezed into Madison permanently, I really began to feel somber and out of sorts. Birdwhistle, an acute analyst, called me the Displaced Person of Love, a term of derision. I did feel like a DP.

"I think you're pitiful," he told me. "Sexual obsession, Henry, I warned you. I'd say it's hopeless."

Hopeless. Just what I wanted to hear. Cheered me the hell up. I stopped dropping by there, knowing sympathy would be absent. I was an irritable little guy: morose and cranky. Gives me the creeps merely in the remembrance. Often, when I walked down the street, I would get the urge to hit somebody. I screamed at young mothers in supermarkets, I tried to climb over the bar to get at a smart-assed bartender in Solon Springs, I carped at Milton for chewing too loudly when we were out for dinner. I was walking a knife's edge during my waking hours and sedating myself with beer and wine near bedtime. I've never in my life been unhappier. It was all due to that Claire Cohen person, a name that was in my head more than my own.

So in the late autumn, I often found myself staring out my window at Gent's house—the man who had an itch he wanted my Claire to scratch—an empty Sangria bottle in my hand, standing in my dark apartment with large, hot tears running down my cheeks. Pitiful creature. Extreme measures were called for. Not knowing exactly what else to do, I began my program of hysterical exercise: tennis, racquetball, basketball, running. I exercised eight hours a day, making a huge loop from one university gymnasium to the other in a pattern that hardly varied: tennis at seven; breakfast; racquetball at ten; basketball at twelve; running at three; dinner; basketball at six-thirty. My canvas rucksack, which carried my gear, soon smelled as foul as a swamp. It was always filled with shorts and socks and shirts that were soaking wet with sweat. The bottom of the bag on the outside had a white, cruddy crust so salty you could rub it on your French fries. The inside was fungoid. On grounds of that bag alone people refused to walk near me on the street. Did I care? I did not give a shit. I was blissfully exhausted. Gradually, after a month of this neurotic exertion, my mental state stabilized. I was so played out I sometimes fell asleep at the dinner table. But I felt better: my eyes cleared and my skin stopped itching. I laughed at jokes and even began to call up Milton just to see how he was feeling. I gave Airy an occasional big hug. (I hadn't yet told her about Claire and me, was in fear of being found out every time Claire's name came up. I wasn't pleased by my duplicity. Not at all.)

By November—a month I enjoyed because of the gloomy overcasts, the relentless north wind, the bare leafless vistas, the white caps on the gray water of Lake Mendota—I was able to eliminate all forms of exercise except my noontime basketball game and my nighttime run. Nothing like running at night in November to infuse you with melancholy. I recommend it. On sunny days I would sometimes feel I was resolving my Claire Cohen fixation; a jog in the threateningly unsettled November night took care of that. It didn't hurt that I was constantly being attacked by Caesar, a German shepherd, owned by "Purp" (an nickname derived from the color of his clothing), a black percussionist (bongos were the core of his existence) with a local rock band. He lived close to James Madison Park, and he would let Caesar run loose there on his evening shitting expedition. Naturally, life being as simple as it is, more often than not, I ran by just as Caesar was on the prowl. He ripped sleeves off my sweatshirts in his attack frenzy.

"Motherfucking bitch," Purp would shout at me, "bothering my fucking dog again. I ought to let him rip your balls off, but he probably couldn't find them."

That's how I came to invent Thunderer, connected eventually with Claire via my breaking-and-entering efforts, but designed, in the main, to stave in Caesar's head so his brains would drip onto the dusty meadow of James Madison. I bought an ash hammer handle and wrapped the headless end with duct tape.

I never had to use it against Caesar. I merely had to show it to him, holding it in front of me like a relay runner's baton. He slunk away, humiliated. I knew just how he felt. Old Purp cooled out a bit, too; he actually didn't have much to say after a while. Sort of settled down to a life of cozy domesticity. He got married, developed a series of sinus infections, was hired to manage a gas station during the day, and played the Afro-Cubano bongos at night. Caesar choked on a chicken bone. You know, the history of everyday life is actually pretty complicated.

I loved Thunderer, slept with it underneath my pillow. And had a very hard time—really hard time, virtually impossible—explaining to Airy what I was doing with a hammer handle in my bed. She accused me of using it with, on, or in Lily Campbell. (It's only with extraordinary self-control that Airy can refrain from appending the two words that naturally occur to her when she mentions Lily Campbell: "that slut.")

Finally, miraculously, just after I had accepted her disappearance from my life (I secretly suspected she was back with Nicky), after almost four months of silence, Claire called.

"Hello," I said.

"Hi, it's wonderful to hear your voice," she said.

"Claire?"

"Yes, It's me."

She was infuriatingly cheerful.

I was so angry I was trembling, and my voice stuck in my throat.

"Henry?"

"Yup."

"What's wrong? It's me, Claire."

Somehow or other I had the feeling she thought all systems were go; that her four-month silence was not out of the ordinary. You want rationality, you've come to the right place. I can be a regular goddamn Descartes. They're probably going to put my brain in a time capsule I'm so fucking above it all and clear headed.

"You've ruined my life," I said (maybe, maybe I was screaming). "You're treacherous and cruel, and I regret the day I ever met you. And I regret every minute I've ever spent in your company."

There, do you see how calm I can be?

She began to cry, not little tittering boohoos either, but sobs that I had to hold away from my ear.

"Claire," I said, "don't cry. Please don't cry."

Eventually, she stopped.

"I really missed you, Henry. Why are you so angry at me?"

"Because you've disappeared for four months. Without a word. Is that so complicated?"

"It's been difficult. I didn't want you to worry about me. I was afraid you'd come out here and do something stupid. You know how you are."

"No."

"Henry, you're strange. Everybody knows that. You scared me with that leaving-Airy-for-me stuff. I won't accept that responsibility. Especially when other people—my family—are relying on me."

She had a point, that was the truly troublesome part about dealing with Claire. She always made a certain amount of sense. So it seems I had managed to make myself crazy for absolutely no reason. I had nailed myself, again, to the cross.

"You could have called me if you were so desperate," she said.

"A point of pride. You said you'd call when things settled down."

"Look, I'm going crazy out here. My father is catatonic, I'm throwing up all the time, I'm bleeding, I'm exhausted. And besides, I've tried to call you. You're never home. You didn't call me, ever. I felt a bit forgotten about too, Mr. Fitzgerald. Did you ever think of that?"

"No. I didn't."

Thoughfulness, calm reflection, has never really been a strong point of mine. Gut feelings are my specialty.

"Henry, you're crazy. You're too complicated. You have a girl-friend. She's pretty and smart. I'm not your girlfriend. What do you want from me? I am pregnant and alone, and my mother just died. Don't I have a right to think about what I should do? I know you made a great grand gesture—offering to leave Tinkerbell for me—but I don't trust it."

"But I really care about you, Claire," I said in a pitiful voice. Henry, the wimpy whiner. If Thunderer had been handy I would have clunked myself upside the head.

"And why would you think I stopped caring about you? You have no patience. None. Maybe I should have made an urgent attempt to get in touch with you. Okay, I didn't. If that hurt your feelings, I'm truly sorry. But this is my life, and it's a mess. And you haven't made it, believe it or not, any less of a mess."

"I'll come to see you."

"No."

"Why not?"

"That's the reason I called. I'm coming back to Madison in a couple of weeks. I might have another job with the Madison public school system, teaching kindergarten. There are some other possibilities, too."

"You're coming back. That's wonderful."

"I'm not so sure it's a good idea now."

"Why?"

"Because you're crazy. I thought we could be just good friends, casual friends. But maybe you're not capable of that. You mean a lot to me. But all we can be is friendly."

"That's great. I can handle it."

"It would have been. But no, I'm the treacherous asshole that ruined your life. How can that make me feel? You hate me."

"I don't hate you."

"I don't want a lot of complicated scenes," she said. "Whoever said it was right, women will always make your life more complicated than it has to be. I refuse to be seen as your victimizer. I have my own problems."

Another life experience for Henry. The truth does come in blows.

"Come back," I said. "I'll be fine."

"You're sure? I really mean it this time. No fooling around."

"No hide the salami."

"Right."

"No nibbling on your neck."

"Don't start, Henry. I'm not kidding."

"Okay."

"Are you living with Airy?"

"No. She has her own place."

"Would it be okay if I slept on your couch for a few days? Just until Franny gets back to town. She's going to be home for break, and I have to be in Madison before she gets back. Don't say yes unless you know what that means. No scenes. Period."

"No scenes. Stay as long as you want."

"Did you tell your girlfriend about our little fling?"

"No."

"That's good. It didn't amount to that much, did it?"

This is the way historians deal with seemingly unequivocal facts in a totalitarian state: revision according to the prevailing circumstances. I felt miserable that it could happen to me, however. Part of my life was being struck out by a Party hack.

"I wouldn't say that at all. I was very happy this summer. I thought it was important."

"But overall, not that important. Not to me. That's my honest assessment of it. We were both unhappy, and somehow our unhappinesses melded. That's what I think."

I had a suspicion that I would be back exercising eight hours a day after this conversation.

"Sure," I said, "that sounds right. A flight to the moon et cetera."

"That's the way we have to think about it. Past tense."

"I got you grammatically, Claire. We had a pleasant summer. We will not pursue our mutual attraction. How's that?"

"Don't be bitter."

"I was bitter. I am not now bitter. Notice the structure of the tenses."

She knew enough to be quiet. In my heart, I was furious.

"I'll call you in a week or so. I think I should get to know Airy. It would make things a lot simpler. Maybe we all can have dinner together. Milton, too, I mean."

"Okay."

We hung up, reassuring each other of the immensely high mutual esteem that formed the basis of our relationship. Blah, blah, blah. I sat down on a straight-backed dining room chair. I used my binoculars to spy on Leonard Gent from this chair, neatly tucked behind a beige drapery. I hadn't bothered to turn on the light. I had the strange feeling I was being irradiated by high-frequency radio waves from an alien spacecraft. (Eventually, sitting in this chair, I believed I was able to interpret those signals and form what I thought was a cohesive plan based on them. A real nutball I became.) The phone rang again. I knew it was Claire calling back to make sure I was all right. I let it ring, and eventually it stopped.

I shucked off my clothes and pulled on my sweats. Thunderer, I cried, where are you? Dog-bane, companion of my unhappy youth. Thunderer! Stand aside; get out of the way. I was going to slip out into the brittle November night and run yet another five miles. Kill a dog or two if I got the chance.

17

Leonard Furioso

I SPENT A lot of time, too much time, looking out my living room window. I had a very beautiful view to the northeast, out over Lake Mendota. In the night ice began to form along the shore, and on windy nights I heard the chunks of ice clinking together, almost musically. November is my favorite month. At least that November, as chilly as a spinster's bedroom, made sense to me.

Often on November mornings, I woke up thinking of Claire. My anger was gone, and so were whatever illusions I might have clung to about a dramatic change—toward coincidence—in our lives. A heavy, white, wintry mist hung over the lake. It was like a picture of Brueghel's—the midwest is full of such moments, such snowy landscapes—and I suspected that I was surrendering to the silence that precedes winter. The red boathouse at the end of James Madison Park burst brightly out of all this whiteness, as bright as a newly made fire. I depended on this landscape—burst of color against a mottled white—to wrench me back into action.

The phone rang, but I'd received only bitter news lately, so I decided not to answer. I hated those precious moods. I'm not really the guy for solemn reflection. I always figure if I'm not dead, or about to be, how unhappy can I feel? Ring, you son of a bitch. To hell with it, I'll be gloomy in another life. Claire is history.

I answered the goddamn telephone, which was on its fiftieth ring. I didn't even get a chance to say hello.

"I'm looking at you, Mr. Fitzgerald, right now. Just the way you look at me."

Leonard Gent.

"Lenny, great to hear your voice."

"Your friend did a very ugly thing a few days ago. I've made some inquiries and have managed to make some discoveries."

Actually, it had been my idea to buy a bucket of chicken livers, embed them in a large dollop of clay with the word "Kaboom" carved in it, and mail it to Gent with a birthday card attached. What can I say? We were bored. It was meant as a harmless diversion, but he called the cops anyway.

"Oh, yeah, I heard about the phony bomb, Lenny. Hey, just be glad it wasn't real, otherwise they'd be scraping you off the ceiling with spatulas."

"I know quite a bit about Norman O'Keefe. Much more than you know about him. He's a liar at the very least. And now I know quite a bit about you. I know quite a bit about your friend Claire Cohen. She's very sweet."

"What do you know about Claire?"

"Where she lives, her phone number. I know about the little purple birthmark under her right breast, Henry. I know she's pregnant. And I know you're a fool."

There was an ugly salaciousness in his voice; it was lousy with vile implications. I have to stop answering the phone. The calls I've been getting have been real gut twisters. This creature is trying to suggest he possesses carnal knowledge of Claire.

"I am a fool," I said. I hung up.

It was a nice try, but Claire doesn't have a purple birthmark underneath her right breast. I should know, because I spent a lot of time this spring with my nose buried at just about that spot. Now, if he had said she has little black hairs growing out of her nipples (which she plucked only after my encouragement because she liked the way they looked), I would have been taken aback. If he had said she had a removed-mole scar just above her pubic hairs, I would have dropped the phone and swooned. Bluffing: he thought I might not notice these things. But I am an avid accumulator of facts regarding the unique aspects of women's bodies.

The phone rang again, and I answered it quickly.

"Henry, I don't know what I've done to you to make you hate me."

The sanctimonious twerp. I hate boring sincerity.

"Fuck you, Leonard."

"Why did your friend want to threaten me?"

"I don't have any friends."

"Norman O'Keefe is your friend."

"Because you killed his babies, you fuck."

That shut him up for a minute. Then he turned really nasty.

"Okay, pal, I'm through trying to accommodate your undergraduate rebelliousness. I don't know what I did to you, but stay out of my way regarding O'Keefe. If you're smart, you won't get involved. You'll just fool around with your various lady friends, and play your games, and pretend you're still a student. I don't like fuckups. And you, Mr. Fitzgerald, are my idea of a genuine fuckup. You're a smart-assed kid. I know all about you. Don't play with fire. That's all I have to say. I'm going to protect myself. Period. If you're in my way, you won't like the results. People get hurt, people have to move away, people end up very regretful. They often make long apologies to me. But do you know what, shithead?"

"You don't accept them."

"That's right. I don't accept them. You're a real smart guy. Get very careful because I have my eye on you. You have your binoculars, and I have mine."

"I have this feeling you woke up on the wrong side of the bed this morning, Leonard."

I must have hurt his feelings because he grew very quiet. Loud, outraged breathing was the noise over the wire. I was in a comfortable free-fall status. I felt bad—abandoned and betrayed—about Claire ending my adolescent illusions about Miss Right and the Propitious Moment. I wasn't afraid of Leonard Gent because just for the moment—who knew how long it would last?—I didn't care what happened to me. That, friends, is liberation. Do not mess with me, Gent, or I will get Norman O'Keefe after your skinny ass.

"Pig lips," I said.

"Faggot," he said.

"You think you know stuff about me, Gent? I could lay a couple of names on you that would cause you to consider the delicacy of your position within the moral and legal structure of this community and this state. Facts, Lenny, have come to my attention that place you and your enterprise in jeopardy. Facts, Pig Lips, which could lead, ultimately, to your being cut down from a telphone pole." I was gathering momentum nicely. "Your records are being examined, Gent. Right now in brightly lighted rooms, filled with books, with high windows that reveal a sun-filled winter sky, righteous men are examining your credentials. They do not move their lips when they read, they do not watch game shows, they do not get their information from the evening news or supermarket tabloids. They don't congregate in the men's room of train stations. They don't stare at their reflection in the mirrors of uriney-smelling barrooms. They are not bullies or fools or cowards. They don't care to whom Elizabeth Taylor is currently married. They are indifferent to the machinations of ward heelers and small-time chiselers. They're about to make a decision about you, pal. They are very close. Count on it. What happens to you won't be in the papers. That's the nice part. It'll just happen, period, kaput, the end, that's all she wrote, Leonard. You'll be strictly on the way out. The just few, Lenny, are keeping their eyes on the unjust many. Among which unhappy congregation you are foremost. They've got tables and charts. Whole rooms are filled with brilliant people checking calculations. Nobody slips by because of a misplaced decimal point, pissface. Logarithms are resolved to vast powers. Expect more bad luck. I've been authorized to say that. Expect the bank to bounce your checks, expect your roses to wither, expect cold sores and mysterious night sweats."

"I think you misunderstand me, Henry. I don't know what you're talking about. What facts? I told you the most interesting things about me the first time we met."

"Scuzzball," I said. I imagined him wetting his pork lips with a tiny pink pork tongue.

"I must have something going for me. Your friend Claire thinks I'm very nice. We talk quite a bit. Did she tell you? Oh, that's right, she hadn't spoken to you for months and months until last night. She

called about ten and gave you some bad news. Claire and I talk a lot,
Henry. She's come to rely on me. I call her just after I go to bed, and
we talk heart to heart. Bed to bed, Henry. I'm really quite attracted
to her. She's a lovely girl. Doesn't understand what you're up to,
though. 'Oh, Claire,' I tell her, 'he's just confused. He wants this, he
wants that. He wants you, he wants the other one.' She's very intelligent, and I don't think she believes your story anymore. She pretty
much sees you for what you are. She doesn't have much to say to you
anymore, does she?"

I felt my life might not be a happy one after all. There was no sense
now in trying to hold myself out of the struggle. I was in it, it was
going to get very funky and weird, and a lot of people would be
chuckling into their beer mugs when they described the crazy things
I would end up doing. Everything that happened, here on out, makes
perfect sense to me. Leonard Gent was evil (see Birdwhistle's description of evil above; in short, it is unbelievably ugly close up), and he
was reaching out his taloned fingers toward Claire. I was not going to
let that happen. Gent was not going to get at Claire. The thought of
him touching her, touching her hair and breasts, the thought of his
penis inside her made me crazy. (Let's be liberal in another moment,
okay? Sexual possessiveness is, for the time being, where it's at. I
think I would have strangled Gent, yes, I mean that, strangled him
before I allowed him to seduce Claire.)

I realized, unhappily, that Claire had become a passive object of
desire. There were some ugly questions to be considered. What if she
wanted Gent? What if he were actually nice to her? What if she were
asked to choose between Gent and me and she chose him? What if
she *lusted* after him? Preferred him carnally? Christ, I would be
unhappy. I'd get stinko with the boys and do something so stupid I'd
have to leave town. No, I'm counting on the fact Gent has misled
and decieved her. Used his black arts. Cunning fellow, Gent; a
genius of darkness. That's what I'm counting on.

"Shut you up, didn't I?" he said.

"Leave Claire alone."

"Says who?"

"Says me."

The quality of our invective had taken a nosedive. I had a stomach ache. I had not actually started out to be Leonard Gent's enemy. I had been warned explicitly against just such a course. Forces over which I had no control pushed me into opposition (it was not a small contingent; the campfires of his enemy would look like those on the eve of the Second Battle of Bull Run). I had been threatened, menaced with the possibility of violence against my person and the debauchery of Claire Cohen (my old-fashioned notion of the low state to which Claire would descend via some sort of emotional transaction with the Demon of Gilman Street). Maybe this was all in my head. Perhaps all of it was imaginary, phantasmagorical, the bewildered fantasies of a young man who was dispirited by his crumbling historical moment. Wait a minute. That's bullshit. Gent was a tramp, and he had damaged a lot of people. Enough of this head-up-my-ass relativity.

Conflict is good for the spirit. Gets you off the dime. Lots of decent people were spinning their wheels on slippery streets while megamonsters like Gent moved straight ahead, pickpocketing blindmen and taking milk money away from six-year-olds. Weakness is only a virtue to the weak, that was the unpleasant truth that Gent had absorbed early on. He wasn't weak. He had a fucking million dollars and had walked away from the clear evidence of his outrageous criminality with a carnation in his lapel. If he had not run across my weird devotion to Claire Cohen (men will do almost anything for the right kind of sex), I might have stayed behind the backstop watching. But the son of a bitch punched the wrong button.

All this exercise didn't leave me limp and unwilling to act. I am strong as a bull. Get me sufficiently angry—just squeeze that bicep, hard as rock, isn't it?—get me sufficiently upset, destabilize me with these extreme provocations, and I'll be all over you like Korean cologne.

If there had been a moon out, I'd have howled at it.

18

Minutes of People's Collective Thought-Rectification Committee (Extraordinary Plenary Session)

A SUBTLE THEME was being expressed in my conversations with friends and my brother: I was out of line; my actions were bewildering; my motivations were fuzzy. Just what did I think I was up to?

"Henry," said Airy, "what in the hell is the matter with you?"

It's really simple, Airy, I should have said, I've developed this intense emotional attachment to a woman, not you, who is absolutely wrong for me. No question about it. None. Now, I like you. Under more stable conditions, I would be perfectly happy to get married and merge our lives and ambitions et cetera. Perfectly stable conditions do not, for Henry Fitzgerald anyway, obtain. I am obsessed with this Claire Cohen. I know that, I do. I know it's not healthy. Other than the fact, the basic indisputable fact, that Claire and I have a remarkable sex life (remarkable is a considerable understatement, by the way), we have absolutely nothing in common. Sex, I know, is only a small part of a well-rounded relationship. But I don't care about the rest. I care about dipping my bait in Claire Cohen's pond. I liked the fishy way she smelled after sex. I liked the fishy way I smelled after sex. The center of my life, almost every waking thought, involved Claire's strong, lithe body. It's awkward to admit to this. I feel myself to be an intelligent person, not a horny hillbilly. Now, the really odd part—from the vantage point of any mature person who examined this obsessional behavior on my part—is that Claire insisted *under most conditions* that she was utterly opposed to having sex with me. Astonishingly, I agreed to that. I saw her point.

Of course, I didn't (not yet, anyway) say any of this to Airy, because she would have shown me the door pronto.

What I said was, "Hey, I don't get on your case when you're in a bad mood, so why get on mine? I'm thinking of what to do."

"How long are you going to think?"

"Until I'm done."

"Maybe I can't wait that long," Airy said.

"For what?"

"For you to decide what to do."

"Look, just because you've got a niche doesn't mean I have to have one."

"Henry," Milton said, "you have to make some decisions about your life."

We were sitting in my apartment on Gilman Street. I had just cleaned the place up, and it smelled of furniture polish and ammonia. The bathroom was spotless: the tiles gleamed (both the black and the white), the toilet bowl had been swamped out so thoroughly it looked like a soup tureen. The kitchen was filled with the intense acidy aroma of my spaghetti sauce (a complicated and secret recipe). Glasses were filled with Chianti, and the prospect of garlic bread had saturated everyone's senses. I had Ben Webster on the stereo (Claire's favorite saxophone player). Candles flickered in their white ceramic holders on the dinner table (an old oak library table I had purchased for next to nothing from a dealer in hot University goods). Airy had on a white blouse, buttoned to the neck. A slender silver bracelet—a moderately expensive birthday present from me—alternately slid down her hand or disappeared into her sleeve as she talked and pointed. She still had a little color from the summer, and her face was flushed from the wine and the heat of the apartment. She was cute as hell, not beautiful after all, but definitely on the cusp. She was fiercely intelligent, and belligerent in the face of condescension, lack of attentiveness, or irresoluteness. Her single flaw from my perspective is that she's not very affectionate; in fact, the Elders treat each other for the most part like commuters on a crowded train.

However, in her own way, she loved me. I couldn't escape that responsibility.

"I have to be with someone I respect," she said.

"So marry U Thant."

"Henry, I'm serious."

I was in a gristly, griping mood. Here were the persons I regarded as my boon companions, eating my food, luxuriating in an apartment I cleaned expressly for this evening's fete, and they were kicking the shit out of me, carping at my lack of direction, my drift, my—I'll say the word that will condemn me—irresoluteness.

Airy unbuttoned her blouse (the top two buttons only, please) because she was overheating. The water was on full boil for the pasta, and the kitchen was steaming, the windows fogged over even in the living room. Outside it was a black and bleak night in November. Leonard Gent was prowling in the bowels of his mansion up to perniciousness. Claire was—who knows what she was up to? Airy pulled her blouse away from her breasts, trying to cool down.

"Can't we open a window?" she said.

"I'll think of something to do," I said, struggling with the center window in my bay. It wouldn't budge, except under a fearful wrenching. "Just give me time."

I groaned, the window frame groaned, and then gave way. Cold air burst in like a Junior G-man; cold drafts can be lovely.

"You'll just waste it."

"Cut me a break here, Airy. I'll admit to being at a loss, but I'll snap to."

"You could live like this for ten years. You could wake up one morning at thirty-five and nothing will have been accomplished, nothing will have changed. This is the thing I really hate about you, Henry, your goddamn diffidence. You get so sloppy and passive. You'll end up sitting in the dark late at night with the TV turned on to Japanese horror films or maybe reruns of *I Love Lucy*."

"Thanks."

The awful thing about Airy's vision of me circa 1982 was that it was depressingly like my own nightmarish projections.

"I've seen it happen," she said.

Confronted by my own ignominy, I stayed off in the dark part of the room, near the bitterness of the open window, trying to figure out how best to defend myself.

Stick and move, I was thinking, move and stick. Don't give them a stationary target. Old Hawk was out tonight roiling among the tops of the trees, chopping up the lake into blurry herringbone patterns.

"I agree with Airy," my brother said, "I think you've wasted quite enough time. You spend too much time with people who aren't your intellectual equal"—code for Birdwhistle—"so you're being brought down a bit. I think graduate school, if only as an experiment, would be a good idea. Shop around for a discipline."

"I don't want to go to graduate school. I don't like graduate students. They all look green in the library. They spit when they talk."

"Be serious, Henry." Airy was annoyed. *She* was a graduate student.

I sat down on the sofa, laid my forearms across my thighs, leaning forward. Once again I had the blues.

"I am serious," I said. And then some really strange words came out of my mouth. I think I must have had one of those drug-related delayed brain spasms that you read about in the dentist's office.

"Let's get married."

"What?" She said that with a mocking, knitted-brow grimace.

"First, and this is my opinion only, before anyone mentions matrimony, Henry needs to find something to focus his energy on," my brother, the village explainer, said. He was weighing in with some relatively fatuous remarks, my favorite kind. My toes were tingling: I felt like going for a run.

"I think Henry is serious, Milton," Airy said. "He's mentioned it before. I think he wants to get married. It makes a certain amount of sense. He loves me after all."

I relish a woman who will rush to my defense. Milton didn't look at me. We shared the deep Claire Cohen secret. Eventually, I was going to have to spill the beans. But not tonight. I mean, I did love Airy.

"But he just wants to marry you because you'll tell him what to do. If you're married, he'll feel like it's okay for him to do it."

"Isn't it?"

Good point, Airy.

"Maybe."

Airy smiled at both of us. She was ready to get married, too.

"I think it would be the best thing for Henry, Milton. He'd have something to work for; someone, me, to help him establish goals and priorities. We would be a team in a way we're not now. It would be a permanent and serious commitment. I think Henry needs a commitment stronger than his own will."

"I don't think I need that," I said.

They looked at me with surprise. I was present after all, and, against their best instincts, they would have to let me have my say.

"What do you need then?" she asked.

"I need . . ." I thought of that photograph of my parents, on Easter Sunday, dressed for church. I thought of my father, and his broad face, and his bristly 19th-century mustache. I knew what it was I wanted, quite suddenly and unexpectedly, based on the iconographic record of my infancy and of my parents; my lovely dead parents whose bones whitened beneath an Arctic sun. It was too sad to say out loud.

". . . another beer."

That didn't go over well. They turned to each other, happy to disinclude me from their calculations. They were sitting on the couch, side by side, quite a handsome couple if you look at them sort of squinty eyed and you swung your head back and forth: my future wife and her brother-in-law presumptive. This was a tiny glimmer of family dinners that made me feel a little queasy. I like to be around goofy guys like Bob Birdwhistle. I like talking about things that have no obvious meaning or global importance, that are sometimes slightly off-color or in downright bad taste. I do not care for the mixing-and-mingling scene, the dinner-party and cocktail-party circuit. (On which circuit, A. and M. were local all-stars.) I would much rather talk to Jack Montana, the Weed Commissioner of Iron County, about sexual perversion in Northern Wisconsin than about threats to the environment or women's rights (I'm against the former and for the latter. What else could I be, a white liberal, in the Age of Bebe Rebozzo?).

I wandered off to stir my special marinara sauce, as savory as ambrosia, a genuine food of the gods. It was a rich red, with a scum

around the top of the pot redder than fish guts. Nice chunks of
tomato followed my spoon to the surface. The garlic bread was
wrapped in its aluminum-foil shroud, ready for a Viking funeral,
soon to come out of the oven delightfully gooey with garlic butter. I
suddenly felt so good, hungry as a grizzly bear on or about April 1
(den-evacuation time), that I did the Fitzgerald shuffle, my feeling-
good dance—half borrowed from the titans of modern choreography
and half sheer exuberance and invention. (Who shall say, Doc, I am
not the happy genius of *my* household, too?) My nearest and dearest
were chattering away in the living room, dosed with red wine and
beginning to feel loose enough to let me have a little lonely fun. Oh,
things weren't so complicated: you eat, you drink, you jump around
in the kitchen, and, if you're lucky, you get your life laid out for you
like a DOA in the uptown morgue.

Airy wandered into the kitchen while I was hopping about. I was
in my stocking feet, so I was silent, not clattering like a Flamenco
dancer. I don't know how long she observed me in my mania, my
mad dance, my happy lopsided juggernautish jitterbug. I had a
wooden spoon in my hand, and occasionally, as I dipped past the
stove, I would stir the sauce and taste it just because it was extraor-
dinarily delicious. I had a glass of beer on the granite-colored countertop and I toasted absent loved ones. The overhead light in the
kitchen, a fluorescent circle, was burning out. It buzzed and flickered like a firefly. Airy leaned against the doorframe, observing her
boyfriend, that troublesome character, frolicking like a leprechaun.
What could she have thought of my lonely joy?

"What are you doing?" she asked. Not sharply, not angrily.

"I'm . . . I don't kow. I'm not sure."

"Are you drunk?"

"Nope." A lie, another brick missing from the Wall of Truth.

"Why are you acting so strangely?"

I wanted to say: because my heart is breaking. But that wouldn't do
at all. Stiff fucking upper lip for the girl with the stiffest upper lip in
our time.

"Strangely?"

"Jerking around the kitchen like a madman. I'd call that strange."

"It was a short, celebratory dance."

"Celebrating what?"

"It's Nijinsky's birthday. I was re-creating 'Afternoon of a Faun.'"

"I'm really disappointed in you. You say something really serious for a change—I consider marriage quite important—and now you're joking around again. What's in your head, anyway? I think you have to see someone."

"Someone?"

"A therapist. You have this compulsion to fail. I won't stand for it."

The only thing Airy will stand for is the National Anthem.

"I won't fail."

"You have to so something other than say that, Henry, you have to do something. Do something. It really hurts me to see you acting like a fool in the kitchen while your brother and I are in the living room trying to thrash things out. It's just embarrassing."

Get your mind right, pal; that was Airy's clear message. I think you're having too much fun.

This is when I should have kissed all this stuff off and resumed my Homage to Nijinsky, danced like a dust devil across the sparkling tiles, freeing myself from Airy's onerous charge (Do something!). Here was a window of opportunity closing, and I had one instant to prop it open.

"I'm sorry," I said, "I didn't realize you would be upset."

I failed; I failed utterly.

"All I want you to do is try, Henry. That would make me happy. Come back to the living room, for me."

When the complete psychic history of the mid-twentieth century is written, this moment will be properly underscored. Henry trudged back into the living room, chastened and apologetic, ready to listen to the lengthy list of his recidivist tendencies.

I confessed to my errors, doctrinal and others, and swore I would cleave firmly to the tenets of a correctly conducted life, if only they (Airy and Milton) would provide consistent and detailed instruction re correct conduct.

Happily, my conscience required me to keep my fingers crossed.

We ate dinner. By the time the pasta was cooked and the sauce ladled out, everybody, including Airy, was a little tipsy. They really got down to it after the antipasto (anchovies and pimentos with capers dressed with olive oil and vinegar). The hounds of propriety heaved themselves onto their hind legs and howled like persons. I was in despair and nodded my weary assents. How could I not? I did see their point. No question I had to motivate myself in some way.

Secretly, I had an image of myself—a sentimental one, I suppose—of Henry Fitzgerald which more closely resembled the unencumbered, unrestrained solitary dancer than an up-your-ass tyro tycoon. That private Henry, happy Henry, walked through a sunlighted landscape with a dark-haired beauty who looked suspiciously like Claire Cohen, in an abandoned apple orchard (the one close to the Northern Lights would do), on one of the last sad days of Indian summer. What I wanted, it turns out, was very simple.

The food was delicious; surprisingly, I'm quite a good cook. I uncorked another fiasco of Chianti and got very quiet. I was filled to overflowing with drink. Airy flirted with me, smiling fetchingly over the clotted remains of pasta and garlic-bread crud. I got the urge to yodel, a troublesome sort of behavior that manifests itself when I drink too much red wine. I started to clear my throat and stretch my neck into yodeling position. Just the way Roy Rogers gets ready to yodel.

"Don't yodel," Airy said. "It's the stupidest thing."

"I wasn't going to yodel," I said, by now, thoroughly whipped. I might have even flinched. "Yodeling is something I don't even try anymore."

Eventually, after dinner Milton fell asleep stretched out on the living room floor. Airy turned on the television and watched a PBS special about the rape of the Alaskan wilderness. I did the dishes, lingering over the sink, with the radio turned so low the music sounded like it was coming from Patagonia. The music was Bach (humming Glenn Gould at the klavier), and I didn't even feel a quiver in my toes. I was miserable.

At about ten I shooed them out, even Airy, who wanted to spend the night. But I was adamant: out, out, let me brood.

"Don't worry, Henry," Airy said to me at the door, bundled in her sheepskin coat and puzzled by my dejection, "everything will be all right. I'll always be there for you."

Then, *sotto voce:* "We can talk about marriage in the morning."

"I know I'm a little high," I said, dead drunk, "but I think it's a good idea. I think we should definitely get married."

There's no question she would be a wonderful mate. Airy, in every respect, was perfect for me, while in virtually no respect was I right for her. The truth is, I may have said this before, she loved me.

Alone, the state I have come to prefer, I turned off the lights and sat in the dark. I thought about a nighttime ramble, a trip down to Birdwhistle's shop or a whirlwind tour of the near east side, but I felt that epoch, the lonesome-traveler mode, was ending. More and more often I was taking up my bay-window position in a straight-backed chair, my binoculars around my neck on a braided leather strap, peering into Leonard Gent's windows.

The lights were out, and the drapes were drawn. It was quiet as a grave at Gent's. I thought my day was over, the seriously damaging part of it at last history, when there was a somber knock on my door. I knew it could be only one person: Norman O'Keefe. He creeps up the stairs, clinging to the wall, so he won't make any creaks. He is practicing, he says, for the Ultimate Moment.

"It's open," I said.

Norman kicked aside the door. He stood framed in the entry, a black silhouette. He peered into my dark apartment.

"Henry?"

"Present."

"What are you doing?"

"Nothing. Thinking."

He walked in and turned on a light. He flung himself on the sofa, stretched out, and covered his eyes with his arm.

"Christ," he said, "what a night I've had."

"What's up?"

"Would you believe that four hours ago I was in a perverts' bar—a genuine hellhole, Henry—just south of the Loop?"

"I'll believe anything at this point, Norman."

"There were dozens and dozens of creeps dressed up like storm troopers, like SS torturers, blood underneath their fingernails. It was horrible. Apparently, if you get slammed up the old kazoo by somebody dressed like Hermann Goering, the effect is especially sizzling. I had to gargle with salt water and Jack Daniel's after I left just to get the smell out of my nostrils. Human slime, for Christ sake. I can tell you, Henry, I'm glad I'm like me and not like them."

"What were you doing there?"

"Field research. Investigating. I finally ran Fletcher Lint to the ground. I cornered him in an alley next to that bar. He's a regular."

"What happened?"

"I held a smooth chrome pistol to his head and said, 'Fletcher, I am who I am, if you don't tell me the whole truth someone will be making sauce Bolognese in your brainpan.'"

"What happened?"

"He wept many bitter tears. He spilled his guts. Jesus, Henry, I would have spilled mine, too. I was on the edge. Only my Catholic school training prevented me from squeezing the trigger."

He held up his chintzy, dime-store pistol.

"Put it away, Norman. Christ, is that thing loaded?"

"It's loaded, but I'm not sure it will fire. It's sort of pretty in a trashy way, though, isn't it?"

"What did he say?"

"He was anxious. He told me a lot. He told me the name of the man who murdered my babies, the monster who lighted the fire."

"What is it?"

"Iggy Pelcho."

"Perfect."

"A Polack, just off the boat."

"Where is he?"

"Chicago. Lint also told me something else. You know, there is no honor among the thieving classes. Gent screwed him out of eight thousand dollars in one of their cigarrette deals via some creative bookkeeping. Lint is furious. He's moving to Brownsville, Texas, to sell condos. Some sort of snowbird-ripoff real estate scam. Before he leaves he wants to deal Gent some serious dirt. He gave me the key to a safety deposit box that he says contains enough lurid info to send Lenny on an extended state-sponsored stay."

"He volunteered that?"

"I cocked the hammer, Henry. Time is of the essence. I'm tired. I can't live like this much more. It has to end."

"Do you believe him?"

"The fact that I found him once, I think, was a disincentive to lie. Also he knows I'm a crazy fuck. He says he has nightmares about my babies."

The lights came on in Gent's room, a pencil-slender beam of light breached the tightly drawn drapes. Norman came over and stood behind my chair. What was going to happen to Claire? Who was going to be in my autumnal apple orchard now?

Norman sighed his sad sigh. He was as worn as an old key.

"It has to be pretty soon, Henry," Norman said softly. "Pretty goddamn soon."

19

True Confessions

SO I TOLD Airy everything. She didn't want to hear everything, but eventually I got most of it out. (I didn't mention the tenderest of Claire-affair details.) Unfortunately, the true confession part of the program didn't terminate with my recitation. She had had a little fling, too, a week's worth of dalliance with another graduate student. Thrashing about naked as dolphins in the azure water of the Aegean, that's the vision I conjured. Her explanation? She didn't think I deserved one. Eventually, "sex starved" was the phrase she used; she was simply fulfilling a basic human need. One tries to understand that, of course, but privately, deep in the heart, one was mortified.

I deserved it all, of course, every revelation, but for about ten minutes, I was absolutely nuts. Eventually, I realized that de facto jealousy was really not part of my new program, so I tried to cool out. I discovered almost immediately I wasn't capable of calm discussion when it came to Airy climbing into the rack with another guy. I felt like the prosecuting attorney in the High Court of Adultery.

"And what was the bastard's name?" I said.

"It doesn't matter. It's none of your business."

"Well, I told you all about Claire."

"I didn't ask for it. I don't care about the dirty details. How many times you did it and so on. We're both adults, and we were attracted to other people, and we did something about it."

"You slept with that jerk."

"You slept with that little scheming bitch."

"Claire's not a bitch."

"And Michael isn't a jerk. He's famous in his field."

Being famous will definitely get you into the sack with Airy.

"So what's the situation?"

"There is no situation. We parted amicably. I haven't spoken to him since. Can you say the same thing?"

"No."

"So what's the situation?"

"With Claire?"

"Of course, moron."

"There's no situation, except friendship."

"And she's coming back and she's going to 'stay with you for a few days.'"

"That's right."

"I don't like that. You'll probably slip it to her at your first opportunity."

"Even if I wanted to—and I don't—she couldn't possibly. She's pregnant and probably big as a house."

"And will you try to be the strong, brave man again and rush to her side. Pat her hand and get her a cold glass of water. Men are jerks. As long as she's here, I won't be around. You can count on that, Mr. Fitzgerald."

"So you're jealous after all."

"No, I'm not. I just choose not to associate with people like her."

"Like what?"

"Your sluttish girlfriends. Like that slut Lily Campbell. I can't believe you get on top of that one. Jesus, Henry, I don't want to be one of your popsies."

It went on like this for quite a while. We were in the Florida room (how I came to despise that ferny and succulent-filled spot) with a modest breakfast between us. The radio was playing Mozart; a pot of tea steamed on the table. We were alone. I hadn't slept very well, guilt finally overcoming instinct, and I had rushed over to the Elders almost at first light to prostrate myself at the feet of my intended. I wanted to testify to the fundamental error of my ways. I got sucked into that maelstrom of ugly incident instead and wound up staggering home with the certain knowledge that I needed Airy a great deal more than she needed me.

"I'll call you when I feel like seeing you again," she said. "Don't hold your breath."

And she showed me the door.

So much for the truth; there *was* a good reason I hadn't placed much faith in it. It was not even nine o'clock, and already I was dazzled with unhappiness. The Elders lived in University Heights, on the highest part of the Heights, and I skidded down the streets (it had sleeted before dawn) amazed, stupefied really, about how long a losing streak can last. I was down to my last silver dollar.

Head down, hands in pockets, a funereal pace: I must have looked perfectly blue. The day was damp, and a freezing wintery haze hung about one hundred feet off the ground. These were the kind of atmospheric conditions which precede a heavy snow, if only a cold front were to plunge into the Upper Midwest from Canada. I was up to an aimless no good when Birdwhistle's west-bound StepVan flailed to a screeching stop. He was on his way to Middleton, loaded with doughnuts, rushing to finish his deliveries.

"You look like you lost your best friend," he yelled, his fuzzy head poked out of the window. Like most Buddhists, he was cheerful in the morning.

"Something like that."

"Airy found out. Am I right? Or maybe you spilled the beans."

"Right."

"You got your balls caught in the wringer. Good for you, Henry, floating like Cleopatra on her barge, right up Shit Creek. Hey, didn't I tell you you were in for some rough sledding?"

"You did. And you don't have to be so cheerful about it."

"You going to stand out there in the weather all day? Get in, I've got some news."

"If it's bad, I'd rather not hear it."

"What day is it today?"

"December second, I think."

"Consider this your Christmas present: Claire Cohen is on her way. She's in the air right this instant. She'll be landing in a few hours if the weather holds."

"Really, Bob, how do you know all this stuff? Why don't I know?"

"Simple, Henry. And I've told you this before. I answer the telephone, you don't. Claire can't get in touch with you, and she knows eventually you will turn up at my door, so she calls me. I'm the recalcitrant bastard who adds the aura of mysterious revelation, second sight, and so on. But life is too short to bore people with details. I'm a CinemaScope personality. Wide-screen spectacular tendencies. You ought to know that by now. Birdwhistle is always down at the end of the bat. None of your choked-up line drives for him. It's a home run or nothing here at Birdwhistle's Home Run Derby. You're slow sometimes, guy."

"Just get on the line to kick the shit out of me, Bob. No charge this month."

"It'll get worse, Henry. But don't think too much about it. Hey, you know about her job, of course?"

"What's that?"

"She's going to be Leonard Gent's assistant up in the House of Mirthlessness. The head matron in the big house. She's going to spoon the treacle into young Nickleby's mouth."

It seems I wasn't the only person capable of delivering an unsavory lie. Claire had disguised her connection to Gent.

"Stop now. I have to get out. I have things to do."

He pulled over near Lombardino's, hopping the curb with two wheels and barely missing a yellow street-sign post. His cargo of plastic five-gallon buckets filled with bags of doughnuts slid to port, pyramiding against the chipboarded sides of the van. (Birdwhistle had lined the interior behind the seats with chipboard, even covering the windows, and he sat back there in this coffinlike environment before going to work, imagining what it would be like to be dead.)

Bob slapped my shoulder fraternally.

"Take it easy, old campaigner," he said. "Patience. It's going to have a happy ending if you can only hang on to the end. Birdwhistle has seen this too."

I was getting very tired of Birdwhistle referring to himself in the third person (a habit I've adopted), as if he were a Hapsburg.

I was farther west than when I had left the Elders, out by the Ag School, as usual, having been led astray and far away from the direction in which I needed to travel. I was shivering, only partly from the cold and the damp. And it was increasingly misty and penetratingly cold; like being on a life raft in the North Atlantic. Torpedoed was not an inapt description of my state.

I had a nasty flashback in Birdwhistle's van: images of a traumatizing pornographic film I had seen in high school. Oh, no, Claire wasn't going to be reduced to spectacle. No subhuman felon was going to write in Magic Marker across her chest and take washed-out Polaroids of the weirdness. No one, I said out loud, this among the first manifestations of a quasi-psychotic episode.

"No one," I said quite plainly while buying a *State Journal* in Rennebohm's, "no one is going to scribble on Claire's chest with anything or force her to take a German shepherd into her confidence. No one."

I was on State Street when it began to snow. The flakes were enormous, saturated with moisture, and they melted immediately after hitting the ground. One of Birdwhistle's many predictions was being fulfilled: Henry caught in a snowstorm, a lost and harried wanderer. (I couldn't help feeling, even in my extreme state, that a vision of Henry walking along in a snowstorm, considering I lived in a northern temperate zone, was not exactly like predicting a comet would collide with the earth at the next full moon. Birdwhistle, as far as being a seer goes, pretty much played the chalk.)

I was wearing only a thin sweatshirt and sweat pants (the pants had been rubbed ragged in the crotch and were leaking cold air very badly). The cuffs of the shirt were ragged, and the laces of my sneakers had become untied. They flopped around my ankles as I dogtrotted home. I was unkempt in the extreme, talking to myself in an agitated way. Welcome to the wonderful world of schizophrenia, Mr. Fitzgerald, we've been hearing splendid things about you.

I turned east on Gilman Street, climbing the almost unnoticeable incline. I was hoary with snow despite my efforts to scrape it off, shake it off, shiver it off. Trudge, trudge, old Henry is marching to his homeland up the hill, Bug Hill, which he shares catty-corner fashion with Leonard Gent, that brute.

I stripped off my clothes at home and dropped them in a damp pile into the bathtub. I sat on the sofa wrapped in a towel and called Airy. The snow hadn't completely melted into water yet, and I was making a sniveling phone call the main thrust of which was to be an apology for any infidelities, indiscretions, or other shortcomings.

"There's nothing to forgive, Henry: you slept with Claire and I did the same with Michael. The difference is you can't sleep with a woman without falling in love with her. I always saw my infidelity, if you insist on calling it that, as my last chance to sleep with someone, just for sex, other than you."

"That's a bit self-serving, isn't it?"

"Probably. But I didn't create a cozy little love nest with everything except a parakeet and a pot of geraniums. My affair was strictly two ships passing in the night. He has a gorgeous body. It was just sex."

"It seems like that should be my line."

"Use it if you like, but I know it's not true. The first time you stayed with me, you were measuring my walls to see if your books would all fit in. It freaked me out."

"I didn't think you noticed."

"You get way ahead of yourself, Henry. Your tendency toward domesticity can be really boring. The one thing I don't want to be is bored."

Out the window my Brueghelian landscape had become even whiter and more like Brueghel. The red boathouse at the end of James Madison Park receded, gradually, into the deep background. It became the sole promise of fire in an icy world.

"Why don't you come over here and we'll make up?"

"No. Not until Claire Cohen has disappeared."

"I'd really like to do the boda-bing boda-bang."

"Why do you have to use those moronically juvenile phrases? Get your duck wet; do the boda-bing boda-bang. You have an entire vocabulary of euphemisms for fucking."

"Why don't you come over here so," and this is Airy's own utilitarian phrase, "we can have sex."

"No."

"Are you angry with me?"

"Yes."

"Will you be angry with me for a long time?"

"I don't know."

"Are we still engaged?"

"Momentarily."

"It's teetering?"

"Yes."

"What's the worst that could happen?"

"It's all relative, depending upon whether or not you want me in your life."

"I do, of course."

"I could break our engagement and never see you again."

"As a result of?"

"Claire Cohen, let me see, what's one of your phrases, 'sniffing around your tree' indefinitely."

"I said she could stay for a couple of days, until Franny got back into town."

"What a guy."

"I can't tell her she can't stay here."

"Oh, I know, Henry, you wouldn't be the fellow in the white hat anymore."

"Claire is a friend, Airy. You can stop this shit any time. You're going over the line. I cede the fact you have a right to be miffed, but Claire hasn't done a dime's worth of damage to you. I made a promise and I intend to honor it."

"Like I said, Henry, call me when she's gone. Then we can resume this conversation."

She slammed the phone down in my ear; crunched it into its cradle.

I went in the shower and stood for a long time beneath the intense barrage of very hot water. Of all the rooms in my apartment (bathroom, living room with a wb/fp, dark bedroom, sun-lighted eat-in kitchen), the bathroom was becoming my favorite. It is black and white, floor and walls, carefully tiled, and when you shut off the light and sit in the dark, a fine place to reflect on your errors and shortcomings. It has both a tub and a shower, and this summer Claire and I often bathed at the same time: she luxuriating in the tub; I, as I am now, head bowed and hands on hips, relaxing under the flood.

I dried off and dressed. It was early afternoon, and I thought I'd just sit and wait for Claire, who was already past due. It was snowing in earnest now, and I calculated that she was probably going to be very late, perhaps she was sitting on the ground in Chicago, in the stuffy plane, waiting to take off. I was just beginning to get warm again. I tried to call Airy, feeling a little less stressed out, a little cozier. I wanted to talk her into coming over for a conciliatory romp. I was remembering her smooth belly, her belly button sticks out and looks like a flower bud, and the burry feeling of her hair against my cheek. Dumb desire is what is ruining my life. The line was busy.

I was not unhappy alone. I sat in the semidarkness of my apartment (the low clouds and snow had squeezed out the available light) momentarily quite content to stretch out on the sofa with a heavy book (the southern voyages volume of *The European Discovery of America*). My squat blue table lamp (shaped like an avocado on end) circled me in yellowish light; the radiators clanged and rasped (full of hot water and turbulent air bubbles). Strike out into the darkness and unknown: now that was the proper way to live. Don't hold back or play the percentages. I nodded out intermittently with the book on my chest, finally surrendered to sleepiness and shut off the light and napped, and when I woke up, the phone was ringing, and I couldn't find it, and in my confusion I thrashed about grasping after the sound.

It was on the end table behind my head, and I succeeded in swatting it into silence with my forearm (knocked it off the table) as I reached back over my head in a stuporous panic. I fell off the couch trying to catch it, failed, but saved my avocado lamp from destruction instead. The phone was on the floor, and I was now on the floor, too, on my back, with the unlighted lamp on my chest and a tiny tinny voice barking my name irritatedly someplace beyond me in the darkness.

"Henry."

I slapped at the floor and finally found the handset.

"Henry. Henry. Henry. Where are you?" said the voice, now recognizably Claire Cohen's.

"I'm here," I said. "Sorry."

"Were you sleeping?"

"No. I was in the kitchen. Where are you"

"Detroit."

"Will you be able to get out?"

"I think so. They're reloading the plane now. We're flying directly into Madison. I should be there in a few hours, I guess."

"What time is it?"

"Four-thirty. I'm exhausted. I've been sitting here since before noon. I think you have to be a mushroom to survive in the Motor City, Henry. It's depressing."

"How do you feel, physically?"

"I've been having cramps. And I've been bleeding a little. It's nothing serious. My doctor said that I could expect to spot. I don't know, Henry, I've been better and I've been worse, but mostly I've been better. I wish I didn't have these cramps. It's uncomfortable to sit on the plane."

"Should I meet you at the airport?"

"No, that's all right, I'll take a cab. Is it snowing there?"

"It's stopped, I think. There's another storm on the way."

"Okay, I'll see you soon."

"I'll be here."

I had a couple hours to kill. I pulled on my heavy boots—my Redwings, lovely maroon ankletoppers—and decided I would take a short stroll. A real aristocrat, I needed predinner exercise to work up an appetite.

Two December 1972 was a snowy day, low ceilinged, winter gloomy. I hunted in the morning and turned wood in the afternoon. I made this innocent, fateful entry in my journal: "Rien."

20

The Spiral Down Commences

I WALKED THROUGH the snowy streets toward the zoo. It was my intention to visit the Elephant House and extract a few words of wisdom from Crystal and Tiny. Two inches of snow had fallen, shag-carpet depth, and after a burst of thawing, the snow and slush had begun to freeze into sleek and crusty ice. More snow was forecast, and behind the snow a wave of Arctic air.

I was looking forward to seeing Claire again after almost five months of no contact. I was also very tense and touchy. At one point, I even tried to run after and catch a Badger Cab that had splashed grimy slush water on me while I was waiting to cross University Avenue. A man on foot on an icy street trying to catch an automobile is, I'm sad to say, a definition of futility.

I made a snowball to throw at the next interloper, the next car, truck, or bus that dared whip a wave of slush at me. I carried it in my right hand and flipped it up and down with a casual practiced motion, like a bullpen catcher during a rain delay. From all external appearances I was perfectly normal; however, if you had stuck a meat thermometer in me, the reading would have been "Dangerous." There was no question that my personality was destabilizing. I see that now. I mean, I wasn't walking around barefooted with a picture of Norman Mailer stapled to my forehead. Now *that's* crazy. But I was filled with a bubbling rage.

It's a long walk to the zoo, and I'm a slow walker. Claire was going to arrive, and I realized that if I proceeded with my current course, I wouldn't be home in time. After about half an hour, beneath the University Hospital power plant on University Avenue, I turned around. The streets were emptying: it was becoming suppertime in the midwest, and most decent folk were gathered around the table forking meatloaf into their mouths. I hadn't eaten anything except a single bite of English muffin at my valedictory breakfast with Airy, and my stomach was rumbling. I was walking, more or less aimlessly, in a frozen cityscape. Claire was due to arrive, and I had to be home to meet her.

I didn't exactly hotfoot it back, but at least I arrived before Claire. I put fresh sheets on the bed and put out clean towels in the bathroom. (The new fluffy ones Airy bought for her showers and which I was not allowed to use for reasons only an anal retentive could conjure. Airy even brought her own roll of toilet paper when she stayed the night. My toilet paper, I gave up trying to tell her, was no more virus laden or infectious than hers.) I opened the bedroom window because Claire likes to sleep in a room with plenty of fresh air and let's not worry about how cold it gets. I checked the refrigerator: beer, oranges, tonic water, and a pot of beef burgundy tinged a bit with green mold. Nothing appropriate for a pregnant lady: dark-haired Claire whose Gentward course I had somehow to obstruct.

I would have to go out and get a few things for Claire: orange juice, whole milk, plain yogurt, whole-wheat doughnuts, a chain and padlock with which to isolate Leonard Gent from the right-living folk of our great republic. I was slipping into exotic reveries. Juice, yogurt, and milk: that's all I needed for the moment. I was feeling nostalgic and overladen with dumb cow love. Moo, I was going in my goofy head; oh, Claire, moo. I was also feeling panicky with the thought Gent would swallow Claire whole. If only she weren't knocked up, things would be simple. Nostalgia and panic, systole and diastole: "No one," I announced emphatically to the interior of the refrigerator (I stood in front of it in a sort of revery), "is going to do anything bad to Claire."

I went to my window and looked up and down Gilman Street for Claire's cab. The street was empty except for my downstairs neighbor, Lucia something or other Italian—Lupinta or Luperna—walking her dog Tickle. Tickle was peeing into a bush, and Lucia was standing patiently smiling like a lover at his uplifted leg. (Crazy dog yelps late on weekend nights had me wondering if maybe Lucia didn't have an unusually intense relationship with her dog or vice versa. It's a slanderous thing to say, but it happens even in the best of neighborhoods, even in the best of times. Neither condition obtained on Bug Hill, 1972.)

Then I saw Claire, on foot, carrying a small bag (a nylon duffle sack she can get almost everything she owns into), walking very slowly up Gilman Street. She paused and set her bag down. She looked up at my window. I stood there transfixed. She bent over but didn't take up her duffle again; she grabbed the backs of her thighs instead, as if she were stretching, getting a kink out of her lower back. I dashed out the door and leaped the steps, crashed from the first landing to the entry, unmindful of the fact that I could have easily broken my neck. I got out into the night air just as Claire was turning up my sidewalk. She had on her beaver coat, patched in the collar and the cuffs, but still clinging to that old irresistible rattiness. Her hair was dark and stuck out from beneath the red beret she wore. She was gorgeous. I leaped at her, and she leaped at me. We discovered quickly the old secret. Despite her incipient roundness (her face was fuller and sweeter) we still made a nice match embracewise; we still fit together as if we were made by the same master craftsman.

"Henry," she said.

"Claire," I answered.

"You're here," I said.

"Yes," she said.

Not scintillating, admittedly.

"Come in. What happened? Why are you walking?"

"I got off in front of the wrong house. There's one a block down the street that looks a lot like yours. I was confused."

She wouldn't look at me when she gave that explanation, though, and I had the feeling she was lying. Leonard Gent's influence was palpable, smelling like singed hair.

I took her bag, which was very heavy, and stepped out of the doorway so she could pass me and go up the stairs. She pulled off her hat and unwrapped her scarf, and all the old inappropriate feelings hobbled back, having broken through most, but not all, of their restraints. She ran her hand through her hair in that estimable Clairish way, untangling her thick black hair from the scarf, lifting it in a hefty handful from beneath her collar. I followed her up the stairs full of schoolboyish longing. We didn't speak until I set her bag on the floor and she had pulled off the weighty beaver thing ("coat" didn't accurately represent its forceful presence) and dropped it on the sofa.

"He picked you up at the airport, didn't he?"

"Yes."

"Why didn't you tell me?"

"I thought you'd be furious. Leonard told me that you threatened him."

"I did. I told him justice would be done."

"He's not like you think."

"I know. He's probably worse."

"I don't want to have an argument, Henry. I'm sorry I lied to you. Leonard picked me up so we could talk about my job. I'm going to work for him. I start on Monday."

"You'll be living there?"

"Yes," she said, "we'll be neighbors again. Won't that be great?"

"No."

"I'm sorry."

"Nothing to be sorry about, Claire. I think it's a real mistake, your working for Gent. He's a monster."

"I don't want to talk about it. He's been very kind to me."

"All right."

"How have you been? I missed you."

"Fine. Great."

"Don't pout."

"I've been okay. I'm getting married." A finger in the eye, passive aggressively speaking.

"So Pixie landed you after all. Good for her. I'm sure you'll both be very happy. Now aren't you glad we were circumspect?"

"No. It makes me deeply unhappy to think of you living with Gent just across the street from me. It makes me deeply unhappy to think of you period."

"I don't want you to be unhappy."

"I don't think what you want for me matters much anymore."

"I can leave."

"Maybe that's a good idea."

"Henry, we have to be able to be friends. I want that. Let's just talk about it. But I have to lie down for a few minutes, right now. I don't feel very well."

"What's wrong?"

"Cramps."

"Are they bad?"

"Pretty bad. It gets bad and then it goes away. Right now it's bad."

"What can I do?"

"Nothing, Henry. Just don't be mad at me."

I went and got a pillow and put it at the end of the sofa. I hung up Claire's coat in the entry closet, jammed it between my down jacket and vest, and put her duffle bag in the bedroom. She was ashen. Remarkable was my lack of sympathy. The sad truth was that I was dog tired of doing things for Claire. I had decided that this was to be our ultimate conversation. My new life would be one of contented devotion to Airy Elder and a triumphant entry into law school. I looked out my bedroom window as I was storing away Claire's bag. The dome of the State Capitol was hung over with mist; the light was absorbed and became an iridescent golden ball. The streets were a glossy black: icy macadam beneath crime-stopping street lighting. The awaited storm was just commencing.

Claire had covered herself with a green and gold afghan Airy's mother had given me (for Christmas, instead of the ice skates I wanted). She was curled into a fetal position, and she had her hand to her face, shielding her eyes from the light. She was sleeping, exhausted from her trip. I sat in an armchair across from her, a sentinel again, admiring her smooth skin and her complicated head of hair. Her mouth was dry, and she smacked her lips in her sleep. She made that sound often, a childlike noise that I had laughed at during the summer when I lay awake and Claire slept. She showed her pregnancy a little, not much, although the full black skirt and the large black sweater she wore I suspected were intended to hide her belly. I sat there for a long time, perhaps I fell asleep too, for I was very tired. My head nodded forward sharply and I awoke with a head-straightening snap. I was hungry, and I was going to suggest a pizza to Clairissa. I looked carefully at her sweet face and her plumpish body, like a wave beneath the coverlet.

It was then that I noticed the blood.

I did not identify it immediately, thinking the black circles on the carpet in front of the sofa were grime from my wintery walk. Then I saw the same stain on the sofa, a blur of blood. Then Claire's left hand appeared from beneath the blanket—she rubbed her eyes with it—and it was bloody, and the blood was fresh and made a bright red streak on her cheek.

She woke up in terrible pain. She grabbed at her abdomen and pulled her legs tighter to her chest. She kicked off the afghan, and then I saw that the sofa was soaked with blood and her skirt and tights were soggy with blood. Claire opened her eyes and pulled back her skirt. She was bleeding badly from her vagina; she was clutched at by terrible pains.

"What's wrong with me?"

I didn't know.

"I'm all bloody. I'm bleeding. Henry, what's wrong?"

Gynecologically speaking, I was an innocent. Of course, what had happened was that, at just under seven months pregnant, Claire had gone into premature labor. Her uterus had opened and spilled out its contents, fetus, uterine lining, and so on. She was hemorrhaging very badly, unstoppably it seemed, bleeding great gouts of blood, volumes of blood, and when she threw off her cover the blood slid down her leg, through her tights, and plopped, plopped, plopped on the couch and carpet like a leak in the upstairs bathroom. Her baby was dead, and Claire was in peril. She was crying, her face scrunched into a grimace. She looked at me for comfort, but I could offer none.

I reached for the phone and dialed the emergency police number. "I need an ambulance," I said, "at One Forty East Gilman Street."

"The nature of the emergency?"

The operator had one of those awful, nasal Sheboygan accents.

"I don't know. I think my friend's having a miscarriage."

"Is she conscious?"

"Yes."

"Stay with her. I'm sending out an ambulance immediately."

I walked to the bathroom and I got a towel for Claire, and I put it between her legs. Her thighs were slimy and hot with her discharge. I wanted to help her take her tights off so she would be more comfortable. She refused. She didn't want to see what was coming out of her. The towel was soaked with blood almost immediately. She grasped my left arm like a tourniquet. Basically, I am a kind man, and I stroked her hair, her thick black hair that always smelled of sunlight and piney forests, but I felt as if I had a heart of stone. I was very calm. I felt a tingling edge of contempt. I knew what I was going to do: walk away. Just like that.

"Henry, help me." There was real terror in her voice.

"Help is on the way. I called the ambulance."

"Hold me, please." Nope, darlin', not interested.

"I don't think that's a good idea. Just stay the way you are."

"Please."

I was already in a different time zone.

"No. You're full of blood, Claire."

"Will I be all right?"

"Of course."

"I'm bleeding so much."

"You'll be okey-dokey," I said.

It was then I got up and headed for the door.

"Where are you going?"

"Downstairs to wait for the ambulance."

"Don't go, Henry. Please stay with me."

"I should go down and wait for them."

"Stay with me."

"I can't. I don't want to."

I left. I turned my back and walked out, despite her pitiable pleas.
I left the door to my apartment open, so there would be no doubt
about where the paramedics should go. I could hear Claire crying,
heaving in shuddering sobs, pleading with me to stay and comfort
her. Comforting Claire, just then, was something I was not a bit
interested in. Let Nicky or Lenny comfort her; Henry was the odd
man out. And Henry was soon enough out the door, jacketless,
abandoning his Claire, in the new snow, running with a sprinter's
stride down the Gilman Street hill toward James Madison Park. I
found a pay phone and called Milton at home. I told him what had
happened and where I was and that I had left Claire more or less in
the lurch.

Milton said only one word to me: "Asshole." I had failed. What
else is new? I walked back up the hill. It was snowing, and the only
sound I heard was the crystalline swish of the wet snow as it fell. I was
sullen and mean spirited, an unhappy creature in a problematical
world. Life is simple if you're brave; complications follow in the
footsteps of cowardice. Complications followed me like a blood-
hound on a hot trail.

I heard the siren. I sat down on the steps of the old Governor's
Mansion, across the street from my apartment. Except for the siren,
which rose like a horrible human voice, the night was dark and
empty. The siren was enough to fill any void. The ambulance arrived, turning red and red and red, for poor Claire, bloody as a
newborn baby. Henry sat on the stoop and watched. Milton arrived
just as the paramedics rushed upstairs and came down with Claire
swaddled in a red blanket. He squeezed her hand and leaned close to
her before they slid her into the back. He kissed her smooth cheek.
Milton went back upstairs.

The snow fell on old Henry Fitzgerald in his thin sweater on the
sandstone stoop. But I was not all sorrow. Claire's baby was dead.
Deep in my heart, deep in my stony heart, I was happy.

21

The Geography of Resolve

IF YOU HAVE deep enough reasons, you *can* run *and* hide. In fact, if the cause is sufficient, you do both. I did.

When I walked into my apartment, Milton was kneeling on the floor in front of my sofa with a saucepan full of soapy water. He was blotting up the bloodstains with a powder blue sponge, and the water in the pan was pink.

For a long time he was silent, daubing the sponge into the bloodstains, clearly unhappy with his little brother. He had blood on his hands and on the cuff of his jacket. Finally, he looked up at me.

"Why did you leave?" he asked.

"I don't know. I didn't feel like staying, I guess. Happy feet."

"I don't understand you anymore, Henry. Here"—and he threw the sponge on the floor—"you do this. It's still fresh." He meant the blood. "I promised Claire that I would go to the hospital."

"Should I come?"

"No. I don't think so. I'll call you and tell you how she is." He couldn't look at me. "It was a really bad thing to leave Claire like that. I'll tell you something: she may be crazy as hell, but this she didn't deserve, Henry. Just for the record."

Just for the record, I acknowledge that Claire, my quiet Claire, didn't deserve what I had done.

Milton left, and I, mechanically, soaked up the gore with the sponge. I whistled perkily as I worked, and no one could have guessed I just had abandoned a woman for whom I had once proclaimed a major amount of affection. Ah, but she had declined my gentle offer for a new life. Subsequently, I walked out on Claire, the object of my former fond aspirations, as she lay on the sofa, miscarrying and bleeding nearly to death (that's an exaggeration, but not by much). Some people cope with rejection better than others. Apparently, it's not one of my strong points.

I got most of the blood up and out, although a shadowy discoloration would always remain on the carpet, and I propped the sofa cushions against the radiator to dry. I took a scaldingly hot shower; the bathroom was as steamy as a boiler room. But I didn't feel anything: I couldn't get the water hot enough to penetrate the cold in my hands and toes. Was I downcast and blue? After all, black-haired Claire Cohen was in an emergency room nearby, the subject of much frantic attention. No, by Christ, I seemed cheerful. Is this the way a madman acts? I think so.

I stood in the shower singing near the top of my lungs some of the tunes Tom Jones made famous; mostly I sang "It's Not Unusual." I actually knew only three words (It's Not Unusual), which was nevertheless no impediment to my desperate vocalizing. Sadly, contradictorily, I suspected that it might actually be extremely unusual; referring, of course, to the prospect of a happy, honorable life.

As I was toweling off (using the proscribed Elderian drying agent), the phone rang. I dashed into the living room, across the damp carpet, to answer it. Milton was on the horn.

"She's okay," he said.

I didn't reply. I hung up and went to bed. Milton was going to be very hard on me for my moral miscue. He, after all, is rushing to one barricade or another, standing against the Descending Amerikan Fascist Silence and Night (suitable topic for one of Crescent Laverno's butch epics). The real Wisconsin night is dark enough for me; ditto the depth of the silence. The snow falls and the city is somnolent. The telephone rang again, and I was sure it was Milton calling back to offer comfort (or maybe to say that sweet Claire had understood and forgiven my bugging out in her moment of bloody panic). I came out of the bedroom barefooted, anxious to be forgiven. The living-room carpet was splotched with damp areas, reminders of my decline and fall.

"Henry," a happy voice said after my quiet hello.

"Yes."

"It's me, Fulmonar."

"Ernie."

I suppose my voice was dense with emotion. It was thick, I know, and stuck in my chest.

"What's wrong?" he asked.

And then for a very long time I couldn't speak. The secret, when you fall, is to find someone to help you up. I rubbed my jaw against the telephone's mouthpiece, my beard stubble scratched in my ears, as if I were trying to rasp away my shame. I was trying to stop my chin from trembling, trying to hide my sorrow. I had been reduced to a very small, very intense point of pain.

"Henry?" he asked after a moment.

"I've done something pretty bad, Ernie."

I spoke that sentence as if I were translating from a foreign tongue.

"Oh, yes," he said with a laugh, "I know. Very bad."

"You do?" I couldn't believe word had traveled that quickly. Henry's shame was moving near the speed of light.

"Yeah, Henry, you've bounced another check," he said. "You keep doing this and I'm going to go out of business."

"Oh," I said, "I'm sorry. It should be okay now. I put a wad of cash into the bank."

"So what did you do?"

I told him, from the beginning to the end, hunkered down on the living room floor, the entire sordid business: my wayward attention, my drift, my solitary nighttime hikes, my misfired affair, my dumb desire, my rejected offer to Claire, my anger, my sorrow, my failure, my grief.

"I wish I were there right now," he said. "I wish I could be with you, Henry." So did I.

"It's bad, though. What I did was bad, right?"

"Yes, I guess so."

"What do I do?"

He laughed.

"Nothing."

"What do you mean?"

"Nothing. You made a mistake. You did the right thing, basically. You called an ambulance. Then you did something strange, out of character, something very sad. I suppose you feel like you betrayed her. But Claire's okay. It happened. Things happen. She lost her baby. You can't be held responsible for that, Henry. You deserted her, that's your phrase, not really in a panic if I understand you properly, more in anger and frustration. That you're responsible for. But look, you have to accept the fact you're going to fuck up occasionally. Nobody's exempt from that."

"I feel like I have to do something."

"Send flowers."

"Claire hates me."

"No she won't. She'll be angry. She'll get over it. Don't manufacture other people's states of mind. Get your own right."

"I don't want Claire to hate me, Ernie."

"Believe me, Henry, she won't."

"I just left her sitting here. She was full of blood and terribly frightened. I don't know what I was thinking. Maybe that she deserved it; she had it coming to her. I'd hate to think it was that. It seems like I was punishing her for not doing what I wanted her to do."

"Look, nobody said you were Gandhi. You're a kid. You'll probably do worse. Look forward to that."

"You haven't."

"Oh, yes, Henry."

"I don't believe it."

"Come up here and I'll tell you about it."

"What did you do?"

"Something bad. Something that made me feel like you feel now."

"What was it?"

"I'll tell you face to face."

Maybe it wasn't hopeless.

"I think I will drive up tomorrow. I'll see if I can borrow or maybe even rent a car. I was supposed to call you today, but I forgot. There's some other stuff I want to talk to you about, too."

"Good. I'd like that."

"Ernie?"

"Yeah."

"I fucked up, didn't I?"

"You did, Henry," he said, as tenderly as an absent father. "But you'll make it up to her."

"I will."

"I know you will, you're a good boy. It will be all right. Just be patient."

Not for the first time and not for the last, Fulmonar had righted my course. Broad-chested Fulmonar, I knew, would be seated at his desk and his ledgers, close to a brisk blaze, calculating which resources he would have to expend, which he would have to conserve. His reading glasses—fragile-looking, silver-rimmed, and chronically dirty—would be jammed onto his face. The fire would reflect brightly on the lenses. It would be silent and peaceful, and after he turned out the library lamp with its green shade he would stand for a contemplative moment and look down from a lodge window on the lunar surface of Lake LaPointe, deathly cold in December. By some secret I had not yet discovered, he had located a latitude and longitude of serenity.

In the autumn, after Claire was long gone and only an increasingly fretting memory, Fulmonar had become a great friend. In the evenings we perched on the porch or on the steps and he told me the places he had been and the adventures he had had: dangerous passages in November across Lake Superior in an ore boat; infantry battles on barren hilltops; building the lodge and the fifteen cabins of the Northern Lights after a wearying battle with alcohol. In the twilight crows would caw—like someone calling from the next life—and Ernie would close his eyes. Lonely sound isn't it, Henry? he would say: lonely sound. Yes, I said, and since I was lonely, I found it truly so. And he would laugh then, with his big handsome head tilted back. He had no secrets. He lived out in the open, and he wasn't afraid.

December second had been a long day. Airy had given me the sack, and I had alienated Claire's affections. Over the course of twelve hours, I had gone from number-one (or so) man to persona very non grata. I was a lump, a bit of doggerel in an era of odes, the burn mark in the velvet couch, the crack in the crystal, a pee stain on khaki slacks. My sofa creaked beneath my weight, the uncushioned springs sagged and snapped at me. I had not washed away all the blood, speckles and spots of it were on the headrest. That blood was Claire's blood, I reminded myself. The tarnished silver thing I had sat on was a barrette my quiet Claire had used to hold back her curly hair: a talisman, an omen, a good-luck charm, a tentative connection with that pretty girl I once cuddled and cooed with here on this precise spot. Here on this couch, she helped me with a hangnail and trimmed my hair. She laughed at my jokes and tucked me in when I took a nap. Fuck it, I was not going down in a humiliating heap: I would fight. North was going to be my direction. I would proceed properly with the Rectification of Names: Oulu, Blueberry, Maple, and Iron River would form the permanent grid of my new life. I would not be burdened by troublesome trifles: mosquito bites, bunions, or a short-term cash-flow situation. I was Henry Fitzgerald, pal. I would sail across Lake Superior in a ferrocement craft of my own design and construction. I would dance with pretty women on sawdusted floors. And I would tell my grandchildren, just before I fell the last time, of how Fulmonar laughed the way the crow cries: unafraid, as a prelude to flight. I'll be full of my own complicated stories about rocky nights on the big lake in my leaky concrete boat, dashing through an abandoned garden brandishing a hammer handle (dog-bane: Thunderer!).

Effervescent with false hope, I borrowed Crescent's Volvo and drove north, straight to the Northern Lights. I intended to hunker down there and get my mind right. After the initial elation and confidence which came in the wake of my cowardly abandonment of Claire Cohen, I plunged—like a member of the Iron River Polar Bear Club into a thawing Lake Muskelunge—into a funk, a depression. I wasn't good company, as whenever anyone spoke to me, my eyes filled with tears and I had to send them away. I was boring.

Then, after two days of mourning, breaking a solemn oath, I

called Claire in her hospital room. She wasn't unpleasant, quite the opposite, just distant. She was perky, and promised we'd have a long talk about what happened "very soon." My attempts to keep her on the line ended with me pinned to the couch with paranoia. I was stammering, with a sorrow-choked voice, an apology, an explanation. But she didn't want to listen to that just then. She announced a visitor, who I believed had to be the Villain Gent, and hung up.

"I miss you," I said, which were among my final words to her, ever.

And from an enormous emotional distance, Drake's voyages were insignificant compared to the New World to which Claire had sailed, she said, "I miss you, too."

By which she meant the very polar opposite.

After that, I lay on the leather sofa of the lodge with a pile of books (Pat let me dig into the bookshelves upstairs). I read *The Red and the Black* in an afternoon. I read seven or eight books in the first two days in much the same manner, remaining rooted on the couch, surrounding myself with Coke bottles and beer cans and plates that held half-eaten Muenster cheese sandwiches. I grew my beard. Actually, that is a rather more active description of what I in fact did. I didn't shave. I grew scruffy and unkempt, exuded the sourish smell of unchanged socks and infrequent showers. It snowed and the wind blew, and I remained alone and aloof, oblivious to the weather good or bad, perfunctorily performed the chores assigned to me (washing the dinner dishes and dragging the garbage cans down to the highway).

Fulmonar would barely speak to me, so angry was he with what he regarded as my indolence and self-indulgence. Directly following dinner he climbed the stairs to his office and called Milton. They discussed capital improvements and the most effective means of making the Northern Lights a viable profit center. From those discussions I was excluded, suspected, rightly, of not being totally dedicated to the bottom line. Pat talked to me instead, patiently, full of affection.

"Henry, dear," she said, "is all this really necessary? If it is, just say so and I'll leave you alone. If it's not, let me help you."

She sat on the couch next to me with her arm around my shoulders. She's a skinny thing, with huge rough-knuckled hands (she works like a stevedore) and a direct no-bullshit manner. She rested her hand on my neck and patted me, gentle little pitty-pats, and clearly although subtly disapproving of my being a geek. I was embarrassed for myself, seeing my reflection in Pat's gray eyes, and although I declined her offer for assistance, I did go upstairs and shower and shave and change my clothes. I put the books away. I cleaned the dirty tableware from around my den; dug the cans and bottles from beneath the couch.

By the morning of day five of my stay, I ducked my head out the door: a cold blue sky and a blinding layer of snow; deciduous trees were bare of leaves (except for the scrub oaks), and the pines were like masts in a crowded anchorage.

"That's a good idea, Henry," Pat Fulmonar said, standing behind me holding my leather jacket, "go for a walk."

She effectively blocked my retreat and helped me on with my jacket and pushed me out the door with a single, graceful wire-biceped shove (she's good at dispatching late stayers and other troublesome guests).

"Come back in an hour or two and I'll make you a nice breakfast. Ham and eggs. Go get the stink off, as Ernie says. Go on."

The sun was pleasant, and I walked down to the main road and turned right, toward Iron River, thinking I might actually enjoy walking there to buy a newspaper. It was a long way. I clomped along slowly, stooping down occasionally to pick up a rock and heave it at a tree. I developed a pattern of rock-heaving on every twentieth step or so, and after a couple of miles my arm was loose and I was clinking birches with fair frequency. I was warm beneath my leather jacket, could feel sweat trickle down my spine. I reassessed my comportment with Claire Cohen, was unpleased with almost every aspect of my behavior (except lending her the money, rollicking in the sleeping bag, naked dancing; those sweet things were okay). Four days as a fungus on Fulmonar's couch had left me feeling sluggish, and after exactly five miles (I had checked the distances this autumn on an odometer when I was creating running routes), I sat down on a snowplow-ruined road barrier that overlooked a frozen stream.

I was a solitary chap. No question about that.

What was to be done? My predeliction for late-night Romantical odysseys was becoming a problem. You couldn't have a normal life with a wife and children, punch the time clock, et cetera, if one's idea of a satisfying evening was to prowl the streets at three in the morning. That smacks, quite honestly, of severe sociopathic tendencies. I was going to have to let go of all that. I framed a plan, plunked down on the hemorrhoid-making cold steel, in a burst of almost mathematical inspiration.

Step One: no more walks after ten, no, nine o'clock CST.

An ugly old crow flew past me. It was the blackest thing in a snow-white world.

Step Two: do something about a career, a profession, a set of goals.

Step Three: abandon all fixations upon sad-eyed, dark-haired beauties and marry you know who.

Step Four: before actually embarking on the preceding three steps, get Claire away from Leonard Gent.

Step Five: don't tell anyone about the steps, especially Step Four, which would evoke a clamorously negative response. Keep my own counsel while preparing for the Final Moment, as Norman calls it, the Ultimate Confrontation, the Battle Royal.

What is brighter than sun on snow at latitude 45 degrees? The light is astonishingly clear: smogless, fogless, fretless. I was bonded to this light and my resolutions. Fuck a duck, life was too short to fall into unsanitary capitulations.

I leaped to my feet, momentarily struggling against gravity (my own and nature's). I started back toward the Northern Lights, realizing I had to commence roadwork and punching the heavy bag. I was going to climb back into the ring.

22

Disappointment

TO THE FACT of Claire Cohen living with Leonard Gent I was
unreconciled. Do I make myself sufficiently clear?

About 13 December I began my observations of Gent's domicile,
not knowing quite what I was looking for: a pattern of depravity,
omens of criminality, Morse code flashed out with a penlight from
an attic window. I saw nothing. I sat in the bay of my bay window,
on a straight-backed chair, half-hidden behind the drapes: a familiar
observation point by now. Hourly, I expected Claire to burst out the
door; momentarily, I expected the phone to ring and it would be her,
ready to hear my eloquent apologia. I would be forgiven, and she
would come away from there. Not with me, that was gone, but back
into the sunlight.

She never appeared; she never called.

I saw Gent, as sleek as a panther, coming and going, arriving in
taxicabs and departing in airport limousines: cashmere overcoats,
Italian suits, Florentine briefcase. He had purchased for his own use
a bright red BMW. He was rich, after all. Bogus cigarettes.

At night, at least in the early days, I sometimes left my perch. In
the evening, I lived more or less normally. Airy started staying over,
and we began the slow process of patching things up.

"I want to fall in love with you again, Henry," she said to me 15 December over my eggplant parmigiana.

"I hadn't realized you'd fallen out of love with me. That's a treacherous concept to absorb, Airy."

"I mean, I felt we lost contact."

"Oh."

"Why aren't you talking?"

"What is this, gargling?"

"Why aren't you listening to what I'm saying and responding to those words? Why are you so self-absorbed? You never used to be this way."

Or maybe you never noticed, I thought, but wisely withheld.

Always after these mid-December dinners, after waiting an appropriate amount of time, I went running, down Gorham Street following the profile of Lake Mendota, bearing left on Sherman Avenue, turning around at the locks in Tenney Park. Stepping out my door, I stood for a moment in the chilly evening darkness, contemplating the home of my great friend and my great enemy. I was as bitter as the winter wind about all of this. I had things to say, finally, and a clear voice with which to say them and I was stuck in silence.

After three or four days of fruitless watching and waiting, burdened by my increasing anxiety, I confessed my mood to Milton. It was around midnight of 18 December, over our third frosted pitcher of beer at Ginos.

"I talked to her the day she got out of the hospital, Henry. She was a little depressed, but you'd have to expect that. I don't want to disappoint you, but she really seemed okay. There was something weird, though. Gent insisted on paying the bill. Claire was just going to send it to her father, but Leonard paid in cash, crisp hundreds, Claire told me. She was very touched."

The symmetry of these cash payments was startling. Milton blushed when he realized that I, too, had given Claire cash in a pregnancy-termination crisis. Gent's actions were not a dumb coincidence, and his motives, I knew, were not benign.

"Did she say anything to you about me?" I asked.

"Just to say hello."

"Did she say she'd be in touch?"

"No."

"Did she want me to call her?"

"She didn't say."

"Did she say anything about Gent?"

"That he seemed very kind."

"Did you tell her about him?" I said that with some enthusiasm, feeling Milton was being far too accepting of circumstances. Circumstances are the things we have to strive to alter.

"No. What could I say? It's not my place."

"Not your place, Milton! Christ, man, can't you'll see what will happen? She'll be taken in by him."

"Taken in by him?"

"Yes. Don't you see?" I was off and running now, straight into the purple shadows of the Forest of Paranoia.

"Henry, you're taking this too personally. That's what happened before."

"Too personally. Don't talk to me about that. You let your wife walk away with all your ready cash, you even help her put your furniture in her rental truck, and you stand in the gutter with a fond farewell as she drives off. Fuck you, pal. I'm not going to swallow that shit. I may be crazy. I may be wrong, but I won't let that . . . creature hurt Claire. Jesus suffering Christ, Milton, the shit's going to hit the fan before that happens. Things are going to get very personal before I'm through."

I was shouting. Gino himself walked over and asked me to quiet down or we'd have to take it on the road. I apologized, because Gino is a true gentleman.

"Henry, I don't want you to go off the deep end."

"The deep end is the best end, Milton. What am I holding back for, the last hundred meters? This is the last hundred meters. Right now."

"Okay. You asked for it, asshole. She said she didn't want to see you right now and that she didn't think it was a good idea to talk to you. She just wants you to leave her alone. She said that you were not a good influence on her. And she said that you shouldn't have walked out. It would have been a lot easier if you had stayed, Henry."

"Well, I didn't. So fuck all, Milton, I didn't. That's not going to stop me. *That's not going to stop me.*"

And it didn't.

I got up and left, the first (and only) time I have ever been so angry at my brother I could not abide his presence. It was then I began night operations as well, only leaving my chair to relieve myself or grab a snack from the refrigerator. I was not in a panic now, I was calm indeed. It was all before me, and I was waiting for the propitious moment, just when the steel was cherry red, and I would strike. I was going to have to do it alone. But what? That was the problem. I was unsure of just what to do, short of a headlong, suicidal rush up the stairs and through the door. I worried my brain for options: letters to the editor, tips to the local television stations, phone calls to the District Attorney. They all seemed too long term and trivial. Inevitably, I suppose, violent action was the only course I could have taken.

What was it I saw, other than the not-seeing Claire?

Gent's house was full of young men who had been in and out of trouble, exhausting the resources of the juvenile court in various jurisdictions. Some were orphans, some were abused, some were there as a result of temporary family crises. There were twenty of them, of junior high school and high school age, a third of them black and two-thirds white. A Gent-leased schoolbus took them away every morning at 7:30 a.m. and brought them back every afternoon. They were all dressed more or less alike: gray woolen slacks, white shirts, blue sweaters. Only their outercoats were not uniform: a variety of leather and down, black and green and blue.

Claire's position, as far as I could observe and intuit, was to make sure everyone got on the bus (I sometimes thought I saw a flash of her hair or her hand holding a clipboard in the entryway in the morning) and everyone returned home in the afternoon. She also did special tutoring, especially in mathematics, and counseled boys who sought her out.

I'm sure she was kind and patient, and under a less perverse set of circumstances, it was a perfect job for her. Milton, upon my insistence, kept in tentative touch. She was always "fine, good." And she was never quite ready to talk to me. Eventually she discouraged

Milton from calling, knowing that I was the ultimate repository of the information he gleaned. During the early, sober portion of my vigilance, I imagined Claire in her new job, explaining square roots with such patience and grace that even the slowest boy with the bitterest heart would turn avidly to calculus at his first opportunity. I missed Claire.

The boys marched in and out. From a diet heavy in starch, they were round-faced and awkward. Gent and Mickey Monahan sidled in and out; a series of frumpy social workers and social services bureaucrats came and went. Claire, dark-haired Claire Cohen, never saw the sunlight. About that I was as bitter as chicory.

What was I waiting for?

Good question, doctor. When, if, I saw Claire exit—on the way to the movies or to buy underwear—I intended to jump out of my chair, rush into the street (making another daring leap from the first landing to the ground floor), and ask for an audience, five minutes of her time, a shared hot coffee or cold beer. In my spare time, I had a substantial amount of it, I made notes toward my explanation, believing with the weight of my eloquence I had a slight chance to undo the damage I had done. I kept a notebook near my left foot, and when a new phrase or an especially telling modification of an old one occurred to me, I grabbed the notebook and wrote it down. The notebook was partially filled with notes from "The Intellectual History of China," a class I took in one of my senior years, I forget which one. Actually, of China's intellectual history it recorded only a few pithy pieces of information; the turmoil that was hard upon the heels of the invasion of Cambodia closed down class and school.

My notebook was decorated on the front cover with a picture of Bucky Badger, bold Bucky Badger, striding forward (Forward is the State of Wisconsin's motto) bravely to an unknown destiny. I stuck a red felt-tip pen into the spiral binding. It was this notebook and this pen, after I forwent my jottings toward an effective plea for mercy, that became a daybook (and a nightbook as well), recording all arrivals and departures into and out of Chez Gent.

On 20 December, roughly a week after I began my observations, Leonard Gent called me. It was a bright day, vivid cloudless sky, and the radio was playing Christmas music. I was drinking a cup of tea and eating a chocolate-covered doughnut, wiping my chocolate-gobbed fingers on the thighs of my jeans. My personal hygiene was breaking down. Gent's house had been adorned with red and green lights (at night it looked like a Portuguese fish factory moored off the coast of Newfoundland); the lights were even strung along the iron widow's walk. And a Christmas tree, gypsyed up with an avalanche of tinsel, crouched pitiably in the parlor window.

"You're still there, I see. Every day, every night, I see you with my binoculars. You're going to get old before your time." His voice was thickened with contempt. The son of a bitch thought he had beaten me.

"Still here."

"She doesn't want to talk to you, you know."

"She will."

"I've been encouraging her to try to forgive and forget, Henry. She's been severely hurt, though, and I'm afraid the wound is very deep."

"The whole truth will be out one day. And if you've done anything unpleasant to Claire, I'll get you, Pig Lips."

"No. No. You can't touch me."

I was afraid that he was right. He was a genius at slipping bonds and manacles. He was too well connected to the corrupt masters of politics to be damaged by my sallow efforts.

"She doesn't want to come out."

"Some day she will."

"And I'll be right next to her."

"I want to talk to Claire," I said. "You can arrange it."

"Why should I do anything for you? Your pal Norman O'Keefe is my blood enemy. You've questioned my honor. Your brother has suggested to the police my history should be looked into." That was new to me. "Claire and I talk about you often, Henry. She said you spin fantasies all the time but that you, personally, don't do much. You're passive, a talker who makes empty promises and emptier threats. A real smartass, too."

"I want to talk to her."

"I know you do. But you're not going to. So sit in the fucking window for the rest of your life. She's not coming out until I say she should go out. She listens to me, Henry."

End of conversation.

My position, literal and figurative, was a tentative one. Ideally situated; right where I had to be. Airy, needless to say, was furious with and bewildered at my conduct. That was not an unjust response. Just as things looked peachy again between us, my old ugly Claire fixation reared its Hydra-head and I was on my weirdness victory lap. What was I doing?

I tried to explain to her that, while Claire no longer meant anything to me romantically, I owed her an explanation, and that I would not rest properly until I did.

"Why? It wasn't that bad. You're making too much of this. It's not healthy."

"It was bad." I was adamant. No one would convince me it was just another troublesome set of circumstances to be forgotten. Unfortunately, monomania—I do have an obsessional personality—was strangling my senses; that would become increasingly apparent. My Abandonment of Claire had achieved a stature in my feverish brain similar to the defeat of the Persian fleet at Salamis or the invention of the steam engine. I was losing a sense of proportion.

"So put your shoes on, Henry. Put your shirt on. Put your jacket on and go talk to her. Is she being held a prisoner in the attic?"

"I wouldn't be surprised."

That was a thought that had never occurred to me: captivity. This would have been 25 December, and we were home after the Elders' annual Christmas-night fete for familyless or stranded faculty. It was a real Dickensian affair with a roasted goose, ghastly plum pudding, and other junk like that. I took no notice of the food, concentrating on the drink. Airy had insisted I come or she would never speak to me again. I did so, but made sure Norman (who loathed Christmas by now) was manning the helm, perched in my bay window. I told him what to do in case Claire came out—run out and hand her the note I had written—although I'm sure he just turned on the TV.

I had too much to drink at the Elders' (my own personal tradition at the Elders' parties). When it came my turn to wish the company a Merry Christmas (another Elder tradition), I proposed a toast to airplane accident victims throughout history instead. I eulogized Wiley Post. I blamed the machinations of world politics, pointing an accusatory finger at the Soviet Union, for the untimely loss of Dag Hammarskjöld. About the gallant aviatrix, Amelia Earhart, I was touchingly to the point. The room was full of tenured professors of so many disciplines that one would need Dewey with his decimals to keep them straight. They smiled at me with embarrassed incomprehension (something I had done often enough in their classrooms). My brother tried to calm me down, but couldn't shut me up, not before I cried, with my Baccarat champagne glass raised to the invisible stars, "Farewell and *bon chance*, O winged heroes of the empyrean!" Heroes of the Empyrean: that's the fate I had in store for Norman and me.

So Airy was, not surprisingly, displeased. She told me to march over to Gent's and ask to talk to Claire. Until I resolved, once and for all, my personal problems, she was going to restrict our contact. I stared at the carpet and muttered a sullen okey-dokey.

Things happen when they happen. A Birdwhistlean tautology if I ever heard one. Until New Year's Day I would say that within the broad range of normality I was extremely marginal but still normal. After New Year's Day, I could no longer make that claim. I had begun to forget just why I was observing Gent's house. I had become slothlike; wrapping my ankles and feet around the rungs of my chair, I was even able to nap. Why didn't I just go across the street or simply pick up the phone and ask to speak to Claire? Because she had forbidden it, and for some reason I saw myself as lacking all rights to do anything other than what she wished. That was the nuttiness that underwrote all my subsequent odd behavior. With options of direct action obviated, I was left with only indirection, caution, waiting. I was an exile from the tiny kingdom of Claire Cohen; uncrafty, unwily, unskilled in contention, I was going to be on the road for more than twenty years, I could sense that. Who could happily bear the thought of such an ostracism? In the end, it was this mortifying passivity that did me in.

One January, in the late evening, after the Rose Bowl—Milton, Norman, and I watched it on my color television, although I didn't budge from my battle station—I began my log of the activities across the street:

> 1 Jan.: Xmas lights not turned on until 9 pm. Gent greets spike-heeled lady alderperson at door. Ks. on ck. [Kiss on cheek.] No S. of C. [No sign of Claire.] Mood [mine]: anxious.

> 3 Jan.: Mck Mhn [Mickey Monahan] begins exercise regimen. Jogs west. Looks like a slug. Waddles like a duck. Cries like a train. Blk Cad at 11 am [black Cadillac, obviously]. Sm., sm. slobber. [Smooch, etc.] No S. of C. Mood: despair.

And so on. Each day's entries resembled the day before's. No more profoundly banal record exists. Gent had a series of visitors, guests, onlookers at his juvenile home, including a busload of psychiatric social workers from North Dakota (I read about their visit in the *Cap Times*). Also logged in were visits from the meterman; the cops bringing in one of Gent's boys after he had been picked up trying to hitchhike out of town or shoplifting at Badger Sporting Goods; bread truck drivers; UPS deliverymen; boiler repairmen; nurses and doctors; attorneys at law and accountants; and so on. Once or twice a week, covered by darkness, I dug through Gent's trash, searching for "evidence of villany." The psychic slope was getting very slippery.

My most common entry was "No S. of C." There was never, except in glimpses I might have only imagined, any positive sign of Claire Cohen.

I stopped answering my phone; by now, only Milton and Gent called anyway. In either case, both parties left me gasping for air: Milton's anger and Gent's mockery.

Milton, goaded into action by my visible decline, had Fulmonar write a letter to me. But Milton wouldn't have been pleased with what Ernie wrote. His message was scribbled on a Northern Lights postcard (Pat places them on the night tables of all the cabins and in the entry of the lodge): "Pat and I think of you often, Henry. Do what you have to do." He signed it "Yr pal, Fulmonar." Confirmation, as far as I was concerned, of the Right Path! Stay out of my way,

small-timers, chicken-shit ameliorators! My trigger finger, in a met-
aphorical sense only, as I had never in my life fired a weapon, was
getting itchy.

Things didn't get any better. They got worse and worse. Norman
O'Keefe moved in, having been evicted from his rooming house on
Williamson Street for smoking in bed. More than ever he was anx-
ious to resolve his Gent obsession.

"I don't know what I have to do, but I have to do something," he
said. "Now is the time to get on with my life."

I advised patience.

"A few more days, Norman, what can it matter?"

"What the hell are you going to do? Sit in this chair for the rest of
your life?"

"What do you expect me to do? I'm waiting for Claire."

"Go get her."

"What do you mean?"

"I mean, you and I go over there and we break the freaking door
down and we go get Claire Cohen."

"That's illegal."

"No," he said, "really? Do you care at this point, Henry? You are
getting loonier every day. Look at the way you're dressed."

I had just arisen from a restless sleep (I camped out on the sofa now
and gave Norman the bed), and I had on chopped-down red sweat-
pants secured with a web Boy Scout belt, a pair of floppy fuzzy
slippers Claire had left in the bathroom (I was attached to them
sentimentally but had busted out the sides because my feet were
much larger than hers), wash-yellowed sweat socks, and a practice
basketball singlet from Mt. Pleasant High School (reversible red and
blue) that I had worn to raggedness. I also was wearing a stocking cap,
I'm not sure why, except in moments of depression I often put on a
cap to reinforce the gravity of the situation.

Norman and I had this chat 16 January, early in the day as he was
making breakfast (oatmeal), and I was attending to my observational
responsibilities. We had been living together for only a few days, and
it was clear we weren't helping each other into the light, to put it
mildly.

Things fell apart in late January. When Norman was away (in

Chicago or who knew where?) my meals mostly consisted of chicken-noodle-soup sandwiches (take a bag of frankfurter rolls, open a can of Campbell's chicken noodle soup, dump out the liquid, fork the noodles and chicken fragments onto the roll—chicken-noodle-soup sandwiches) which I washed down with Coca-Cola. Simple starches were what was keeping me going (physically, my metabolism was virtually shut down anyway), and I was bound up as tightly as a big bass drum. It would have taken the proverbial drug-addict's corkscrew to unplug my colon if things hadn't ended when they did, how they did.

Twenty-three January, I decided to suspend my journal keeping. Who cares when the meterman came and how long he stayed? In a lucid moment I had that insight. My handwriting was illegible anyway. Not even the CIA's crytographic computer could have made sense of it. Sadly, the one notation I could always read was this: "No S. of C." There was never any sign of Claire. No one had heard from her or seen her for over a month. She refused to speak to Milton; Mickey Monahan's message was that she "was too busy to talk."

It was a cold winter, cold especially for me during the day, when the landlord shut off the heat, and I was stuck near a drafty window. I took to wrapping myself in the green and gold afghan and rocking back and forth. With my cap on and my beard sprouted on my face unevenly (I made half-hearted attempts to shave but wouldn't, toward the end, leave my chair long enough to do a thorough job), Norman said I looked like an especially devout yeshiva student. This is not what I wanted. I had intended to become the middleweight champion of Gilman Street, not a davening adolescent. I felt futile and foolish, an object of amused contempt. I didn't care for that mode at all, victim, as I am, of overweening pride. I had not yet managed to pull down my vanity. If there is to be in my life a sadder, more hopeless moment, I don't want to think about it.

Burning with embarrassment, I decided to end my vigil and get on with the dicey business of restoring Claire's acuity; an acuity in which I believed myself to be a singular believer. ("Restoring Claire's acuity," I suspect, meant helping her penetrate the heart of Gent's particular darkness. Who was going to restore my acuity?) I was

almost certainly nutty, of course; an antipsychotic drug should have
been administered intravenously at this moment. In more ways than
I care to recount, I was truly now in a dark woods, awaiting, no
longer with any patience, the affirmation of light. The Ultimate
Moment—Norman's phrase has a sort of tradesman's poetry about it,
doesn't it?—was at hand.

I was tired of passivity, tired of gloominess, tired of waiting. I
decided upon a direct approach. I pulled on my down jacket (ripped
somehow and hemorrhaging feathers) and marched across the street.
Gilman Street was empty of people. It was late afternoon, in the
instant of winter dusk before darkness. The lights in Gent's parlor
were on and shone through the unshaded windows onto the snow.
The light was a pale bluish white and picked up the irregularities and
odd concavities in the drifts. I was happy, as one is always happy
advancing toward the enemy. The front door was an old-fashioned
one, oak with a fragile pane of glass set into the upper panel. Through
it I could see a dimly lighted foyer and beyond that a panel of light
on the carpeted floor. It was too dark to make out any details. A fire
burned in a fireplace with a guttering, exhausted flame. I punched
the door bell, and it rang shrilly down deep in the bowels of the
mansion and up high above me on the upper floors. I expected that
malevolent shrimplette Mickey Monahan, with his puckered puss
and his sniveling manner, to open the door and turn away my request
to please see Claire Cohen with a hideous cackle. But my prayers
were answered, and Claire herself answered the door, and we both
stepped back in surprise.

"Henry," she said.

"Hi, Claire." I was casual. Why not, my brain was in lunar orbit?

"What do you want?" she said, and she looked over her shoulder
apprehensively. "This is not a good time."

She edged outside; I edged inside. We stood, as if it were at the
single solid belaying point on a dangerous ascent, on either side of the
door saddle. It was dark inside. She pulled the door closed enough so
no one could see to whom she was talking. I stood in the cold and
what was left of the wintry afternoon light.

"We're having a counseling session now."

"Is there a good time?"

"No, I suppose there isn't, Henry."

"Do you feel okay? Milton told me that you were fine, physically, I mean. No long-term problems."

"There was something wrong with the baby. The doctor said miscarriages, stillbirths, occur when there's a problem, a defect, or whatever. It's a natural way to prevent monsters or something from being born. He said I can still have children. That's not an issue. Thanks for asking, but it's a little late. You can understand how I feel. You left me all alone, after I practically begged you to stay."

"I know. I'm sorry."

"You hurt me. Sorry doesn't mean that much."

"I can't say I'm sorry anymore."

"Is that all you wanted? They need me inside."

"I worry about you, Claire."

"You shouldn't. You shouldn't think about me. I don't want you to."

"I feel awful about what I did."

"Henry, you don't have to do this. I'm all right."

"Do you hate me?"

"No, I couldn't. It's just painful for me to remember."

"Are you happy here?"

"I have to go in now. I'm cold."

"Are you happy here?"

She kept her head down, avoiding my gaze. Her hands were behind her back, tightly grasping the doorknob.

"I probably wouldn't be happy anywhere. I'm useful here. That feels good to me."

"I'm worried about you. It's distracting."

"Henry, I have to go."

"Claire, just tell me. Come on, this is Henry, not a stranger. What the hell, should I be worried about you?"

She shook her head. She didn't seem much interested in forgiving me, and wasn't I after forgiveness? I couldn't blame her; she was the one who had been abandoned. Yes, yes, it's a dark world, folks—I know I've mentioned that before—but the evidence just seems to keep accumulating. In certain bittersweet moments, though, the blackness is not complete.

"Hey," I said, "just remember if it weren't for me you wouldn't know a fungo from a fungus."

She laughed. At least I could still make her laugh. Sweet memories were like seeds beneath the snow, and Claire touched my arm with a tender Claireish gesture which recalled a lost, happier time: nestling and nuzzling in various venues, the rattling fan used on furious summer nights while we thrashed about on sticky sheets, a slender brown arm across my chest, postcoital walks and perching on crumbling piers talking about Tolstoy, and sad old Nat King Cole crooning in the dark. I hoped that I might not be such a bad guy, after all, because Claire looked at me with something resembling the old affection.

"Oh, maybe you should worry a little, Henry," she said. "Maybe just a little."

23

Rescuing Claire

THE CONDEMNATORY TAPES and damning documents were in a safety deposit box in the Wacker Avenue branch of the First Illinois Bank, just as Fletcher Lint had indicated. There were two of them, one original and one copy, both labeled "I.P.Fire/Do Not Erase." Norman was gray-faced—heartsick, of course, is what he was—as I put the tape into the tape deck of my stereo. Norman was badly in need of a resolution. He had traced with dogged, rage-fired patience the tangled trail that connected counterfeit cigarette tax stamps, his father's trucking company, Fletcher Lint and Leonard Gent, the Polish arsonist Iggy Pelcho, his family's incineration, his heartbroken rambles, his fierceness for justice, the chromed pistol he held to Fletcher Lint's head, and this sentence which he uttered with absolute conviction: "Tell me who killed my babies or they'll be making sauce Bolognese in your brainpan."

We were alone, Norman and I, on the afternoon of 1 February. We knew an unsavory, wholly burdensome amount about Leonard Gent, Fletcher Lint, and Iggy Pelcho. It was time, at long last, to do something. Included with the tapes were canceled checks, one of Gent's appointment books, figures and percentages scribbled on a sheet of notepaper, telephone numbers in Florida, Chicago, northern Wisconsin, and Southern California. None of the odd scraps of paper told much of a story, although, I suppose, if the information were collated and studied, it would be very revealing. So, seemingly, Fletcher Lint thought. All Lint wanted to do was punish Gent and make his getaway to Brownsville, Texas.

The tape recording was a nightmare. On it, Iggy Pelcho, dumb as dirt, told his sad story, responding to Lint's questions. Acting on Gent's instructions to give "O'Keefe a good scare," he set fire to a bunch of paint-thinner-soaked rags. He sobbed, describing how he watched the fire explode throughout the top floor. It was all a terrible miscalculation. When he realized how bad it was, he ran to a fire-call box and broke the glass window with his fist.

"Here," he said in a thick Polack accent, "here's da fuckink skart."

Halfway through the tape, Norman shut it off. He was now beyond the beyond, in nutball city, a true professor of revenge; a thin, shrill look of hysteria flashed off and on across his face.

"What are you going to do, Norman?"

"What do you want to do?"

"I'm not sure, Norman, I'm really not."

"Nothing, in other words."

"I guess that's the short answer."

"Nothing is always a short answer. Okay, Henry, I'll do it alone. Look, no hard feelings. You and Milton have been a big help. Honestly, I would have dissolved into absurdity. I was a sad sack of shit. What Gent did was wrong, however unintended were the results. No one wanted my family to die, I know that. But it doesn't matter."

"Where are you going?"

"Get a beer or something. I'd invite you along, but I have to be alone. I've got to get it done, Henry."

"Come back for dinner. Airy's coming over and I bought some steaks. There's plenty for three. Baked potatoes and Airy's bringing dessert."

"'The condemned man ate a hearty meal.'"

"Norman, don't do anything stupid. What about Joan Montana and all that?"

Joan Montana was a woman he had met at the Northern Lights; the daughter of the Iron County Commissioner of Weeds.

"She doesn't mean much to me right now."

"Just come by for dinner. About seven."

"Okay."

"Promise?"

He promised, crossing his heart.

"I'll be here," he said.

For one of the very last times, I settled in my bay window, watching Norman's glacial progress down Gilman Street. The day was springlike, a February thaw was transforming snow and ice into black pools of water, widening into lakes near intersections where sewer grates were blockaded. I was worried about Claire just a little. In fact, I was worried about her more than a little. She had suffered loss after loss in the past few months. The people she had loved and relied upon had vanished, and she was left to minister to the needs of twenty miserable children under the direction of a notorious liar. I longed for Claire. I wished she could be here now in my living room so that we might sway together, under the musical influence of Nat King Cole. Henry was happy when he was dancing, he discovered that, and he's certainly not happy now.

Gent's house was quiet, the delinquents were away tormenting their teachers, and the drapes were drawn on the upper floors. Behind the house, which really was elegant (sand-colored brick and elaborate 19th-century ironwork, capped with a Beaux Arts mansard roof), were a large garden (a rectangle of black mud in thaw time, punctuated with the exclamation marks of tomato-plant supports) and a garage (home to a new blue Dodge van and the new red BMW). The garden and the garage (a late addition to the property, a functionally clunky balloon-frame carholder) extended from the back of the house to a crumbling bluff which overlooked Lake Mendota.

Gent, I will grudgingly admit, had done a beautiful job in supervising its restoration. Gent and the house were greatly admired by writers for slick regional magazines. A typical illustrative photograph was of Gent, in a carbon-black suit, seated in his upstairs study with its plum walls and snow-white ceiling. Light reflects off the polished mahogany of his partner's desk (rescued from the loft of a carriage house on Gorham Street). His expression in these carefully posed photographs is like J. P. Morgan's in the famous Sargent portrait: irreducible and as arrogant as Xerxes.

I was a sad boy, let's face it. I yearned for Claire, I suppose, the way a homebound seaman yearns for the sight of land. I missed the sound of her voice and her laugh. I really had lost the edge. Better to do something than nothing; doing nothing was making me weird. One way or the other, Claire had to evacuate Gent's premises or I was going to have to evacuate mine. Long-term, I thought, the best plan was to extract Claire from her current circumstances, to deliver her from her deceiver (such was my estimate of Gent's role). In short, and this is a measure of how far off the path of sound judgment I had strayed (what arrogance, what icy condescension), I believed I had to rescue Claire. We were at the end of the road.

I had just come to this conclusion when I spotted Claire coming out Gent's front door. She had jettisoned her beaver coat (a step in the wrong direction) for a rust-colored down jacket. She had her purse, a tattered woven Guatemalan bag, over her shoulder. (I bought it for her this summer to cheer her up during a period when she was barfing at every change of barometric pressure.) Claire looked hesitant to leave: timid, afraid of the cold, worn down. This was not the little powerhouse I knew who threw me out of her car. So what was she doing out there, afraid of the fresh air and the brilliant winter sunshine?

My instinct was to leap up and rush to her, make yet another gruesome apology, recounting my many shortcomings and failures. But I was suddenly very tired of being the bad guy. I sat there and merely watched her walk down Gilman Street, probably to State Street to do some shopping, maybe just to get some air. Then Mickey Monahan appeared at the door, just as Claire would have completed her escape, just as she was turning west down Gilman Street. He beckoned her back with an impatient wave of the hand.

Sadly, she accepted his summoning.

"Another bullet in the Body of Reason," I said. I'm not sure exactly what I meant, although if one were to dig deeply enough, a shard from Birdwhistle's philosophical pot would very likely be uncovered.

"Count your minutes, Monahan. Henry Fitzgerald is reviewing your file."

I knew I was not going to fail again; I was not going to be turned away by a Munchkin. I marched to the bathroom and drenched myself with icy water, slopping it on my shirt and my jeans, leaving a treacherous puddle beneath the sink. I walked into the kitchen and opened the refrigerator, scanned the vegetable crisper full of pale green lettuce, the rude rawness of the beef, the buoyancy of a single green olive afloat in its jar of murky water. Dinnertime was approaching. If the condemned men were to eat a hearty meal, Henry was going to have to cook it.

So, and this is the good part, happy men we were, when just after midnight, Norman O'Keefe and I slipped from my apartment building into the February night. It was a starry night, a black starry night: cloudless, moonless, just right for mayhem.

Airy, and Norman, and I had had a jovial and relaxed dinner. Contrary to my expectations, Airy liked Norman and was happy, genuinely it always seemed, when the three of us were together. At his best, Norman was funny, kind, and very charming. He treated her like a kid sister and was always asking questions about her dusty digs and what was beneath the Greek soil. And we both listened to her raptly, while the radiator pipes banged and the steak slime congealed on our plates.

Airy went to bed and read with her serious tortoiseshell glasses perched on the end of her nose. About ten-thirty I crept into the bedroom, took the book (*Archaic Times to the End of the Peloponnesian War*; she complained about the poor quality of the translation, having peered at the originals one time or another) from her fierce grip, slipped the glasses off her face, and kissed her on the cheek. She was peaceful and very pretty; really an extraordinary woman, my intended. I left the light on because she hates to wake up alone in the dark. (She's troubled by nightmares, and I often have had to comfort her coming out of a gruesome dream. That's a good moment for us: when she surrenders her terror to my calm affection. And a rare one.)

Norman and I sat in the living room, slipping an after-dinner brandy. No, this is not true. We were drinking the remainder of the three bottles of Hungarian wine—Bull's Balls or Bull's Blood—he had brought. We were not totally sober. (Lack of utter sobriety was only a partial explanation of our subsequent actions.)

"I'm miserable, Henry."

"Me, too."

Right in the middle of the third bottle we got our coats. With a final glass, we toasted ourselves, new men and about to be unburdened. As an afterthought, I sat down and scribbled a brief note to Airy. "I'm going," it said, "for a walk with Norman. Be back soon." Such was my intention and expectation. Who would be in hot pursuit, of course, I had no idea. As an additional afterthought—it was propped up in the corner by the door—I grabbed Thunderer on the way out.

"What do we do?" Norman said. We were standing on the sidewalk in front of my building, and now, outside, a little tentative.

"Something final, Bub."

"He killed my babies," Norman said. "What are we going to do?"

"He stole my girl," I said. "Leonard Gent is devouring her brain. Only Goya could paint him properly. I hate him. Let's just see how far mindless violence will bring us."

"Good idea, Henry. You get Claire, I'll get Gent. You go in the back. I'm going to break down the fucking front door. Give me that thing. I'll crack a few skulls."

Norman badly wanted to be a bloody feint, to storm the house with Thunderer in his hand, and, playing the part of the grief-doomed madman (not so distant from the truth, by the way), engage in an act (or a series of acts) of distracting violence. While he was out front, I was to break into the rear of the house, find Claire, and take her away. I believed that these drastic steps were now morally condonable. Something of the oddness of our psychological disposition (and perhaps of the actual effect of the wine) is suggested in our thinking this plan could have worked. It did work, partially.

"Thunderer stays with me, Norman. I'm afraid I'll have to insist on it."

"Okay."

"So what are we going to do, Norman?" I asked.

"I'm not sure," he said, "maybe we should just make it up as we go along."

We went for a leisurely stroll up Gilman and down Pinckney, toward the lake. Once, phantomlike, lost in the shadows, we ducked past Gent's garage into his backyard. The night was black. We were on our own. No sirens screeched, no alarms blared, no bullhorns warned us to come out with our hands up. Yet. We were kneeling in the muddy garden behind Gent's manse. My neck was being scratched by a low limb of a shrub, and I had an urge to pee.

"Hey," I said, "are we together on this? This may be the end of civilization as we know it. We have gone too far, Norman. There's no doubt about it. So let's go right to the wall, right to the fucking edge. What's the difference between serving ten years or twenty? For sure we'll get out early with good behavior. This may be the moment in our lives we remember the longest. In there, that house"—I was pointing with Thunderer—"is a man so vile maggots won't feast on his putrefying flesh. Have you got the picture? Are we going to shake him up or not? I have just been handed a message from a secret source. It says 'you can't overdo it when it comes to getting Gent.' Hey, Norman, let's roll."

"We've gone too far to return to normalcy."

"I'll go in the back," I said.

"I'll go in the front."

We shook hands. Soon we would hear sirens in the distance and the upstairs lights would flash on. The unsavory, starchy inmates would be up and scrambling about in their pajamas any time. Gent would be on the telephone calling for reinforcements.

"See you in a bit, Norman. I'll meet you at Claire's room."

"I'll have Gent's head under my arm."

Brave man, he dashed out of the garden and back into Pinckney Street. His destination was the front door. I had nothing else to do, really, but get Claire. I ran to the back of the house and broke a basement window with Thunderer, a series of quick snaps of the wrist and the glass was sharded and knocked onto the floor. I slid feet first through the window, scraping my forehead on a jagged piece of glass. I jumped down to the floor, and the glass crackled beneath my feet. I was in a laundry room, which smelled of soiled sheets and plugged drains. I opened the door and peeked out into a brightly lighted room. Some sort of commons area, with ping-pong tables, blue plastic chairs, long lunch tables, and a Coke machine. It was empty, although a steaming bucket of water and a mop were abandoned in the middle of the tile floor. Gone to check out the commotion upstairs, I guessed.

For some reason, I started to hum an especially favored passage from the Bach Double Violin Concerto. It made me as happy as hell to be undoing a monster whistling Bach. Tell me, if you can, what monster can stand up to a liquored-up boy with a broken heart, armed with Thunderer, for Christ sake, yodeling Bach? I'll answer for you: nobody, not one smirking fiend, no one! I was in my Nijinsky mode, suspended in one of those feet-twittering leaps for a breathtakingly long moment. I was bleeding from a head wound, blood slithered onto my jacket and my blue chamois shirt. They weren't going to stop the fight because I had a cut. Then I heard the pleasing sound of a riot upstairs, cries of dread and encouragement, and Norman screaming at the top of his lungs: "Justice." (An answer, I would learn in an hour or so, to Gent's nearly rhetorical question: "What do you want from *me*?" Justice indeed.)

At the front of the room was a staircase. A rectangle of bright light and urgent shadows of the upper-floor struggle sat on the floor before me. I could see three or four carpeted steps. A room near the top of those steps, I knew, was Claire's. The noise of footsteps was like the tide coming in and out. Seemingly thirty or forty people would rush from one side of the house to the other, shifting ballast in a sinking ship. I climbed the stairs two at a time toward that noise and light, Thunderer in front of me, on the lookout for watchdogs or razorblade wire. Nothing. Blood dripped onto the steps in front of me; my shirtfront was covered with it. (It looked worse than it was, unfortunately—I would have loved to have had a 15-stitch gash. How did I get it, curious folk would ask. "During the commission of a felony," I would have told them.)

Most of the action had shifted to the second floor. Gent had run into his bedroom and locked the door behind him. The hellacious thumping I heard wasn't a recording of moose mating but Norman battering away at the door with his shoulder. Eventually, it gave way.

A few feet from the top of the stairs I had just climbed was a door that carried a small brass nameplate: *Claire Cohen*, it said, *Private*. I rapped at the door softly; no one answered. It was unlocked, and I turned the knob tentatively. Mickey Monahan appeared behind me, that loathsome toadie.

"Get out," he said to me. He walked past me and nearly slammed Claire's door in my face. Only Thunderer jammed in the jamb prevented his gambit. Dog-bane received a nasty cut. I kicked the door open with my foot.

"Go away," I said to him.

"You don't belong in there, you bastard," he said.

Foul little man, you fucked up big-time when you tried to stop me from seeing Claire. For the sheer joy of it, I conked him on the head and shoulders, solid slaps with Thunderer, not damaging but the potential was there, just a little beyond the three-quarters force he was tasting. He ran past me down the hall, routed by Thunderer. Remember, Mickey: regardless of who you know or who you blow, there will be no one to protect you in the funky days to come. You've heard of shit storms, Mickey? Count on softball-size turds. I turned and snarled at the creeps who stood at the end of the hall. Mine was a bloodcurdling cry from prehistory. Lord, I felt well. I was dripping blood on the carpet.

Claire's rescue was at hand. Okay, so maybe I didn't expect Claire to leap in my arms (these were extreme circumstances), but I wasn't expecting total chagrin. She had sat down on the edge of her bed, wrapped in her terry-cloth robe, with her hair dryer pointed like a pistol in my general direction. She was a bit surprised; perhaps "mortified" catches her expression more accurately.

"I'm here," I said, assuming she'd know what I was here for.

"Yes, you are."

More sirens, louder shouts. "Upstairs, upstairs," the bug-eyed boys were crying. I had only a few minutes, I realized, because the cops had arrived. Bullhorn and tear-gas time, I was going to have to make my retreat, with Claire of course, immediately.

"Well?"

"What are you doing? Just what in the hell are you doing?"

I should have expected this. I really should have.

When I actually began to say the words out loud, like a child describing an irrational fear, I realized, somewhat unhappily, that I was way off the beam.

"I'm here to rescue you."

She laughed at that.

"Rescue me? me?"

"You. Claire. Right. Take you away."

"Oh, Henry. I tried to call you all afternoon. Your phone's been busy. I wanted you to have breakfast with me in the morning. I'm leaving for New York tomorrow. My father needs me at home. And besides, this job isn't working out. Gent gives me the creeps."

I had taken the phone off the hook and buried the headset in a pillow. Sheer petulance was the motivation.

"You don't like him?"

"He's disgusting. He's a shit."

Concrete poetry: happy words to a desperate man.

Large black drops were still rolling down my nose. I was sweating, too, and the blood and sweat were a slithery slime on my forehead and face. The racket upstairs had grown measurably in the last few minutes. Norman was acquiting himself with distinction, that was the inference one could draw from the noise, the constancy of sirens from outside, the unabating football scrimmage grunts.

Claire took a towel off her bed, it was still damp, and she held it to my forehead. She leaned against me, put her hand to the back of my neck, and blotted the blood off my face. Her eyes were full of fat, salty tears.

"Henry, you're an idiot."

But she said that as in the old days, when she was my quiet Claire, when she loved the weird dude who stood before her. She put her arm around my shoulders. She leaned against me as in ancient times, lithe Cohen against sturdy Fitzgerald. Just for old-time's sake, I gave her neck an affectionate nibble.

Then the door burst open, and a whining Mickey Monahan screamed over the shoulders of two cops, "Him, too. He tried to kill me."

The cops took Thunderer away from me and manacled my wrists behind my back. They shoved me out of Claire's room. I didn't get a chance to say anything else to her. Norman was at the end of the hallway, his shirt and pants torn to shreds, missing a shoe, bleeding from a multitude of scrapes and cuts. Ambulance attendants hurried past us up the stairs.

"He's all right," Norman said to me bitterly. "He was still breathing when the cops pulled me off. Maybe a little brain damage."

We were led to a police cruiser and dumped in the back seat. Airy was across the street on the curb, dressed quickly and her hair uncombed. She looked at me and mouthed the word: "Why?"

She wasn't happy.

I didn't get to say anything more to Claire. What was there to say? "Claire didn't need to be rescued after all, Norman."

"I figured. So what? We touched all the bases, though, Henry. What is it that Birdwhistle says?"

"He says it's a home run or nothing, Norman, here on Home Run Derby."

We rode in silence to the City-County Building as the majestic wheels of justice began to grind. I have just this one thing to say as a summation of the night's activities—you may underscore this if you wish: if ending up in jail turns out to be the culmination of my relationship with Claire Cohen, that's okay. Really, it's okay.

Beneath us, in one of the cell blocks, I heard the well-oiled slide of a steel door slamming shut. Outside in the hallway I heard the vanquished archfiend, Leonard Gent, shouting at the cops. I had seen him, as we were being de-belted and unshoelaced, strutting about with an evil grimacelike grin on his face. He was banged up a bit about the eyes, the result of Norman's end of our evening. He had pulled a camelhair topcoat over his pajamas, which were the color of the summer sky. His pajama bottoms were tucked into heavy black boots, the kind that members of motorcycle gangs kick their victims to death with. He probably had a wire-thin stiletto stuck in one of them as well.

Milton arrived, anxious but not terrifically surprised.

"Jesus Christ, you guys did all this in one night? This is like a month of felonies."

He held a carbon of the charges against us, a flimsy wraithlike piece of pink paper.

"Conduct regardless of human life," he said. "I always liked the sound of that one. You had the hammer handle?"

"Yup."

"What did you do with it?"

"I used it to fight my way to Claire's room."

"That's my brother. He used it to fight his way to Claire's room. You mean the Claire Cohen we were supposed to have breakfast with in about four hours? The Claire who was trying to get in touch with you most of the afternoon and evening? The Claire who finally called me in exasperation to find out where you were and/or why your phone was off the hook? The Claire who wanted to have a long talk with you about 'stuff'? That Claire?"

Sarcasm was not Milton's true métier, and I was too happy to take offense.

"Yeah," I said happily, "that one."

"Did you do any serious damage?"

"I don't think so."

"I tried though, Milton, I really did," Norman said.

"I believe you, buddy," Milton said gently. He slapped Norman on the shoulder affectionately. "Okay, okay. Let's think about this. What did you do, really? Harmless prank gets out of hand, et cetera. I know Gent's out there calling for blood, but I think I can get the charges reduced. Nobody likes Gent, and I can maybe squeeze somebody."

"What if Gent decided not to press charges?"

"It won't happen."

"Just tell me," I said.

"The cops might charge you anyhow, but I doubt it since Gent is not beloved by the P.D. Since nothing serious happened, you'd probably walk out of here. But don't count on it. He's foaming from every orifice."

Preplanning, as Birdwhistle says, preplanning is the key.

As raveled as we were in the consequences of our wrongdoing—we were guilty of serious crimes, I admit it—I could whiff in the stagnant jailhouse air the sweet smell of freedom. Earlier in the evening I had typed a name and a short declarative sentence on a sheet of expensive bond paper, folded it neatly, and put it in my pocket. Insurance, I thought, against the inevitable.

"Give Gent this," I said.

Milton was skeptical, but he went anyway. I think he was rather looking forward to defending me against the felonious charge of

"Conduct Regardless of Human Life"—which had a distinctly By-ronic sound to it. Milton came back after about half an hour. He had his coat on.

"Let's go, boys. My vehicle is out front. Quickly, before reason seizes the moment," he said.

It was early in the a.m. The streetlights illuminated iridescent patches of ice, silver against the asphalt. Milton's car was an expen-sive Buick, navy blue, midnight blue, the color of a starless sky. With Milton behind the wheel, it roared and rumbled; in it we hurtled through empty streets unhindered. We zipped the short trip back to my house in an instant.

"Get some sleep, boys, will you," Milton said, idling at my door-step. "I'll call you later."

Norman was out of the car and headed toward the door, utterly exhausted.

"Thanks, Milton," I said. I looked over at Gent's house and my stomach tightened. I believed Claire still to be a captive (captive: the old instincts die hard).

"She's okay, Henry. Believe it or not, Airy took her home with her. She called when I was arranging to spring you boys. They were going to have hot milk and brandy, steaming showers, and turn in. Airy said she was going to go with Claire to Gent's in the morning to pick up her stuff. Henry, I don't know if I've told you this lately, but you are weird. Absolutely weird. Hey, and I like Airy."

I nodded an agreement. Truly, I was weird and Airy is a lovely woman. She is as solid as Sam Huff in a crisis. Red Dog Elder, filling yet another hole. I was going to have a bit of explaining to do, of course; that flash came across the psychic wire service.

"That's great," I said. "Good old Airy. Good old Claire."

I was too tired to say much more.

"I'm falling over. I have to go to bed, Milton."

Milton smiled wickedly, for not only does he dig dirt, he loves to dig it.

"Henry, one more thing, *muy importante*: who the hell *is* Fletcher Lint? And why did Gent wet his pants when he read that note? Fletcher Lint: I've never heard of the guy."

I decided to let him puzzle over that a bit.

"Just some slime from the bottom of the slime barrel. I'll tell you the whole story later. Goodnight, Milton."

"Goodnight, Henry. I'll call you."

It was a bitterly cold morning in Brueghel's midwest. I stood in the cold, on the cusp of a new day. The snow was white, the sky was black, and my red boathouse hunkered down in the darkness before me. So much depended upon it. Finally, I looked at Gent's Perversity Palace, scanning the windows for a malevolent face, but the joint was shuttered and dark.

"Ha," I said in Gent's direction. "Ha."

I was going to catch bloody hell in the morning, I knew that. It would be like going over the top at Verdun: grinding artillery fire in my face. But I didn't give a shit. I had blood all over my clothes, Thunderer was missing in action, and I was worn to a nub. Of my old life I remembered very little. In the new, the only certainty I could claim was this: Claire Cohen, black-haired Claire Cohen, my Claire Cohen, was asleep safely, beneath a heavy quilt, behind a locked door, rescued, at last. Rescued by me.